WHO TRESPASS AGAINST US
AGAINST US

A Novel
by

Peter Cunningham

CENTURY
LONDON SYDNEY AUCKLAND JOHANNESBURG

First published in Great Britain in 1992 by
Random House UK Limited
20 Vauxhall Bridge Road, London, SW1V 2SA

Random House South Africa (Pty) Ltd
PO Box 337, Bergvlei 2012, South Africa

Random House Australia Pty Ltd
20 Alfred Street, Milsons Point, Sydney, NSW 2061
Australia

Random House New Zealand Ltd
18 Poland Road, Glenfield, Auckland 10,
New Zealand

ISBN 0 7126 56782

Typeset by Deltatype Ltd, Ellesmere Port
Printed in Great Britain by

WHO TRESPASS AGAINST US

In London, in a street near Paddington station, on May 17th, an IRA bomb claims its victims: a girl on her way to visit her parents.

Two months later her father, Adam Coleraine, a highly placed civil servant in the most sensitive department of the Home Office, disappears. So too does a top secret report on the IRA, never meant to have been there in the first place. Terrified of the consequences of Adam Coleraine being captured and debriefed, the British Government turns to Dublin for help.

Told by Brian Kilkenny, the Irishman sent to find Adam Coleraine and the author of the secret report, WHO TRESPASS AGAINST US is a passionate, tender and gripping portrait of men and women in love, in grief and in war. In a story as old as the two countries themselves, and against all the odds, the seed of forgiveness is sown and finally comes to flower.

Peter Cunningham shows himself to be a master of dramatic narrative, and gives the reader a rare insight into the hidden depths of the human heart.

Who Trespass Against Us

For Carol

Contents

So, reader, I am myself the substance of my book, and there is no reason why you should waste your leisure on so frivolous and unrewarding a subject.

Michel de Montaigne,
this first day of March 1580

Events in London, 17 May

My darling Gilly,

The things that happened at that time have never been properly recounted. Today, through the haze of the years that have passed, all that remain are impressions – mainly, I would say, the work of media and politicians. But I cannot allow history to be written for you by men for whom expediency is king. That would be to lose the heroic, which, in my humble view, would be to lose all.

History, of course, is the big, lazy, inconvenient dog that lies across the threshold and, depending what side you are on, you see it with passion or indifference. We have had seven hundred years of forcible restraint in which to form our view. In such a position you come to understand everything about the wearer of the boot, every minute shifting of his weight, his follies and caprices, and the length of time he hung the game he ate the night before. The lads would not see it like that. The lads would not admit to something visceral at work when laws and treaties now govern everything – and if a judge of the Dublin District Court rejects a British extradition request on the grounds that the name of our country was incorrectly spelt, then the lads would simply shrug. 'Lads', by the way, evokes comradeship, rural origins, the image of a hearty bunch of fellow officers thrown together by fate and doing a tough job for the common good, doesn't it? But I recall an occasion when our Special Detective Unit was involved in a cross-country manhunt for men who had shot dead in cold blood a postmaster in Mallow and his wife and were headed north; I recall receiving word at night from a guard in the midlands, and he said: 'I think the lads are headed your way.' He meant the killers, of course, and equally, of course, I understood what he meant. Only afterwards it occurred to me that in his mind there had been a spontaneous fusion.

I apologise if I have left the track on which I started. I was trained as you know to reconstruct events, but even so what has come through to me in here, first in slow drips, then steadily like a stream, then in a flood, has threatened to take me with it. It is sensible therefore to put a time and a place on things, particularly at the beginning, and so my place on Wednesday morning, 17 November that year, was as usual at my desk in Harcourt Square, Dublin, in the special Detective Unit of the Garda Siochana. You never saw my office. It was on the first floor, the walls were an anaemic yellow, the carpet grey, the furniture cheap chipboard and sheeted pine. The doorway through which I ducked proclaimed by means of a decent, metal sign affixed on the corridor side: 'Detective Superintendent B. Kilkenny.'

That Wednesday was, I much later realised, exactly six months after the bomb. I remember walking to the Foreign Affairs meeting at Iveagh House and leaving ten minutes in hand to take in St Stephen's Green. It was bright and crisp and the bust of Joyce had acquired a laurel wreath of ice. By Newman House I passed an old woman walking slowly, a very young boy, her grandson he had to be, held by the hand, each of them drawing, it seemed, their entire strength from the other. Maybe it was that fond scene that made me think of retirement as I crossed for Iveagh House. But returning to Harcourt Street two hours later, retirement had vanished from my horizon. I read my notes once in my office and again that night, at home. Nothing was clear, everything had been obscured by years of mistrust. Only one thing was plain: never before had there been a meeting like it.

The previous afternoon in heavy traffic I had driven to Ryans, Parkgate Street, where in the back snug Arty Gunn was installed. Wide and butty, always the boxer, the Assistant Garda Commissioner in charge of crime and security was round and bald of head and massive of chin. His brow puckered, his small, blue eyes flickered and one large hand gripped a glass. 'Pint?'

'Thanks.'

At the foot-square hatch, the waxy face of a man appeared and disappeared.

'The thraffick is wicked.'

Arty still said 'thraffick'. They were a special breed these people reared in the west who came east in the fifties. They had great, strong trees of bodies. They had – and still have – a great tradition and capacity for hard work, as Arty's career had shown. Aged fifty-four, rising to pay for and deliver down my pint, up to five months before Arty had been my chief superintendent, in charge of the Special Detective Unit, but had then been elevated to his present position, a keeper of the nation's secrets.

'Slainte.'

'Slainte.'

We drank sweet half moons of creamy bitterness.

'Dere's a bit of a meetin' tomorra,' Arty said, crumping his lips.

I put my glass on a little shelf. Although we had never in twenty years exchanged a cross word, I had come to learn that Arty's allegiances were to himself and to his country, strictly in that order.

He said: 'A wicked crowd altogether comin' down from Belfasht – and over from London.'

'NIO?'

NIO, the Northern Ireland Office.

'NIO, RUC,' Arty nodded, his brow wrinkling up and down. 'Home Office.'

'Home Office.'

Like a farmer, you get to know the signs.

'Tice,' Arty said. 'Permanent Secrethry of the Police Department.'

'Is it a Trevi?'

'No.' Arty sucked stout and leaned back. 'We had a Threvi in Portagil three weeks ago, in Lishbin. They tried it on there. Dis is the next assault. Big guns, boyo, Iveagh House.'

So three weeks previously Arty had been to Lisbon; and a meeting had taken place there of the Trevi Group, an informal gathering of European security chiefs, called after a fountain in Rome. Where 'they' had tried it on.

'Dey're neck to the bone, the Brits,' Arty said grimly. He finished his drink in a swallow and put up his glass. 'It didn't shtop at me, boyo, let me tell you.' He pointed up at Ryans' skylight. 'It didn't shtop at me.'

Hands twined in his lap, staring plaintively at the floor, he looked for all the world like someone's favourite uncle trying to comprehend the passage of time. Hard to believe that one night a

3

year before I'd seen him bat a Provo until blood had flowed from the youngster's ears.

'Have they no shame? Have they no sinse? Do they honestly expect us again to deliver them our own, asleep in deir beds? Like eighteen months ago?' Arty shook his head, as if more from bewilderment than indignation. 'No sinse, no sinse at all.'

Eighteen months before there had been great successes, North and South; Armalites and mortars in great numbers and three tons of Semtex had been captured and there followed between the two countries a climatic aberration: genuine warmth. This wondrous change in nature led to a rush of optimism, impossible expectations and agreements entered into that even the most hopeful men on both sides must have known they would come to regret; and when the RUC requested of us a report on republican paramilitaries I argued against giving it for weeks. I knew the Brits, how they operated, their ruthless downgrading of a problem which to us is paramount. I understood them; I understand them. I was uncompromised, in a unique position to refuse. For fifteen years I had delivered intelligence of unparalleled quality from a source known only to myself. But faced with stark choices, to my eternal regret I eventually complied with my orders and wrote my report with a mixture of fact and obfuscation worthy of a man forced to make a written defence of his own adultery.

In the spring of the year whose autumn we were now in, Ulster republicans were shot in their beds, or off their bikes, or in their drinking clubs, and often the only thing they had in common was their names in that report. And when in July a Dublin newspaper purported to know something of what had gone on and briefly the murder of Irish innocents by British government-paid terrorists became a ringing issue, you could hear the sound of the RUC shredders from Dublin. Relationships between the two countries fell from brimming to very low tide, which in the case of the Liffey smells like a bad conscience.

Arty rose busily to the hatch where two pints had appeared by wordless requisition.

'By the way, I shoulda asked before, how's Gilly?' he asked.

'Grand, thanks.'

'An' the children?'

'Grand.'

'How many now?'

'Seven.'

'Seven! God bless ye.' Arty leant towards me and grabbed hold of my arm so fiercely that I thought I was going to hear one of his state secrets. 'Dey're what matthers, boyo, dey're what matthers. All dese things we're made do, the likes a you an' me, all this dirt we're up to here in, dat's nuttin'.'

It was not impossible that his remarks were genuinely felt; most of his life had been spent reducing problems to a parochial context and then butt-heading his way through them. He was under pressure. Something was happening in the wider context, the political context, some deal or breakthrough was on the cards and butty little terrier Arty Gunn had been sent out to bring home a bone.

'Tice,' he said, frowning.

'Who else will be there?'

'The head of the RUC Special Branch and the Permanent Secrethry of the Police Department in th'NIO,' Arty said. 'The Assistant Secrethry in charge of th'Anti-Terrorist Division of th'NI Police Department.'

'Counsell's replacement,' I said.

Arty's brow rubbered up. 'Ay, Counsell's replacement.'

'What's going on, Arty?'

'We're playing it low key,' Arty said blithely. 'St John Flanagan from Foreign Affairs and that bitch Moriarity from Justice is as high as we go. She'll have a legal advisor along with her, probably Dick Jennings.'

'What's going on?'

Arty gave me his corrugated, punch-drunk look, then glanced away, chewing at the inside of one cheek.

'Politics,' he said to the closed hatch.

'Ah. Politics.'

'You know, you know.'

Coyness was a new part of Arty's armour.

'A lot of behind-the-scenes goin's on,' he winced. 'Anglo-Irish shtuff. Concessions to Dublin on consultations, promise of direct talks shortly, that sort of shtuff. You can't believe what you hear . . .'

'Arty.'

Arty looked at me steadily. 'Talk of a Brit declaration to take deir army out. A timetable.'

I raised my eyebrows.

'Just talk,' Arty warned.

'But . . .'

'But . . . There's a lot a activity and, well, you know the Brits, they want to see the colour of our money.'

'Oh, I thought they might want something of value,' I said, tired of this game.

'Dey're after you,' Arty said defiantly and suddenly went red.

'They' again.

'Go way.'

'I'm serious.' He took out and unfolded a crisp white handkerchief and wiped his forehead.

I said: 'You know my position.'

Arty slammed his glass down. 'I bloody well do! I bloody well do! I said to that Moriarity one: "D'you think Brian is goin' to shop his sources to any Etin-educated hape a shite with a rifle stickin' outa his arse pocket?" I said.'

'Were my sources requested?'

'No.'

'Did they say, "We need another report", or an update on the last report, in order to advance their intention to withdraw, or in order to advance something – or anything – to Ireland's advantage?'

'No. Definitely not.' Arty made a show of coming out of his corner to the rescue. 'Moriarity – Jaysus, that one'd trample her own litter to get to the trough first – she says: "Everyone will simply follow his orders, Assistant Commissioner." I'm not leavin' this one resht, Brian, believe me, no way, not for a man who's been as close to me as you have.'

'And what are our orders, Arty?'

'To attend dis meetin' tomorrow, boyo,' Arty answered with all the innocence of Judas.

Leaving Ryans ten statutory minutes after Arty, I walked in sheeting rain halfway up the steep start of the North Circular. Instead of west and home to you and the children in Palmerstone, Gilly, I drove north into the Park. I never did want to come home after an absence of twelve hours and withdraw myself. I wanted to laugh with Simon, talk with Oisin about football, see which of the twins would kiss me first, Sorcha or Naomh, and creep up behind you and press you to me and marvel that this tantalizing woman of mine was a grandmother.

I came to a halt after some minutes on the grass beneath the Papal Cross. As distant headlights made strange crystals of the rain on the windscreen, I was pierced by a shaft of utter loneliness that only a person in my position cound understand. To tell anyone what I knew – anyone – would put not only their lives at risk but mine as well. I had known that for fifteen years. A long time, but that's how long it was since he first set me up.

I had seen him. Tall as me with a long face and jaw, one eye bright and on me, the other smeared with a birth stain the colour of port wine, from his eye to his ear, the deep red thumb mark of God. A fine, June evening over on the north side. I think it was a new Fianna sports club being opened with all the optimism of the early eighties.

'They say you're the man who keeps the peace around here.' A slightly crooked smile. 'Vincent Ashe.'

'Brian Kilkenny.'

'Kilkenny, Kilkenny. Who was it who wrote about "Kilkenny in the rain"? The Marble City, Kilkenny Castle, Kilkenny beer, Medieval Kilkenny. People go to Kilkenny – they just don't pass through it, isn't that right?'

I laughed. 'I couldn't tell you. I'm Dublin born and reared. So was my father, and my grandfather was a schoolteacher from Roscommon.'

'Roscommon. West of the Shannon, like myself.'

Out the clubhouse window a large, blue sign with 'Ashe' in white letters sat on scaffolding.

'You're Ashe Brothers?' I asked.

'Oh, the junior, very much the boy,' he smiled. 'Our poor father always told me: "when the man upstairs was giving out the brains, he never saw you." ' He looked down at my empty glass. 'What's that?'

'It was vodka.'

He took my glass and made of' to the bar, recognising people on his way. Ireland is a small place: the same success stories do the

7

rounds of everyone's lips. There were four brothers: Tom, the driving force, who came up barefoot from Clare to a Dublin builder; and saved to send home for his brother, Jim; and that eight years later it was Vincent's turn. The fourth was a priest, a missionary somewhere. The blue sign became increasingly noticeable on new office blocks and on the extensions to airports and hospitals. Blatant republicans they were of course, but in Ireland republicanism and success in business are frequently consanguineous.

'Isn't this wonderful?' He handed me my drink and swept his around the room to embrace everyone. 'It gives you some idea of what we could be.'

I must have looked curious.

'As a nation,' he elaborated. 'They're all so young, so bright – it's bloody infectious.' He touched my arm and smiled. 'I'm sorry. You know what I mean. For centuries we populated the armies of France and beyond, the workforces of Britain, of America, the civil services of umpteen colonies. But always with our culture intact, mercenaries with our inner values never lost, do you understand me?'

'We are always Irish.'

'Exactly. And think of the potency, the undeveloped potential left behind.' He shook his head like someone who has tussled long with a problem. 'The Irish nation has always existed, here in our hearts. One day we will be able to let it out – when we have an undivided country to let it out to. Then the Irish nation will be more than something of our hearts – it will be physical and indestructible.'

'You're certainly doing your bit to build our nation,' I said with deliberate lightness.

'Thank you,' he smiled and dropped it.

We chatted on. He was cultured and intelligent and highly successful. He was unmarried. There were Ashes in New York, he told me, both from his father's time and now, from his sister's marriage to a man who owned bars. Vincent had an office in Dublin, in the Ashe Brothers headquarters, and in a light engineering company outside Belfast that Jim had purchased in the seventies, he had another. In Clare he'd hurled as a youth, in the centrefield, he told me. He must have been an apparition as

8

fearsome as our warrior ancestors, this charging boy, *sliothar* balanced firmly as a rock, his opponents thrown into check for a vital strike by the sudden, awful sight of his haemangioma.

Later, driving home to you all those years ago, something struck me: it was all about himself; never once did he ask anything about me. Of course, I realised much later, this was because he already knew.

I opened the car window and heard the rain falling in perfect tympanic over every inch of the Fifteen Acres. I could not understand why current, in-depth information about the IRA would be wanted by the British Home Office in the context of the diplomatic breakthrough blurted by Arty. Such matters would be the preserve of the Northern Ireland Office and the British Foreign Office. Sir Trevor Tice, the Home Office Permanent Secretary, Arty's 'Etin-educated hape a shite', was an icy, Whitehall grandee, known to me only by reputation. He was the type of Englishman whom many Irishmen regard as transparent and therefore irrelevant. This was a mistake. Tice's position between the vast security apparatus of Northern Ireland and its relationship with the anti-terrorist divisions of the mainland police was geocentric. In our border counties and in Dublin, his MI5 boys operated without restriction, as did his grey little tele-communications spooks from Cheltenham who came in on the early Monday flights and went out from Dublin again that evening leaving red-faced men high in their Dublin offices worrying the tops of their Bics and cursing the fact that we had been born poor.

The gossip Arty had passed on was not something he would have had the imagination to invent, so its origins had to lie in higher ground. If the political plum of a British intention to quit the North had truly appeared on the Anglo-Irish sideboard, nothing would be allowed to stand in the way of its winning: to survive in a setting of such political predacity you would either have to be absent at feeding time or have the appearance of being non-digestible. For me, matters could only get worse.

A gale came at midnight, eastwards over the midland plain, and blew the rain squalls out of Dublin by first light. Iveagh – Guinness beer to landed peer – House in nowadays home of the Irish Department of Foreign Affairs; it is a house of generous halls, wide staircases and upstairs rooms designed for dancing. I walked in fifteen minutes before ten, half-expecting that Arty might bluster into me, but waiting instead on the first landing was the Assistant Secretary of the Anglo-Irish Division, a man in his mid-forties named Harold St John Flanagan. Dressed as if his tailor had always longed for a man so smooth of contour, tall and slim with sloping shoulders that crept up to the bole of his fine neck, he came forward, all tucked of smile and long of linen cuff. 'Detective Superintendent.' My hand was caught between his and squeezed. '*Nice* to see you.'

'Mr St John Flanagan.'

'Harry. Harry.' Down a wide corridor his hand cupped the point of my elbow, dictating a crawling pace. 'It is so kind of you. We are all *most* appreciative.'

We paused, if that's the word. His face was set in an attitude of intense admiration and his small, brown eyes made me his forever.

'We *appreciate* it.'

'Appreciate what, Harry?'

'You're helping us out,' he whispered, doing all the smiling with his lower lip. 'Your helping us out.' He drew me into a window as a secretary passed although had she been riding a charabanc the measure would have been equally unnecessary. 'We are in the foothills of history, Detective Superintendent,' he murmured with little sideways motions of his head.

I could see through open doors into a room ten yards away where a mighty table was laid out for a meeting.

'Shall we?' Harry asked and initiated the resumption of our passage, smirking at me every few slow strides.

Dick Jennings, the white-haired and red-faced advisor from Justice, was sitting, writing, and Arty was standing, dressed in a new blue suit. Arty opened his mouth and said something but it was Janet Moriarity who moved first.

'Detective Superintendent.'

'Assistant Secretary.'

'A moment, Harry, please,' she said and brought me to the white fireplace in which burned real coals. The Assistant Secretary of the Department of Justice was tall and wore skirts that showed her knees. Her hands were big and ringless and her eyes behind oval-shaped lenses were wallflower blue. Somewhere in Carrick-mines was a Mr Moriarity and children.

'This is not the type of situation I would normally put you in,' she said. First-class degrees in law from universities North and South, together with an intimidating reputation within Justice circles for proficiency, had made Janet Moriarity into something of an icon; but I had always found her voice with the occasional vowel from somewhere north of the border unforced and husky. I smiled and so did Assistant Secretary Moriarity, but then she seemed to regret it and said: 'I believe that the Assistant Commissioner has informed you of a recent approach.'

'Arty mentioned Lisbon,' I replied.

She nodded impatiently, whether of Arty or of me it was unclear.

'Two approaches in Lisbon, as far as we can make out,' she said crisply. 'One, from the British Home Secretary to our Minister. Along the lines: "We need to dust our cupboards out, old boy, clear the beaches of old mines, what?" To be honest, our man didn't take the fly until he was halfway home. Two.'

A counsellor in the Department went up to Harry and both men left on the trot. Janet Moriarity looked at her watch.

"Two. The Assistant Chief Constable of the RUC approached the Assistant Commissioner at the same meeting and floated the idea of the mutual destruction of sensitive, historical security data as a way to foil future leaks of the "shoot-to-kill" variety.'

I must have looked amused.

She said: 'I know. Arty stonewalled – he's good at that – and said perhaps they should talk about it again over lunch, before Christmas. That obviously wouldn't do. Next thing we know we're all on parade here this morning.'

'What do they mean, "old mines"?' I ventured, innocently. 'If they pull out, we're left with the mines, Janet, not them.'

Assistant Secretary Moriarity's sharp look suggested that Arty had overrun his brief the evening before, then she softened. I liked the ever-present contrast within her.

'I don't know, Brian,' she said quietly. 'All I do know is that Merrion Street is standing on its head.'

'This is a fishing expedition, Janet.'

'But for what type of fish?' she asked as the doors opened and Harry St John Flanagan led in a group of dark-suited men.

Sir Trevor Tice would always dominate a delegation. Tall and angular as a crane, his face was that of a good-looking man ravaged by malnutrition. Sharp cheekbones and jawline, jagged Adam's apple, blonde hair straight in its fall to deeply-recessed eyes, he had elongated hands with fingers too long to have been composed of three conventional joints. Harry guided him to us, where we now stood in a bunch. To each of us he said, 'Hello. How do you do?' in an accent that a stand-up comic would hesitate to try out.

Our people had frequent meetings with the RUC, and with the two NIO men, who were cheerful and dour respectively; but the presence of Tice and his Home Office Terrorist Division man brought tension and formality to the occasion. We sat one side of the big table, Harry first, then Janet and Dick Jennings, then Arty, then me, our pecking-order assumed naturally. Sir Trevor Tice, on the other side, told his people where to sit and placed himself in the middle, the RUC and Terrorist Division men at each elbow and the NIO men one further out. Tice had cleared his throat and was about to speak when the doors opened once more. I saw two lads from our Special Branch with Uzis out in the corridor then the counsellor seen earlier wheeled in a trolley crammed with crockery and silver dishes and tea and coffee pots. Dick Jennings seemed pleased and although the RUC chief and the NIO men all smiled at what was, I'm sure, well-established tradition, I saw Tice toss restlessly as Harry and the young counsellor unloaded mats and pots and jugs and silver bowls with tongs and linen napkins and cutlery and cups and saucers and silver dishes with sandwiches and biscuits from the trolley to the table. And Tice's long, spindly fingers danced on the tabletop like the legs of an impatient grasshopper as the counsellor left and Harry and Arty saw to the napkin distribution, and the pouring of tea and coffee, and the passing of milk and sugar up and down the table, and the offering of sandwiches and biscuits, until at the end of six or seven minutes everyone, including Tice, was served and everyone, except Tice, was slurping and munching.

'Of course you'll stay for lunch, Sir Trevor,' said Harry warmly as if success in this business was measured by the quantity of food you got into the other side.

'Thank you,' Tice responded, 'but I am back to London.'

The NIO Permanent Secretary nodded and munched, but I was

sure that a good lunch without Sir Trevor Tice would have appealed to him far more than an RAF flight to Belfast.

'Nuttin' like a cup a tea, is dere?' asked Arty happily of no one in particular.

Tice propped his elbows on the table and joined his hands in a cat's cradel level with the top of his head.

'I first would like to thank everyone, no less my colleagues from the Northern Ireland Office, for facilitating this meeting,' he began crisply. 'I think it speaks for the climate of trust between our two countries that such things can be achieved at such short notice.'

Dick Jennings and the Terrorist Division man from the Home Office were waiting.

Tice said: 'We find ourselves, all of us, in a situation not dissimilar to the East-West rapprochment of the late eighties, albeit on a tiny scale. That process was made vastly easier then by the candid declaration by each side of its arsenals, and then, of course, by their agreed, mutual destruction. In the case of Northern Ireland, madam, gentlemen, I would suggest that our arsenals include submerged mines and time bombs in the form of sensitive, security information.'

Except for Harry, whose face was set in an expression of perpetual indulgence, no one on our side displayed any emotion.

'History is bunk, as we know,' said Tice, in a show of banter, 'and I don't propose we waste time on it this morning – except to say that I know of no other issue that enflames passions and threatens rapprochment to quite the same extent as when such mines and time-bombs go off.'

'Quite so,' said Harry, with reverence.

'Are you suggesting, Sir Trevor,' asked Janet coldly, 'that there has been an information leak of some kind from Dublin?'

I saw Harry cringe.

'In order for there to be a leak anywhere, Madam Assistant Secretary, there has to be, *de facto*, something which can leak,' Tice replied, matching Janet's ice.

Dick Jennings looked down at his writing pad, but I could see his eyes slide left and right looking for someone to tell him what was going on.

'I make the point simply to illustrate a far more wide-reaching issue,' purred Tice in a warmer gear. 'Let us be absolutely frank. There are political decisions to be taken which will require immense bravery. It is not for us to anticipate such developments, rather to create an environment in which they can flourish. Certain information, if leaked, however inadvertently, can be used by the enemies of society to cut the ground away from beneath our political masters and render their high objectives impossible.'

There was a period of silence, broken by the chiming of someone's wristwatch.

'Are you suggesting,' asked Janet firmly, 'that we . . . jointly declare, as it were, what information we hold on Northern Ireland security matters – and then agree to destroy such information?'

'There are undoubtedly items of particular sensitivity that have come into existence over the recent years, madam, which – let us be candid – both sides may have to come to regret,' said Sir Trevor with sweetness. 'We would all be better off without them.'

'Items such as your own report, Detective Superintendent,' said the Terrorist Division man to me quietly.

If there was an alternative to my being mute and expressionless, I could not think of it. Inwardly I prayed no one would take the bait and for a moment it looked as if my prayers would be answered.

The Assistant Secretary from the NI Police Department's Anti-Terrorist Division spoke in a deep, Welsh accent: 'No one's accusing, no one's suggesting. What's done is done, the dead can't be brought back. But when you decide to marry a girl, you get out your old address book with all the telephone numbers and you chuck the damn thing away.'

'Quite so,' simpered Harry on cue, but I could feel Tice hovering.

'I think it would be very wrong to concentrate on any one item that might or might not still exist,' said Janet coolly, showing why she was top of her profession. 'We absolutely reject any implication that Dublin is any less leak-proof than Belfast or London, or that a leak of any kind has taken place, if that also is inferred, and I am very surprised, Sir Trevor, that you would see fit to bring up such a suggestion.'

'At the same time, no one is taking a stance, no one is sticking their spear in the sand,' Harry murmured.

14

'Indeed,' said Tice. 'Reciprocal is the key word, isn't it? Neither of us needs to have around all these potentially leakable items, whatever they are, that might lead to grief.'

Of course it was Arty who then said: 'So what are ye suggestin'? That Detective Superintendent Kilkenny here should take out his report and that you should take out a sim'lar document and that we should burn them?'

'You have it exactly, Assistant Commissioner,' said Sir Trevor Tice angelically.

'I'm sure Brian don't have dat report anymore,' Arty frowned. 'All the information is in his head.'

So it was. The meeting that must have cost the British taxpayer well into the high hundreds of thousands ended and the RAF pilots out at Baldonnel switched on their Harriers and everyone flew home. Granted, there was agreement that it was early days to be specific but that in principal the two sides were really not far apart; and as everyone stood up, waiting for the cars, it was like nothing had happened, with Arty and the RUC Branch head chatting in one corner, and Janet Moriarity and the NIO men smiling to each other at the fireplace, and Sir Trevor Tice asking me some searching questions about the Irish weather with the interest of a well-bred, British tourist come to, say, Peru. Out of the corner of my eye when he thought I was otherwise pre-occupied, I saw Trice's Terrorist Division man glance across at the NIO Permanent Secretary and nod once in a gesture of triumph that confirmed my worst suspicions. Then we moved out and down, our Special Branch hitching their coats up around their sub-machine-guns, as Harry ushered the British delegation out on to St Stephen's Green and into the cars and away.

Janet Moriarity and Dick Jennings both had meetings in Government Buildings and I walked through the Green with them. People were breaking for lunch, circumnavigating the flower beds under the eyes of the park keepers.

'So, what do you think of that, Dick?' asked Janet.

Dick joined his hands so that his slim briefcase sat up on his stomach.

'I'm just a simple lawyer, not a psychiatrist,' he said and looked at me. 'The Brits have a problem, right?'

'A major problem of some kind,' I said, 'and when they have, we have too, usually.'

We crossed the footbridge where Simon and I still came to feed ducks.

'Still, they must be clapping each other on the back, don't you think?' Janet said to me. 'They went home with what they came to get.'

I nodded.

'I'm not with you,' Dick Jennings said.

Janet said, 'The meeting had nothing at all to do with plans to protect or destroy security information, but was designed to establish whether or not Detective Superintendent Kilkenny's report still exists, and if it does not, to see if he will deliver them a facsimile copy.'

'Why didn't they come out and ask us straight?' Dick asked. 'Why didn't they try a bit of this new trust that's meant to be on the go? I mean, as Arty said, I thought that report of yours was shredded and forgotten ages ago, Brian. Wasn't it?'

I envied the waterborne ducks their grace and mobility.

'That's not a question I would ever ask of Detective Superintendent Kilkenny,' said Janet and strode purposefully for a gate in the railings.

*

That first meeting in Iveagh House was six months exactly since the day of the bomb, since the explosion of the seed pod. Nothing for him would ever be the same after that day, I understand that now, not even the past.

At twenty to seven on the morning of 17 May Adam Coleraine, the Grade 6 of the anti-terrorist division – known as F4 – of the British Home Office, came up the stairs of his house in Sidcup. The spare room shared a bathroom with the master bedroom which meant he could shower after jogging without having to meet Alison, his wife. When his father, Pom, came to stay, Adam used the shower unit in his daughter Zoe's bedroom across the hall for the same reason. Fitness was the thing those days in the Home Office – was he under or over average weight for a Grade 6 of forty-three? He was a huge man, gone a bit heavy over the hips

16

and his beard, which like so many permanent events had started out as a temporary affair, now hid a chin too many; but he jogged because he liked it. He hated categories of any kind: black or white, thin or fat. Soon it would be circumcised or not. He'd been done at three months. Was the man whom Zoe lived with circumcised?

Sidcup brimmed. Eating fibres from a bowl, in suit pants and shirt, Adam overlooked the dereliction of the back garden from the kitchen step. Starved, unpruned box had grown to resemble urchins queueing for soup, if that sort of thing still existed. A procession of cracked paving-slabs gave the impression that a lorry had shed its load in transit. It didn't worry Adam. He addressed a lone, dwarf conifer for the purpose of the lines he was trying to memorize: ' "Be careful, be careful, Donal Davoren. But Minnie is attracted to the idea, and I am attracted to Minnie. And what danger can there be in being the shadow of a gunman?" ' 'Gunman' made him think of Counsell: loose, white, jowly, puffy – shadowy. Why did he do it? The kitchen radio announced seven twenty-nine, news text. ' "Be careful, be careful . . ." '

'Adam, I want to say something.'

Alison had arrived. Striped robe, knuckles white from the way she was pressing them on the white, pine kitchen table.

'Yes?' Adam enquired.

'Do I ever enter your scheme of things? Do I? Ever? Do you ever pause to think about me anymore? What event have I just interrupted, or could I possibly know, or if I did would I understand?'

'My lines, that's all.'

'I asked you, do I enter your scheme of things?'

'Alison,' he said with tired reason, 'it's seven-thirty. The train from Sidcup leaves at eight-o-six. There is no time for the philosophical discussion you propose.'

'Not this time, not any time!' she said tightly. 'Do you know what I've been doing upstairs? Lying awake, thinking: do I know the man I'm married to? What do you think of that, Adam? Do you know me?'

Adam ventured, 'I know your face so well.'

'Adam, our marriage is bust.'

'The truest word is oft spoke in jest.'

'This is no jest – I'm serious!'

Adam looked at Alison's face: like her heart it had been wound tight over the years by some inner ratchet. They had married in a Catholic church, beautiful, intelligent Alison, clever, confident Adam. Alison had travelled, had lived six months in France, she knew what a *baguette* was, even in those days; Adam, by night, had studied political economy. When Adam went each day to climb the rungs in QAG, that is Queen Anne's Gate, that is the Home Office, Alison's smile lit up the art department of a publisher. Then the thunderbolt: a fruit in Alison's womb! That night, topped with a Turkish fez snatched from the head of a ridiculous porter outside a restaurant in Soho, he cavorted for an hour in the middle of the road like a circus elephant, with the result that over twenty years on certain people in Sidcup still didn't salute them. Mother of his child. After Alison's fourteen hours of incredible, never-to-be-repeated forcing, when they brought Adam the skew-nosed, red blob of warmth with jet hair like a wet kitten, he had said: 'She's Zoe.'

'I must go,' Adam said and heard letters plopping into the hall. Top of the broken fan as he stooped was a postcard of the Severn Bridge.

'Oh, Zoe's in Bristol. "See you Wednesday evening." Today's Wednesday.'

'He's thrown her out.' Alison pulled with fervour at a cigarette, pulled even tighter the belt of her robe, and knotted it. 'Why else would she condescend to visit Sidcup?'

'Dear Mummy, I'm making an effort . . .'

'She's selfish, Adam. She only comes here when she wants something.'

'. . . Yours sincerely . . .'

'You're blind to that.'

'. . . Zoe.'

'I can tell you something for nothing. If she's pregnant then it's her lookout. I'm not wasting what I've left on a bastard.'

'One of us should be here.'

'Tonight's my last film society.'

'Our only daughter, in fact our only child is coming home for the evening, okay? I have play rehearsals for two hours after work, okay?'

18

Alison's face was a bayonet fixed. 'She's got a key. She doesn't exactly need to be held by the hand, unless of course the person doing the holding is a greasy rag-merchant over forty.'

Adam said, 'I know I can depend on you, Alison.'

'I'll come back and see her in,' said Alison tightly. 'But then I'm going to the film society – why shouldn't I?'

Adam cut along the footpath in sharp heels made of her bitterness. Spite. Awesome performance. Playing a full season. With the legendary sisters, Envy and Bile. Sabin, their neighbour, slicing out discs of engine noise as he tried to start his 25 y.o., as new XJ6 4.2, looked up from his coaxing and spoke. Shibboleth. Zoe's homeward trips had petered out under the ever-curdling sourness of Alison's regime. And, you could not see your daughter, as it were, on the side. So, if you would not leave your daughter-hating wife, how could you see your father-loving daughter? At the other kerb a minicab gurgled and at a halldoor Adam glimpsed a youngish man in shadow, unshaven, and then stepping down the path on stupendous legs a gloriously cascading blonde. He wondered . . . *was* she? At three minutes to eight in the morning? O'Malley sorwe she was.

'Hi.'

'Morning.'

She ducked for the cab, all legs and bum, and under navel Adam twitched. O'Malley swore it was a twenty-four-hour business. Adam thought of Angie.

It wasn't always like that. Times were – When? Misty '73, the Yom Kippur war. Surface-to-air missiles, tanks screaming, Israeli gunners in foxholes on the Golan heights pang! pang! pang! pang! They watched it all from Sidcup in a three-dimensional aurora of Mary Jane. On the rope carpet Alison was pliant, come on, come on, she had on some silk things and each ripple of her body through them was like hard water. She had to have him straight away, delicious, Jesus! Adam!, and he was like the big gun on a tank, holding fire for hours and hours as Migs rolled and popped in the white sky. The best, yes. Next day his knees had been raw as rumpsteaks.

With twin cams roaring Sabin passed, beard rigid over the steering wheel as Adam joined the road which joins with Station

Road, Sidcup. What would leaving her be like? Financials aside. He wondered if he had the stamina for trauma. What about her position? She had her mother, Ella, God, with whom she got on, and her perfectly normal sister, Sara, with whom she didn't. At Christmas she got invitations to the parties of publishers she once worked for. They had friends. In Bexley, the Luptons. But the Luptons made a foursome. She had a friend in Cornwall named Joy, a crime writer, God help her. O'Malley's wife, Mary, a born-again-Christian, New Yorker, a mouse, also devoted to the Sidcup Film Society – which the world knew ended its season that night, 17 May.

'Good morning, Mr Coleraine.'

Behind knobby fists holding up her handbag like a shield, shuffled Mrs Littlejohn, neighbour on the other side.

'Good morning.'

'How is Mrs Coleraine?'

'Better than ever. Vanished, in fact.'

'Very well, thanks ever so much.'

On the wide station approach Adam bought the *Guardian*, went through at eight-o-three and three minutes later was whisked away by the half-full, faded-blue, dirty-floored Dartford to Cannon Street train.

They swayed by way of Lee, by Hither Green, by dreary, weary Lewisham. Past blocks of flats and blocks of flats the wheels said flats-in-blocks and flats-in-blocks; and cem-et-ery cem-et-ery cem-et-ery. Adam looked out at a water tower and thought of his penis; of the blonde girl on the road, query hooker; of Angie; of Zoe; of Zoe's suddenly possible but previously unconsidered pregnancy. He took up the paper which told of murder in Belfast and brought him back to Counsell. Why did Counsell do it? When Counsell went out before Christmas with his gall bladder, Adam as the acting Grade 5 had had to be given the lock combinations of Counsell's metal presses and filing cabinets. Not only why did Counsell do what he did in Belfast, but why did he then bring the damn report back with him to London – into the Home Office! – where in all likelihood it still was? Adam just could not fathom Counsell. O'Curry, O'Daly, O'Dalaigh. Adam saw blue hoops around their names like the so many nooses of a hangman. O'Donnell, O'Donovan, O'Dee. Counsell had hopped them! The

British Home Secretary had put his hand on his heart and had sworn it could never have happened, and all the time it was Robin Counsell, now the Grade 5 of the anti-terrorist division, who'd been feeding Loyalists and off-duty reservists with names from a report he should never have had. Clyne, Hyne, Ryan. Dead men. Rochford, Rossiter, Roche. Adam could see the names on their tombstones.

Coming up into May morning light at St James's Gate, Adam saw fifty yards down Petty France, combat-geared and webbed, Coldstream Guards, some stage of security alert or equally perhaps a drill. He took out and showed his pass and saw in his wallet the picture of Zoe that he liked. Young, tall and ripe. Black, glossy hair that came to her shoulders, just, persuasive lips, big, almondish, upward-sloping eyes. Structures existed for Zoe to live within; she was not concerned with creating structures. She was going to be a Vogue model, she told him, and had tried to describe the boundlessness that came with such ambition: 'New York; L.A.; you use the world, Adam! You just . . . go!' Zoe was not selfish as Alison insisted, just beautiful and young. She told him how she wanted to get both arms around the world, how she wanted to jump in the air and yell to everyone, 'Hey! I'm where happiness is! I've been told the Earth's inner secrets!' Now Adam had been made to consider that she might be pregnant. Adam nodded good morning around the lift. No way. As he got to his office, Rose, his secretary, followed him in and said: 'We've got an IRA bomb gone walkies.'

*

Two weeks had gone by since my first summoning to Iveagh House. A man with less experience might have assumed the amelioration of circumstances but I knew better and Janet Moriarity's request that I come and see her in St Stephen's Green proved my point. Janet's office was on the top floor of the Department of Justice and took in all of St Stephen's Green from its two windows. Dick Jennings was with Janet and gave me a friendly smile on his way out. At five it was already dark.

'They're coming back, in two days time, 8 December,' Janet said. She began careful steps up and down her ample office, hands clasped before her. 'Can we speak privately?'

21

'Certainly.'

'This government has six months left in it, eight at the most. Their record on the economy is a stretcher case, fifty thousand people a year emigrating, Irish agriculture is a Third World set up. But what they have got – by fortuitous timing, nothing more – is the real possibility of a change in the British position on Northern Ireland and the chance to put it over as their own achievement.'

'A timetable for a British Army withdrawal?'

'It began at the British Tory Party conference last summer,' Janet said, unwilling to be rushed. 'A motion calling for troops to leave Northern Ireland, narrowly defeated. There's a widespread weariness with the whole Irish question, not to mention the fact that Labour's talk of quitting the province is suddenly a vote winner.' Janet spoke to the Green. 'So, embryonic commitments to even and universal franchise, to constituency redrafting for achieving this, to real power-sharing. Even a blueprint, however theoretical, yes, for a withdrawal.'

'The Unionists will never wear it.'

'The Tory Party has suddenly tired of the Unionist Party.' Janet came over and sat down on the other end of the sofa. Whereas the various parts of her were angular – her big hands, her glasses, her knees – all together they somehow combined to make her warm and desirable. 'I hate this part of the job,' she sighed, 'the party political dimension, the pursuit of power above everything else. It's pitiable to see the likes of Harry St John Flanagan doing somersaults – or our Minister.'

Although the pursuit of power was commonly thought to be the principal which guided Janet's every move, I had not realised the extent to which she was prepared to be my ally. She crossed her legs and cupped both hands around her knee.

'They appear to want the report you wrote on the Provos, so clearly, although the report was written for and delivered to the RUC, they no longer have it. In the light of the current shoot-to-kill rumpus, perhaps that is entirely understandable: your report might constitute a very embarrassing link.'

'There's talk of yet another enquiry,' I said, meeting her eyes.

'Yes.' Janet was looking at me but seeing the logic unfold somewhere more distant. 'But why do they want it? What's the wider context? What happened that might be relevant, around or

22

just before the time that Arty was first approached in Lisbon?' She went to a sidetable and switched on a smart, white kettle. 'For example, early September, the head of Home Office F4 division, Sir Robin Counsell, suddenly resigned. No explanation, no golden handshake, nothing. Why?'

'He's ex-NIO,' I said. 'He was in the sort of position to have delivered republican heads.'

'Of course,' Janet said vigorously, 'of course. But scapegoats are needed in these matters, moral victories are required. If Counsell's the victim, why haven't we heard?' She brought over cups of tea with milk and a sugar bowl. 'What else?'

I scratched my head. 'We refused them an extradition back in June. Could that have led to anything?'

'A crabby judge with a bellyful of sour port refused a request because the Brits spelt "Eire" wrong,' Janet said dismissively.

'These things rankle, although hardly at this level, I admit.'

'The idiots have lost your report, Brian,' Janet said quietly, 'but why they want it again is frankly beyond me.' She drank her tea. 'The Minister sent for me this morning.'

Some sins you pay for forever.

Janet was frowning. 'I don't think he knows any more than I do, I don't think so. But he has an election to fight and he desperately needs a Northern Ireland.'

'What if he were to learn that the report no longer exists?'

'That's the point, Brian. He knows of you. He knows you could write the whole thing out again word perfect.'

The china cups were at odds with Janet's world: delicate, fluted things with tiny handles.

'I'm too old to repeat my mistakes, whatever the reasons may be,' I said.

'That is, of course, your decision,' Janet said.

We stood up as Janet's secretary, a man in his fifties, came in with a wire tray of papers.

'They'll have to kick me out,' I said. 'I'll go down to Ballyvoy and pick mussels off the yellow rocks for the next ten years.'

Unexpectedly, Janet burst out laughing. 'The next thirty by the look of you,' she said warmly and again I saw the woman in her. 'Brian . . .'

'Yes, Janet?'

'No matter what happens, I hope we can be friends.'

'You can take that for granted,' I said and I thought for a moment, but for the secretary's presence, she would have given me her cheek for kissing.

*

That day is now equally slow and fast for Adam Coleraine, each second has its place, yet he can recall everything in a single, trembling second.

Late afternoon, back from the Yard, climbing between colour-coded floors overlooking St Paul's, he felt irritation: that morning the Yard had raided houses in Cricklewood and captured bomb-making equipment and lists of targets, but no players – they'd moved out three hours ahead in a van which had been missed. Now the van was said by the lab to be likely as not full of nitroglycerin. Counsell had been briefed: his Yorkshire voice on the phone had had wind in it like a bellows.

Rose tramped in. 'Sir Robin's been on again. He's put tomorrow's meeting with the permanent secretary back to ten.'

'Anything else?'

'Ashby wants to talk about Syrians.'

'I'm sure. What about the Press Office in case this thing blows?'

'They're briefed. Working on a couple of statements. They've promised to let you know.' Rose's voice shifted down an octave. 'And a lady called on your private line but didn't leave her name.'

Adam looked at her; Rose knew Alison's voice.

'Thank you, my Rose.'

Ample Rose, gathering papers, glancing back, saying 'good acting', Rose knew Alison's voice; but who knew Adam's private number? Just Alison. And Angie, but she had never once called. He dialled out.

'If you *do* call, I'm in London for the afternoon . . .'

Alison's voice could be honey or vinegar; the message for that evening was, repel!

'It's just your husband calling,' he said flatly, then added with a touch of vengeance, 'at ten past five.' He dialled again.

'Hello?'

'Happy birthday.'

24

'Adam.' Angie always said it businesslike in her clipped, correct accent.

'Slippery slope, huh?'

'Don't make it worse,' Angie laughed. Then, without expression, 'Do you have a problem? Do you want to call it off?'

'No.'

'How is England?'

'Chipper. Burping now and then. Aglow with health, actually.'

'Thank goodness it's in good hands.'

'See you in a couple.'

Adam cleared his desk and locked away in cabinets and drawers everything that could move and fit. The contrast between the two voices sucked the morning up to the minute – the fact that Alison's venom was taped seemed to confirm the person she had become and Adam thought briefly of life where all dialogue between them was transacted by means of recordings. Everything existed as a possibility except leaving. 'Leaving' for Adam existed in a vision of Pom, nose and eyes red, rambling on and on; in the words 'glandular fever'. Tall and lithe and flat chested. Coolly beautiful. On a big, wooden frame, slowly a tapestry was forming that would go on to win a prize in London. Slowly it formed no matter how much Adam screamed for it not to. He stopped screaming when she looked at him, but her cool, sloping gaze through the drift of her cigarette smoke made Adam's heart turn. It was the strong part of her that Adam saw in Angie and liked. She was in Zoe, in eyes that had looked for thirty years from a leather-framed photograph. The second leaving involved no murmur, no ripple. He left Pom in smoky Carlisle like you glide out a punt on a still day. Two amputations that should have been gaspingly horrendous, both occurring in their own ways with brutal casuality. In matters personal, Adam sought to avoid a third.

Walking to the lifts it occurred to Adam that Angie never said it was she who called. But he never asked. The doors glided open and an executive officer from F1 walked out and held them.

'Did you hear about a bomb?'

'Bomb?'

The doors shuddered; the man took his hand off.

'We've just heard a bomb's gone off in central London.'

25

Adam was prisoner the twenty seconds the lift took to reach the top deck canteen. There is a phone by the cash register.

'Ashby,' a voice snapped almost as soon as Adam rapped out the code.

'Coleraine. What's happened? Where?'

'Paddington. We're this second on to the Yard.'

'Is it a big one, do you know?'

'We don't know for sure but we don't think so. Where are you?'

'In the canteen.'

'Give me half a minute,' Ashby said.

The Drama Society members were gathered in a semicircular cast, all eyes on him.

'What does it look like, Adam?'

'Paddington,' he replied. 'But not big, they think.'

There was that realisation that history in the making is a peculiar vacuum. Adam grabbed the ringing phone.

'Coleraine.'

'Very preliminary, okay?' said Ashby, clipped. 'From a plod at the scene. Bayswater. Worth Street. It's our van alright. A man and a woman seen leaving it forty minutes ago. Chaos at this point but no fatalities.'

'None?'

'That's the word. They're saying because the nitroglycerine was loose it lacked punch.'

'Warning?'

'No. Bastards. Another twenty yards they'd have got people coming out of Paddington.'

'The Minister . . .'

'We've said we'll get him the information as soon as the Yard decided to talk to us. Whenever that will be.'

'Find Sir Robin, patch him through here. Set our committee up for a meeting. Keep the information coming.'

The Dram Soc had been sorting itself out on other phones; two higher executives from the Fire and Planning department asked to be excused. Adam thought of going down to Ashby, but then, with no casualties, Ashby was gaining experience.

'Very well,' said the lady from Statistics who rose twice a week from the confines of her profession to flower as producer-director of the QAG Dram Soc. 'Donal, Seumas. Your best, please.'

Two chairs and a small table had been set apart; Adam and a youngster from F4 took up their positions with scripts.

' "The cold chaste moon . . .",' prompted the director at Adam.

' *"The cold chaste moon, the Queen of Heaven's bright isles,*
Who makes all beautiful on which she smiles;
That wandering shrine of soft yet icy flame,
Which ever is transformed yet still the same."

Ah, Shelley, Shelley, you yourself were a lovely human orb shining through clouds of whirling human dust. *She makes all beautiful on which she smiles.* Ah, Shelley, she couldn't make this thrice-accursed room beautiful – '

' "Ac-cur-sed!" ' the lady director spat. 'Spit it out!'

' "Ah, Shelley, she couldn't make this thrice-accursed room beautiful. Her beams of beauty only make its horrors more full of horrors still. There is an ugliness that can be made beautiful, and there is an ugliness that can only be destroyed, and this is part of that ugliness. Donal, Donal, I fear your last state is worse than your first." '

'Donal is a poet, remember, Donal.'

Adam wrote on an imagined pad:

' *"When night advances through the sky with slow*
And solemn tread,
The queenly moon looks down on life below,
As if she read
Man's soul, and in her scornful silence said:
All beautiful and happiest things are dead." '

'Wonderful, wonderful power in that,' raved the lady director-producer. 'Don't forget how these lines will come back to haunt him. On we go. Seumas.'

The telephone at the desk rang.

'Ashby. I've got Sir Robin, Adam, but to fill you in. The van went off just before five. Anti-Terrorist confirm a lot of people with shock, cuts from glass and so on, but no fatalities. Emergency procedures are up and running smoothly, although Bayswater and Paddington will be sealed off for bloody hours.'

Adam asked, 'What about the Minister?'

'Tice has briefed him. A short holding statement will go out soon ahead of a full statement tomorrow in the House. Here's Sir Robin.'

Counsell knew the responses in his sleep. 'Got the gist. Sounds it's limited.'

'Sounds that way.'

'Post mortem in morning,' Counsell said. 'Anticipate flak.'

'We're meeting shortly.'

'Do you need me in there?'

'I really don't think so, Robin.'

'Good lad.'

'I'll let you know how our meeting goes,' Adam said. Counsell clicked off and Ashby floated back in again, but Adam could tell he'd always been there.

'It's coming faster now,' Ashby said. 'A massive traffic jam north of Oxford Street and building. Media in full cry, of course. Committee ready to meet here in fifteen minutes.'

'Keep it coming.'

'Seamus, "I don't know . . .",' prompted the director-producer.

' "I don't know how a man who has shot anyone can sleep in peace at night," ' cried Seumas.

Adam returned to this bed/chair: ' "There's plenty of men can't sleep in peace at night now unless they know that they have shot somebody",' and he thought of Counsell.

' "I wish to God it was all over," ' said Seumas.. ' "The country is gone mad. Instead of counting their beads now they're countin' bullets; their Hail Marys and paternosters are burstin' bombs—" '

'Buurrstin' bombs!' burst in the director-producer, exploding air with little hands. 'Burrstin.'

"—burstin' bombs, an' the rattle of machine-guns; petrol is their holy water; their Mass is a burnin' buildin'; their De Profundis is 'The Soldier's Song', an' their creed is, I believe in the gun almighty, maker of heaven an' earth – an' it's all for the glory of God an' the honour o' Ireland." '

The phone rang.

'We're getting numbers now,' said Ashby. 'One fatality, I'm afraid. Two serious but not critical, up to a dozen with nothing to worry about but cuts and shock.'

28

'One fatality?'

'Definitely only one, they say. A woman. Could have been a hundred times worse.'

'A woman?'

'Evidently hit by a flying particle. Fell under a parked car which is why she wasn't spotted.'

Woman, he thought; he thought, repel! 'Who? I mean, her name.'

'We haven't got a name yet, I don't think. No.'

Little pins, thousands of them, began to bother Adam's head. Ashby said, 'The Yard say things are almost back to normal.' Mere nettle rash assaulting the bulwark of his reason.

Ashby said, 'Everything's go for the morning, except the Perm Sec now wants it at nine instead of ten.'

'I'm on the way down now,' Adam said. Name. All over London men wanted a name. He stabbed for the external line and twice fluffed Sidcup. One ring. *If you do call,* I'm in London for the afternoon . . .' 'I'm sorry, I must call it a day,' Adam said to the lady director-producer.

He chose the stairs to gain time. All his brain could chatter was numerics. Five, ten. He called. Her. Van went up before five. Ten minutes. Between five and ten past. Five. At six-o-five, now, she should be home. Great, warped gulps of bitter time surfaced everywhere like night toads, yet already, in ghoulish self-defence, structures of justification were springing girder-like to fortress his crumbling ramparts. They had loved. They both had changed. Was it natural for a mother to reject her own flesh and blood? Fourteen hours tearing did it. On the fifth floor Adam walked towards Ashby's office, light-headed, praying to be mercifully granted feelings of decency. Ashby and four other executives from F4 looked up as one at his entrance. Her name. They knew. It.

'Adam.'

Professional. Considerations.

'Adam, for you.'

Ashby held a phone. Which Adam took.

'Yes?'

'It's me, Adam. It's Alison.'

A gentleman in the mould of Mr Salman Rushdie carefully tucked long-stemmed, tulip glasses into folding tissues of paper. Peace flowed through his slender, deft fingers. Peace dwelt in his oak wine bins and shelves. Peace smiled lazily outside on the smooth white masonry and pretty pediments of Victoria. Even in the abandoned *Evening Standard* billhead – 'Carnage!' – askew in the trellis of its empty corner box was there peace. The two wrapped glasses were wrapped again like swaddled babies. Between the first mention of a woman dead and his arriving in Ashby's office, every shadow in Adam's mind had crystalised with fiendish starkness. The twins joined their mother bottle in a brown bag.

'That will be twenty-six pounds altogether, please.'

Then her voice. For a moment, like someone just awake who has not yet remembered rancour, Adam's fondness had surged. 'You're alright.'

'I'm in Oxford Street, Adam. There's been a bomb somewhere as I'm sure you very well know and the trains are all delayed. I'm calling to say that there's no way I'm going to have time to go home now – I'm going directly to the Film Society.'

Bowed out through the shop door into diminishing sunlight, on a kerb, Adam paused. Relief fast fading he had neglected to ask Alison was it she earlier who called. But Rose knew Alison . . .

Three white steps marched up to a brass buzzer.

'Push the door.'

A long, dim, hall led to stairs with lights strung along the banisters like on a runway. Out came the bottle and, from their tissue, the glasses. Uncaging, twisting, silently outslipping, he brought to each rim a puff of froth.

Da dah da dee do

'Da dah da dee do . . .'

'Glasses!' Angie in shorts that showed long, brown legs, in a sleeveless halter that showed long, brown arms coated with sheens of fair hair, took a glass and kissed him with lingering precision. 'Hmmmm.'

'Happy whatever.'

'Thank you.'

Air, trapped years ago in Epernay, bubbled for the skylight. 'Delicious!'

'Just a marrying of sweetnesses.'

Angie's face was square and strong and her hair was cut to just

30

below the line of her jaw. She linked Adam into a rectangular room that overlooked through generous bow windows a garden. Varnished floorboards were brightly rugged; the walls were whitewashed and brightly hung. Angular lighting devices on skinny stems leant over the chairs of lowly-slung designers. A white cat arched primordially by the leg of a square table on which were set out the tools Angie needed to fulfil the peripatetic ambitions of young ladies: a telephone/fax, a computer and printer, a Filofax index, and a thick volume of airline schedules.

'How goes the slave trade?'

Angie rested on the edge of the table, crossed her ankles and sipped her champagne as the cat sprang to join her. 'I have a little tart in upstate New York who claims she's being raped by a man of eighty. I have an anorexic in Lyons. I have two homesick Italians in Utoxeter – you're good at languages, want to take them off my hands?'

The contrast to Alison, Angie's strength, was what Adam loved.

'You are the only person in the world I know who bothers with birthdays – that includes me.' Angie tossed her head as if to dismiss the entire calendar. Gently Adam fed each glass and the cat purred his erect tail across the ripple of Angie's arm. '17 May. We lived in Bournemouth. My father always brought me for a donkey ride. Each year the man said the same thing: "You'd make a regular little jockey, luv." Once he let the beast go and it trotted out on an outgoing tide through half a million seagulls. I screamed all the way.'

Adam frisked on all-fours. 'Hee-hah! Hee-hah! Up! Up!'

'Don't be ridiculous!' Angie laughed.

'Hee-hah! Hee-hah!'

Tittering, Angie mounted, clinging with her knees. Unsnaffling his collar, Adam directed her hands. The cat, with jungle knowledge of things awry, crouched.

'Adaaaaam . . .!'

Adam plunged. Braying hoarsely he cantered to rise in mid stride over a pouffe.

'Ayeeeeeeee . . .'

Stumbled, but a fine recovery. With knee-thumping concussion the partnership loped over colourful sward, little to choose for bawling and screaming between jockey and ass. Reedy lights were scattered like trodden cow parsley, an ottoman was crossed.

'Adam . . .!'

Adam stopped in mid-canter and caught her softly as she arched out on to her hearth.

'Aik-aik-aik-aik.'

She gasped. 'What's "aik", for God's sake?'

'Seagulls.'

She pulled him down to her mouth. Slow urgency guided her tongue. Adam slid the straps of her halter to bring lips to her shoulder, to the wide, smooth splay of her breastbone, to the rise of her small breasts with their tight berries.

'Not here.'

Standing Adam scooped her and she encircled with her long legs his waist so that even in transit they could kiss. At the bedroom door with new vividness she explored Adam's head, inside it with her delving tongue, outside with her racing fingers. Adam lowered them onto soft patchworks. Adam's thumbs softly polished her nipples; Angie's mouth-feasting begot a slow rotation of her hips. Commandeering Adam, despite his size, she ground into him with intense tongues of inevitability. All her ribcage was in Adam's hands. Adam and Angie rocked in crashing waves of bed lurching. Never once did she relinquish Adam's mouth as the crazy room dived and reared ship's cabin-like and items of domestic furniture overturned and fell tinkling. With all Adam's power he gleaned into her bare loveliness with a massive thrust to the headboard and in great gasps of soft shuddering pleasurement they sank with a crack of ruptured timber to the floor.

In towels Adam followed the damp path of footprints to a sunny cushioned corner of the living room where Angie and her cat lay, feline sisters. Adam sprawled between them and squeezed the last two half glasses. 'I have been meaning all day to ask you.'

'Hmmm?'

'Did you call? My office, leave a message?'

'Did I . . . ?'

'Speak to dear Rose?'

'Of course not.' Angie rubbed together their feet. 'Did the play go well?'

'There were interruptions.'

'What's it about?'

'It's O'Casey.'

'You, of course, have the lead.'

'With Burton and Olivier dead . . .'

'What's it about?'

'A pot, who pretends he's a poltroon. He tries to gain the respect of a girl.'

'Tell me the poetry he writes.'

'He prefers to recite Shelley.'

'Recite the Shelley he prefers.'

'To be honest, I can't remember.'

'Adam, who made the world?'

'What?'

'Adam, I asked you something,' said Angie at the sharp end of her voice. 'Who made the world?'

'It came from nothing, a meeting or melting of gases, a gigantic, cosmic fart.'

'And man?'

'Eels and things.'

'Pain and pleasure?'

'A huge zero sum. One man's loss, another's gain. Useless to worry.'

So intelligent her face, relentlessly so.

'I sometimes fear for you, Adam.'

'Nonsense.'

'You have this unhappy knack of taking nothing seriously.'

'Angie . . .'

'Shush. I owe it to you to tell you.'

'Dear girl, "owe me"? Why?'

Angie arched lightly her whole length in the sun, a cat. 'Because I love you.'

Two hours on the road of identical houses became quieter the further from Station Road Adam walked, leaving behind youngsters on skateboards leaping fluid bridges of air. Compared with Victoria, a living village with its shops and movement, Sidcup seemed more a place to park in, not live, life garaged overnight. Adam turned left, the familiar, last leg of his morning jogging circuit, and felt suddenly out of breath. What had started a couple of years ago as lust good and simple had wound vinelike around them and although never had Angie asked anything of him or demanded that he make a choice, equally never before this evening had she affirmed love as a motive. Adam felt tired, all the bomb business taking its toll and then on stage again next morning for the post mortem. Counsell must be chortling that he bagged as many as he did when he did. Why did Angie turn him on so much, even when she was, in fact, berating him? Why did he like that? Strange. All those years ago it had been the other way around with Alison, her size, his, she used to say he was impaling her. Liked that, at the time. Power. Now the other. Couldn't bring himself to touch. Too weak. Might break. Strange, because once exactly that had been the turn-on. Like Sidcup, small and neat. Submissive. Victoria dominated. Age. What would it be like to leave Sidcup, Adam wondered as he reached his front door? To relocate, preferably near water?

'Hellooo?'

On the train he had wondered if he would find Zoe alone, or Alison and Zoe, or Alison alone if Zoe had gone out because when she had got home Alison was out, or none of these possibilities.

'Hellooo?'

The TV room was empty. So was the kitchen. There was no note, no evidence of recent cooking. Adam took the stairs in threes; he stopped at Zoe's room; he knocked. Opening the door, he peered in, trying to discern her sleeping head by windowlight.

'Zo?'

Opening the door of their own bedroom he went through to the bathroom and relieved himself of champagne. Coming back downstairs now he could see the green eye of the telephone answering machine blinking fretfully. Adam rewound it and the tape clipped its full length in a staccato of little squeakings as Adam reminded himself to ring QAG.

'Hello, you two.'

Zoe never played up Adam's and Alison's differences.

'Dad, I called your office but you were at a meeting. I don't know if you got my card, I'm coming home tonight, for the night, okay? Don't worry about food or anything. I'm in Bristol now and

I'm just about to get a train to London, okay? So I'll see you both later.'

The machine whined. Adam had heard her every word and was now stooped, mesmerised, as the words gelled to produce another word, the name of a place that he could not bring himself to say.

'It's just your husband calling – at ten past five.'

The sound of his own voice, at ten past five. Into the hall were now playing a wailing succession of tones and disconnections, muffled background chatter, the acoustic of someone calling and calling but declining to speak. And this stomached him. The tape was rewinding having run its course but Adam stood in the same position. He cast around him as if to verify that he was in the right house. To move was disaster. To speak was to break the safe spell of time suspended that he had spun around him. And then, following the sound of a car, up the path came footsteps and in the frosted panel was the outline of someone tall. Zoe.

'Zoe?'

Adam's voice, and the bell, broke the bittersweet crust of the moment, recreated past and present. Adam lurched forward.

'Zoe? For one dreadful moment . . .'

But Zoe had her own key.

The older officer's hair was white, his cap held deferentially under his arm.

'Mr Adam Coleraine?'

'Is it. . . ?'

'Sir, I'm very sorry, but I'm afraid we have some very bad news.'

*

Christmas decorations were up at the top of Grafton Street as I made my way to Iveagh House. Harry St John Flanagan's assistant had been assigned to receive me: we walked up stairs under a gilded clock, chiming.

'Not a bad day,' the youngster said. 'Cold but at least not wet. The new year will be on us before we know it.'

He led me to a small, overheated room got up in expensive fabrics and appearing little used. A single, high window revealed the back of the Department of Justice. The counsellor took my coat saying he would tell them of my arrival; a reappearance by 'them'. Almost immediately Janet came in. She was dressed up this morning: in a navy blue outfit, a fluffy, white blouse, even eye shadow.

'Good morning, Detective Superintendent.'

'Assistant Secretary.'

As the counsellor left us, Janet sat opposite me, forward in her chair. 'It's the same line-up as last time, except this morning the Minister is here and the Garda Commissioner.'

I had never met Cyril Maguire, the Minister for Justice. A slick forty year old from the midlands and a recent cabinet appointment, he had inherited the seat from his father in the manner of these things.

'The Brits want the report,' Janet said simply. 'They say they're within sight of indicating an unspecified number of RUC officers for unlawful killing but that they need your report to bridge the gap.'

I have always found the term 'unlawful killing' amusing in a macabre way.

'Do you believe them?'

'Whether I do or not is now irrelevant,' Janet replied tersely. 'I've been in there for over an hour arguing our position. Sir Trevor Tice is simply adamant that they must have it. Fundamental to the "overall current position", as he puts it.'

'Maguire can kick for touch.'

'He's tried to, half a dozen times, but Tice is having none of it. They withdrew to a private room thirty minutes ago. Tice knows the political situation here. He knows he's got him.'

I said nothing; there was nothing to say. They must have remembered my opposition the last time to have mounted such an attack; but they must also have remembered my capitulation.

At a soft knock the young counsellor put his head in: behind him I saw the recognizable face of Cyril Maguire TD and that of Commissioner Joe O'Keeffe, a humourless stick in uniform of whom I'd always made a point of seeing as little of as possible.

'Ballyvoy, remember,' I said under my breath and Janet, once again unexpectedly, gave a warm laugh as the minister walked in. Joe O'Keeffe, an arid miniature, came busily around his minister's elbow. Word had it that they viewed one another with equal distaste.

'Superintendent.'

'Commissioner.'

'Minister,' said O'Keefe, 'this is Detective Superintendent Kilkenny. You haven't met him, I believe.'

'No.' The minister was smaller than he seemed on television and had learned to make a big thing of eye contact. 'Detective Superintendent Kilkenny.' Much groomed, nonetheless his power was too new to him to be carried inconspicuously. 'Sit down, sit down,' he scolded and propped himself on a little stool although chairs were not in shortage.

Commissioner O'Keefe spoke: 'Detective Superintendent, I think you have a good idea of the reasons behind our meeting today.'

He awaited my reply, a headmaster's trick.

'Yes, Commissioner.'

'I have personally reviewed a British request for a copy of a report already delivered to the RUC. I have been assured by Minister Maguire of the absolute propriety of the same request. Therefore I am authorising you to release to me for onward transmission the information asked for, whether in original form or by way of redraft.'

Neither Maguire's nor Janet's eyes left my face.

'I'm sorry.'

O'Keeffe drew in his breath. 'Detective Superintendent?'

'I'm sorry.'

Sudden blood livened up Joe O'Keeffe's face, but Minister Maguire kept his footing. 'Detective Superintendent Kilkenny,' he said, holding up one hand, 'I've spoken with Leinster House. you with me? We're satisfied that the circumstances of the British request are very exceptional, in more than one sense, let me add.' He smiled to put himself and me bravely in the same little boat headed for tricky rapids. 'The commissioner's directive to you is non-appealable.'

No point that I could see in making a defence: my stand had up to this morning been the policy of the Irish government.

'Very good,' said O'Keeffe, all business. 'I assume twenty-four hours will be time enough?' He took out a little card. 'Ring me direct if there is anything else you wish to talk about.'

'Nothing has changed, Commissioner.'

Joe O'Keeffe's top plate snapped out and in again like the cuckoo in a clock. 'You've – been given – an order.'

'With which I'm not complying.'

Breathing noisily through his nose, the commissioner jumped for the door and snatched it open. The counsellor had been hovering but skipped when we appeared. Twenty yards on down the corridor I saw the usual Special Branch outside the room of the last meeting.

'Who in God's name do you think you are? Eh? Just who?' Joe O'Keeffe hissed. 'Never in forty years have I heard such insubordination – and in front of the minister!'

'I didn't mean to put you in that postion, Joe,' I said, 'but I was faced with no options.'

'Let me tell you this much, Mr High and Mighty, I don't care who you are or what you know, I'll break you, I swear to you. I'll strip you of everything. I'll hang a bell around your neck. Is that what you want? Ruin? For your children and your grandchildren to be tinkers, is that it?'

'Fuck off, Joe,' I said. 'Mention my family again and I'll kill you.'

'You're suspended, you bastard!' Joe O'Keeffe gasped.

I could see Arty shuffling up like a man short taken. 'Well, that suits grand,' I said. I left him with Arty and passed the counsellor at the top of the stairs.

'Your coat . . .' he diplomatically began.

'Post it,' I said.

Down in the hall, the guard gave me a strange look.

'Brian!'

Janet was at the top of the stairs, the light from Iveagh Gardens behind her. The way she stood, the way her body was arranged, was feminine and vulnerable.

'The minister would like a word.'

Janet and the counsellor looking down; myself and the guard, the hall door open, looking up. I wondered if she would disappoint me with a direct appeal, saying something such as, 'For me, please'; but Janet, as I was learning, rarely disappointed. I went back up.

Joe O'Keeffe and Arty were not to be seen; neither was Minister Maguire going to let it show if he'd been ruffled. He looked over my shoulder as Janet came in behind me and closed the door.

'Thank you, Detective Superintendent. Brian, isn't it?'

'Yes, minister.'

'Brian.' We Irish have a great penchant towards first names. 'Brian, Janet tells me that no one in the force can touch you for ability. Isn't that so, Janet?'

'Yes,' said Janet coolly.

Even then, I still felt free.

'The three of us here in this room, Brian, are all intelligent, successful people,' Maguire blustered as if he was wary of anything he might say in front of Janet. 'I'm not going to bullshit you or threaten you. What I am going to tell you is that of this minute my political future depends on you.'

There must have been mockery in my eyes.

'Very well. Will you wait here a moment, please, Brian?'

I watched them leave the room, Janet and the minister for justice. I had been the exception, Gilly, I had almost finished the course intact. I had been downstairs in the hall, I'd been at the door when she called me. 'Brian!' I could have kept going, taken the Dart to Sutton, skimmed stones over water for the rest of the day and when I came back, although I'd have had problems to face, equally Tice and his lot would have been gone. With a proper knock the door reopened and in they came.

'I believe you have met Detective Superintendent Kilkenny, Sir Trevor?'

'Yes of course. Hello. How do you do?'

'Thank you, Janet,' said Maguire curtly.

As she left the room, Janet gave me a look of genuine curiosity that made me wonder whose side she was really on. What I really would have liked to do was to follow her, but Sir Trevor Tice had folded himself into a deep armchair and had laced his hands in their usual position. He looked at home, one knee peaked sharply over the other.

Minister Maguire, sitting said, 'I have decided that the only way to be absolutely fair, Brian, is also to be absolutely frank. I'd like you to hear what Sir Trevor has told me this morning.'

Sir Trevor Tice lowered his hands. 'I believe you have your

reservations about our intentions, Superintendent,' he smiled, one clubby old chum to another.

'I don't believe I said that.'

Tice gave a short, workmanlike sigh. 'Events in London, 17 May. A van with nitroglycerin was detonated in Paddington by the IRA.'

I remembered the bomb.

'One person was killed, a young woman. Her father worked as a Grade 6 in Division F4 of the Home Office Police Department. Her name was Zoe Coleraine.'

*

'Mr Adam Coleraine?'

'Is it. . . ?'

'Sir, I'm very sorry, but I'm afraid we have some very bad news.'

Adam staggered, sank.

'Grab him, Colin, there's a good lad!'

The two policemen ducked and hoisted his shapelessness.

'Walk him around in the air,' instructed the older man. 'Blimey, he's heavy.'

'Agh . . . agh . . .'

'Keep him moving, Colin, that's it.'

'Agh . . . gok . . . gag . . .'

'He's trying to be sick . There you are, sir, it's alright, just lean on me and we'll walk about a little.'

'Bla . . . blo . . .'

'Shouldn't we get a doctor, Bill?'

'He'll be alright,' Bill said.

Wheeled in a ring dizzily, juices oozed from new crevices and spurted into his angles and other devices, and he looked out from behind skull pits and said, 'Oh God . . .'

'That's better, sir.' Bill winced in concern. 'You're never going to get a worse shock, if I may say so. Tragedy, a beautiful young girl like that. I'm sorry I had to be the one to tell you.'

'Ahhhhhhhhhhhh . . .'

'He's trying to say something, Bill.'

'Just keep walking him, Colin, keep walking him.'

Dragged in an unending circle of freezing night summer.

'You're shivering, sir. If you feel up to it, we'll go inside now and make a nice cup of tea.'

'Noooooh!' A bog monster assaulted in fossilised sanctity. Adam reared.

The two policemen looked grimly to one other.

'Mr Coleraine.'

Adam lurched around at the woman voice, he pitched under curiously peeping stars.

'Mr Coleraine, we want to help you.'

Shapes grew beside the policemen: a glorious young woman, a dark young man.

'Adam, isn't it?'

'Adam gaped.

'Adam—' She stepped forward. 'My name is Becky. I want to help. This is Ricky. We live across the street. We know what's happened. We're heartbroken for you.'

'. . . Zoe . . .'

'I know, Adam,' this girl called Becky said and he could see tears on her fine face. 'I know,' and she caught him there and then as he fell.

'Where is Zoe?' Becky asked the constables as they helped her with him.

'St Barts, miss,' panted Bill. 'There we are now, sir. Like an angel, she is, miss. Could be just sleeping. Can you stand, sir?'

'Someonesgottofindmywife.

'We've tried to, Adam,' Ricky said. 'We've tried the Film Society but they were through there an hour ago.'

'Zoe!'

Lights were going on in other houses and a peculiar silence was descending on that part of Sidcup.

'Zoooooooo . . .'

The policemen exchanged looks of intent and made to step forward but Adam sprang back, quivering. 'I want to go to Zoe!' he shouted, knowing he could prove it all a huge mistake.

'We'll take you there directly sir,' said Bill. 'That's if you're sure you . . .'

'Oh, no, no, God.'

Becky linked Adam and, softly rubbing his hand, said, 'We should go now, constable.'

Out of Sidcup they reeled wailing in blurs of phantasmagoria. Very soon at any moment in just a second everything would snap into atoms of daylight and Adam would spring from bed and leave sleeping Alison and run come back and shower the whole, impossible thing away. He gasped '. . . did she suffer?'

Becky kneaded Adam's hand as Bill squinted in his rearview. 'Died instantly, sir.'

'Who . . . found her?'

'I did.'

Policeman Colin was little more than a schoolboy. 'You. . . ?'

'I was on duty in Paddington, sir.' Colin turned in his seat and lights from oncoming cars showed fair stubble on his young, uncertain face.

'Go on.'

'I heard the explosion. Like someone hitting a wooden box. I was the first into Worth Street. There was smoke, water shooting straight up into the air from a pipe, people crying and standing around with their faces cut from broken glass. All . . . all the parking meters along one side had been flattened.'

Adam hadn't grasped it yet; he hadn't grasped anything. 'I began to evacuate people from Worth Street in case there was another bomb. I was terrified, I must admit. The whole place felt so dangerous, you know?'

'Oh my God.'

'Then I saw her shoes.' Bill negotiated an intersection with the lights against them. 'She was lying beneath a car, fifty yards away from the point of the explosion, at the Bayswater end. I didn't want to pull her so I got down and crawled in beside her.' Young Colin's eyes checked with the wheel. 'She wasn't conscious.'

'But . . . not dead.'

'She was unconscious, sir. She was dying.'

Becky's eyes released pearls tumbling down on to her's and Adam's hands.

'All my other feelings, of fear, everything, just went. I put my arm around her and got her, got us, out so that we were lying half out from under the car, on the footpath. But I didn't leave her, sir.' With a snort not out of keeping with his dignity the young policeman began to weep. 'She was perfect, you know? She was so pretty and I could see she was slipping away and there was nothing

42

I could do, there was no wound I could see. Her breath was getting it hard to come. She had her bag around her neck, I opened it and I found her credit cards and things with her name on them. I imagined her as my sister, sir. I brought her head into me so that her ear was beside my mouth. "It's alright, Zoe, it's alright, Zoe", I kept saying. I didn't want the ambulance people to move her until I knew for sure she couldn't hear me, sir.'

Adam still could not grasp why these new people were all at the dead centre of his life. It was beyond grasping. They had pulled up under a door canopy. A woman in blue stood there beside Alison's brother-in-law solicitor, Ronnie. God knows how he got there, Adam thought. As Becky got out of the police car, Ronnie dived in.

'Adam.'

Ronnie's long nose was a ski jump, Adam and Zoe used to laugh at it. God what a time to think of that, of how cross Alison used to be at them. But Ronnie's presence was a further filled-in square of darkness.

'Adam, what can I say?'

'. . . so it's true . . .'

'Adam, you don't have to do this. I can do it. I've seen her. Seen Zoe. From the point of view of formal identification, it's done.'

'Ahhh, God.'

'She's . . .' Ronnie's face dissolved without warning, tumbling in all directions from noisy, streaming nostrils. 'Oh, Jesus, she hasn't a cut, God help you, I'm so sorry, I'm upsetting everyone. I'm sorry.'

'Who . . . How. . . ?'

'Alison,' Ronnie babbled, 'Alison rang me and told me a few minutes ago. Oh, God help you both.'

Very much a group now, policemen included, they clip-clopped down corridors of linoleum into the pungent vapours of rooms presided over by a man in a short-sleeved, green smock. The blue woman smiled a jaw-splitter. 'I don't think we've ever seen such a beautiful girl,' she said. 'She's perfect.'

'Never,' green smock assented, 'no mark.'

Bill crossed himself as the blue woman looked at Adam with professional expectation.

'God help you,' whispered Ronnie.

Adam went on alone. He was gripped by raw terror and in half a dozen strides was coated every inch in ice-cold film. He stopped. Through a door, whiteness, and a baffling scent, not unsweet. In the centre of the whiteness, in more whiteness still, grew a body shape out of the white litter it lay on.

Adam stumbled back. 'No.'

'There's nothing to be afraid of.'

'No!'

Becky detached from the grim little knot and hurried to him.

'Mr Coleraine,' said the hospital woman with practised kindness. 'Come on now. For the little girl. She really is beautiful, you know.'

Adam looked at blonde Becky who was all at once as familiar to him as any other woman he had ever known. 'The day Zoe was born, that night, she'd taken fourteen hours to be born, gave Alison hell, tore out of her, Alison never forgave her.'

'It's alright, Adam, it's alright.'

'That very night I held her, a little thing, Alison didn't want her wouldn't feed her although everyone begged her to she'd suffered too much although it's nothing to what she'll suffer now.' Becky put her arm through his. 'That first night I said to Zoe I can't feed you sorry and she smiled to say up to me that's okay. Do you know what I thought at that very moment when I was meant to be stupid with happiness? I thought one day little girl you'll stand watching them lowering me downwards when your own kids will be either side to help you over the old man's going.'

His arms flapped up and fell back again, several times, like a big bird, rooted. Then up and down in uncontrollable stammers went his shoulders.

'The queenly moon looks . . . down on life below,
   As if she read . . .'

'Adam.' Becky reached up tenderly to wipe his eyes.

'. . . Man's soul, and in her scornful silence said – '

His hand struggled with his twisting face.

'*All beautiful and happiest things are dead.*'

'She is beautiful,' smiled the woman, 'and she is far, far happier than we are.'

He wept five minutes in that spot, in Zoe's marble vision. Then Becky wiped his face with a paper towel.

'We're going home now, Adam,' Becky said.

Time was neither friend nor enemy to Adam, neither rigid nor plastic. Zoe had died a lifetime ago in the last few seconds the year after the year after next. People came and went below him like faces passing a reviewing stand. An undertaker who said, 'Sorry to have met you, sorry.' At the grave, ten or a dozen young men and women, Zoe's friends, some of whom shook his hand, and Pom, out of place, embarrassed evidence of natural order stood on its head, floating along like someone hired for the day from a waxworks.

Standing in his house, in a room swirling with people, Adam saw Danny O'Malley angling for him.

'Adam.'

Danny was a very big man, as a big as Adam. He manoeuvred Adam into a bear hug. 'Adam, I don't want you to say anything, but what I have to say can be said in a minute. Zoe is alright, okay? I know this. We are the ones in pain. I knew today in that church, at that grave, that Zoe is happy. She's laughing! She's praying for us, Adam. She's lucky because she's free. Beyond hurt, alright? We're hurting. I say we, of course I mean you, because my hurt is a bruise but yours is a massive gash, an amputation, an arm – you know? – a leg, gone, it can't grow back, but the hurt won't always be there. Zoe is always there. She's with Christ. She's so . . . so lucky! We're unlucky. We're left in a deep hole that we can't get out of. But if you look up you can see the sky! Christ is the sky, Adam. Find Christ and you will find what you have lost and the courage you need to go on. I love you.'

'Danny . . .'

He hid from them in Zoe's room. With its long-forgotten music contemporanea it was really the room of Zoe years ago, of Zoe before she left. The bed seemed small as he lay on it, his feet propped on the endboard, staring as she must have done at the sky, looking for some sign. Everything was gut. Blood boiled and pounded, the sky he knew was blue he saw through a prism rinded. Exhausted by his sheer inability to attempt understanding, he began to search for clues to what had happened in Alison.

She was different. She had left him in the pew that morning and when she asked from the lectern in a voice rock steady, 'Death, where is thy sting?', the great yearning for such strength among the gathering of casual believers had been palpable. She had caught his hand when he came in from Barts and said: 'Poor Adam.' Other women in the room had wept but Alison's face had shone with the brittleness of shells. He and she had entered a new world whose creation had come with the first words of the policeman. Everything had changed, had become unendurable.

'Adam?'

'I must have nodded off.'

'Adam, Mr Counsell's downstairs and asks if he can have a word before he goes,' Alison said from the other side of the door.

They squeezed between withered box to stand by mounds of rubble and in sunlight Counsell's skin seemed to have acquired an even deeper pallor, as if called for by the occasion.

'Not to worry about QAG, now,' Counsell soothed. 'Minister's thinking too, let me say. Four weeks, five. Six. Whatever you need.'

'Thank you, Robin.'

Counsell's voice dropped, 'Can only conjecture how you must feel about those who did it, Adam.'

Adam heard for the first time a voice within Counsell's voice. 'I haven't thought about them,' he said.

'Your point taken,' Counsell murmured. 'Beneath consideration, they are. Know dirt we do, don't we, Adam? Know what must be done with dirt we do, don't we?'

Adam stared into Counsell's blue eyes of the pattern willow.

'Don't we?'

Words burst from their chrysalis in Adam's belly and fluttered upwards, naked butterflies of admission to what he knew of Counsell's deeds, words somehow beautiful in their innocence. But a mere embryo of reason pleaded within him to hold. Then shoes drifted into his vision. A goateed, small-sized man, and a woman wrapped in fur stood there in the stone and splinter.

'Mr Coleraine.' The man was holding a hat. 'We're from next door. Sabin.' Rich perfume wafted out from the Levant-skinned coziness of Mrs Sabin's unseasonably mink-lined bosom. 'We are sorry, we want you to know that.'

46

'Thank you.'

'My wife remembers your girl.'

'I remember her from when she was, you know, a child,' thickly said Mrs Sabin to Adam, to Counsell. 'I said to Mr Sabin that little girl next door, for her own good she's too pretty, I told him.'

'Mrs Sabin said that to me many times.'

'Every day she comes home from school, I used to just look at her. Good for your eyes, she was.'

'You're kind.'

'When we have a daughter, I said, I want her to look like that little girl in next door.'

'Mrs Sabin always wanted a girl like your little girl.'

'But I never had a child and now it's too late.'

'Has anyone offered you some tea, a drink?'

'Tea we have had,' Sabin said, putting both palms up. 'We must be on our way. If there's anything at all in the way of soaps or perfumes you think might cheer Mrs Coleraine up, you may not know this, but I got an extensive range, feel free, anytime, just call me up, if I'm not there Mrs Sabin always is, my pleasure, you understand.'

'Thank you,' Adam said, 'very much,' as the Sabins picked delicately their retreat.

'You were about to tell me something,' said Counsell softly.

'Just that this alters nothing, Robin,' Adam replied. 'Nothing at all.'

What were those days to Adam Coleraine? Parched of mercy, that is all. He functioned: rose, ate, drank, retired with an oblong shaped and purple coloured pill as birdsong rang over Sidcup, awoke to the same birds' singing as if they had never slept. From being unable to think at all of Zoe, now he could think of nothing else. He had failed in every way: failed to make safe the streets Zoe walked on, failed to bring her safely to motherhood. When she had called his office he had failed to be there – who knows what might have happened, what change in her plans for that day might have resulted had they spoken? Adam skimmed the seas of his memory for the one extra sprat of Zoe that he craved. He hovered and plummeted for the infinitely expandable instant when Zoe crossed the line; for the moment between her striking and her falling; for the twilight between her light and forever darkness. He replunged for that vital moment that seemed to hold in its slippy shell all the essence of what Zoe and he meant to one another. He panned and panned for that priceless speck of time. Each day there came a point where his love was so much pounded it had to cease. He took the pill and night came for him as for all men, unmindful of their tears or of their joy.

Alison was another matter. From his cushioned chair by the back step Adam could see Alison on the go. She had an old tautness to her that had made her good once at tennis. Writing a letter and speaking on the telephone at the same time, she moved in a blur as if each second without movement or physical purpose was a snare to be avoided. She ate little; her new dynamic was fuelled other than by food. She never mentioned It. She swirled in a cosmos of which Zoe was just a part, not the centre; in an hour she would leave for two nights in Cornwall. Adam preferred the Alison of the old world whose life had been marked by a desperate frankness and whom he knew he had made unhappy.

From the back step Adam heard the telephone ringing in the empty house. It took a moment to remember that for two weeks Alison had dealt with telephone, with the rush of hospitality on offer, with the priest's persistent kindness, with the daily calls from Ella, Alison's mother, and from Pom; it took another moment to remember where the telephone was: the combination of telephone, answering machine and hall held associations that Adam was not yet ready to face.

'Hello?'

'Adam, Robin.' Counsell's voice sounded rich and confident. 'Some good news. Police in Dublin this morning arrested a James Pierce Doyle on a charge of being a member of the IRA. Three months ago this Doyle was resident in Cricklewood, they think in the house the bomb came from. Our key, he is.'

'Yes.'

'Irish promise us a hearing in the next few days and a swift extradition.'

'Thank you, Robin.'

'Thought you might like to know that we're all working for you. How are you, lad?'

'Taking it easy.'

48

'Envy you. Your wife?'

'Very positive.'

'A lesson. Should you feel like a chat, Adam, feel there's anything you want to tell me . . .'

Alison returned from Cornwall with a cold. Daylight filtered down a culvert between the bedroom curtains as Adam stood at the bed's end and Alison's larger-than-normal eyes turned to him unblinkingly. Her hair fell limp and greasy, and about her, hands clutched at bedclothes, there lay an air of seige.

'Is there nothing I can get you? You haven't eaten today.'

Alison coughed and Adam went on one knee. There was something of old Alison in the coughing frame. 'Alison, I . . . people say one should talk.'

Her eyes were empty, hollow. Like a top that had lost it's motion, she was a-tumbling.

Downstairs he ambled from kitchen to back step and out of breath sank into the chair of plumped cushions, unbuttoning the waist of his trousers so that the sun was presented with flesh and pubis. His beard after two weeks immunity sprouted fuzzily. He felt exhausted by the practicalities that had come to chafe him: Alison's need of care that he could not give, the food that needed to be bought, the undertaker's prompt invoice that needed to be paid: waxed special American oak, raised lid, preparations. He was letting go: decline had its own sweetness that Adam was learning to savour. He thought of Angie, wondered where exactly he was and what he was doing the moment Zoe died, tried to imagine if he was thinking of Zoe at that moment, wondered if Zoe was thinking of him, remembered a dream he had either the night before or ten years ago in which he and Zoe had shouted at each other. Realising piercingly and afresh how impossible was the reality he was now drowning in, Adam heard a rapping sound. Repeated.

In the hall Adam saw the silhouetted someone rap the front door again. Rap rap. He opened the door and peered unsurely. 'Yes?'

'I'm wanting Mr Coleraine, please.'

'Yes?'

'Mr Coleraine? I'm Giorgio.'

A steel-flecked mane of tar ringlets coiled by sallow, coal eyes down over the white collar and purple tweed shoulder pads of an open-shirted man on the doorstep.

'Gior. . . ?'

'Giorgio. Zoe's friend, see?'

'Zoe's friend?'

'We met at the funeral, remember?'

'We did?'

'Yeah.' Giorgio's hands came together, hairy as moles, and he fiddled around a gold ring. 'I got her things.'

Suitcases either side of burnished shoes. There swelled in Adam sudden recklessness. 'Please come in.'

'Can't.' Giorgio turned in the direction of a car with a woman at its wheel. 'Sorry again about everything, you know? Are you getting over it?'

'Please. For a minute.'

'Well . . .'

Adam stood, holding his trousers, as Giorgio dipped and brought the cases in. Through the kitchen Giorgio's hair bounced lightly and expensive oils lingered in his wake. In the back place Giorgio opted for the chair with cushion and crossed dun-flannelled knees and fingered a gold crucifix as his eyes roved wasp-like. Adam stared. He smelt Giorgio's sweet-smelling body with its clothes so far from the world of Adam but so near Zoe's. He wondered if by inhaling this man something of Zoe might come into him, or by touching him. Giorgio had finished buzzing the untidy kitchen, the furniture, the outside dereliction and looked at but did not meet Adam's mouth-drooping stare.

'. . . I think of her all the time,' Adam said eventually.

'Yeah. So do I,' Giorgio said. 'We talk about her.'

'We?'

'Yeah, I mean Zoe's friends as well as myself, you know.'

A long sigh came from Adam and he appeared to suddenly be asleep. The new thought that Zoe had friends whom Adam would never know seemed to threaten his memory of her. 'Such a beautiful girl,' he said without warning.

'Unbelievable,' Giorgio agreed.

'Skin like a young apple.'

'She had class had Zoe.'

'So full of life.'

'Yeah. Very popular.'

Adam sank again and Giorgio snapped a look at his watch, just as Adam relooked at him.

'I was in Milan, see?' Giorgio said.

'We were two of a kind, you know.'

'Spoke to her that morning. Called her in Bristol. She was happy, I can tell you that.'

'I can still feel her skin.'

'Flew home the Thursday, they give you British papers up front, you know. Jesus, couldn't *believe* it.'

'I know every inch of her. Her throat, her breasts, the small of her back, her thighs, her knees, her feet.'

'Don't know how I wasn't sick there and then. Talk about a shock.'

'I see her in the shower, I stretch my hand out to her wet skin and touch it. She smiles. My fingertips are still tingling.'

'Went straight from the airport to the hospital, you know, thought there might have been a mistake. Christ.'

'In a perfect world a father could marry the daughter he loves.'

Giorgio went still. 'Yeah?'

'Do you know the feel of her skin?'

Giorgio shifted uneasily. 'Yeah.'

'Unconsciously, subconsciously, oh God, who knows what is love between a father and his daughter? It's unique. It's perfect because it's unconsummated, incomplete, but how can something incomplete ever be perfect?' Tears ran down Adam's face. 'How do I know now if she really existed? I never was consciously aware of any incestuous thoughts. Now I don't know. I'm sorry. Do you despise me?'

'What you do is your business, my friend.'

'What was she like . . . in the hospital?'

'I like, you know, never saw someone dead before.'

Adam offered his pouring face to the sun. 'So . . . she was dead . . .'

'Sorry?'

Without sense or prospect there had come with Giorgio a window of mad hope, an untouched patch of reason holding out

51

that Giorgio might be able to deliver where all the laws of God and man had failed. 'Was she dead?'

Giorgio had decided to call it a day. 'Do you have anybody here to look after you, like?' he asked, getting to his feet.

'Please, answer my question . . .'

'Yeah,' Giorgio said, moving to the kitchen. 'She was dead. She was in a coffin, you know.'

'Wait!'

'Look, ah, ciao, mate, and mind yourself, alright?'

'Please! Please – don't – leave – me – please – take – me – '

Over the house came the sound of a car revving and squealing away. Adam could not move from where he had fallen kneeling with his hands emptily clutching the air between him and the deserted kitchen. With Giorgio sweet and seductive had gone the last hope of Zoe, nothing could have been easier than to curl up like a cat beside Giorgio, whatever else that might have entailed, to breathe him in, Adam would not have interfered, promise. Dismay, temporarily suspended, crashed back with impact loaded. Adam stumbled to his feet, face wet, hands out blindly. He had to talk, had to tell, he could not keep to himself what he had just heard without feeling the warm touch of another person, even a sick one.

He rattled up and in by the spare bedroom, old habit, sat panting on the bed, kicked off his shoes so that if she was sleeping his heels on the bathroom tiles would not awaken her and on stockinged feet eased in the bathroom door. The shower's whoosh met him. With a shout of terror he fell back. He crashed in again and down, mouthing bawls to Alison's bare body.

'Alison!'

Alison's head was forward dipped so that through steam her shoulder blades reared in twin gibbets. Either side of the shower's outer base her legs splayed like a cut-throat razor.

'Alison! Alison!'

Adam cupped through hair her forehead and propped her wetly back as water bounced out and down his sleeves. Clambering up he brought her slitheringly with him, trying to give her head some form but her went heavy hair everywhere defied him falling down, forward, bringing with it her head, her face. Sodden in his socks he splashed for their bedroom door, kicked it back, pulled her in

through, her heels eddying, water pouring from her head and from
her groin. On carpet he lay her sprawling, mouth round as an
apple. To her chest he rushed down but above the toil of his own
ears he could hear nothing. He battened with his mouth to hers
and with two massive contortions, first blew, then sucked. *Again!*
He scooped and dropped her on the bed with frantic gaping at the
breasts in their flaccid hanging, the wire ribs, the jut of primal
bone. Shouting, yelling out for someone, he upped and straddled
her, and with strung hands drove down their hard heels into her
chest and wondered would she shatter. Again. The water from her
hair ran down the pillows and onto the sheets and blankets and to
the floor. Forcing with a big finger and thumb into her mouth past
sharp teeth down into her throat he plunged his index tip and dug.
Alison spasmed and retched. Adam rocked back and saw a neck
pulse. Shouting anew, jumping off, he ran for the stairs.

'Hello?'
   'It's . . . Adam.'
   'Adam.' Angie sounded calm. 'Where are you?'
   'At. Home.'
   'Are you alright?'
   'My wife . . .'
   'Yes, Adam?'
   'She took sick a week ago.'
   'My God! Are you alone?'
   'Yes. I've got . . . to get out.'
   'Of course. When?'
   'Now.'
   'Of course. I knew you'd call.'
   An ambulance had come that day. Men placed Alison softly as
feathers on a stretcher, pumped her arm up and hooked a drip in.
Alison's removal greatly simplified Adam's isolation; contact with
her had taken him from the raw wire music of his soul. Reality to
Adam became a timeless, dream place. Out of soft whiteness Zoe
came running to be with him, shining. They roamed as now like
two puppies, yakking, never worrying that for company they
would only ever have each other. Adam left in his slippers.
Towards him around a once-familiar corner came the bundle of
shuffling Mrs Littlejohn. She looked at Adam sharply, then

stepped off their footpath and crossed the road, head averted. Adam's eyes blurred. Up the wide approach to Sidcup station he swayed. Head humming, he boarded the first inbound train.

Angie put him in a big chair by the window and put the cat out. Kneeling between his legs she grasped his hands and looked up at him, her square face taut. 'You know I couldn't ring.'

'I found myself praying to a God,' Adam mumbled. 'Is there such a thing? If there is a God, what is His purpose in allowing evil? If there's no God, can Zoe still exist?'

'If there is a God, to my mind He has some explaining to do,' said Angie tightly.

'All my assumptions in life have been wrong,' Adam said, 'all my expectations. I have no meaning.'

'Please, Adam, for Zoe,' said Angie. 'Were Zoe here, she would never see you in terms of no meaning.'

'Life has no meaning,' Adam trembled. 'It cannot be happy so why take it seriously? Why not laugh? Yet what is more serious than a dead child? How can you laugh?'

Angie stroked the ridges of his knuckles and the wide backs of his hands with their mattings of gingerish hair. She looked grimly out the window as Adam, his sprouting beard laid at her cheek, wept.

'On the way here, a woman, a neighbour, an old bag I've spent years being civil to, she crossed the road.'

'The world is full of inadequate people, Adam. The thing is not to let them upset you.'

'She did it because she's guilty of being alive.'

'We assume that suffering has some basis in logic,' Angie said and laughed bitterly. 'What fools we are!'

'I know how she feels.'

'Adam, you must allow time to do what it does best.'

'Why?'

'It's nature's remedy. Time. It solves everything.'

'No!'

'Adam . . .'

'You don't understand! How could you? I don't want time! Time is a thief!'

'Adam . . .'

54

Adam wept. 'Time separated Zoe from me. Time will finish her off. You see this head? On my knees I beg the real God if He exists to chop it off in exchange for one minute back of the time I've lost with Zoe. One minute!'

'God help you.'

'Time, time . . . Stop! Oh, Jesus, stop . . .'

Angie let go of him. At the sideboard she poured two tumblers from an amber decanter. 'What kind of people would plant a bomb?' she asked. 'If they could only see you now, the people who did it.'

Shaking his head, Adam said, 'They don't exist.'

Angie brought over the drinks. 'Filth.'

'They don't exist.'

'The trouble is they do.'

'You're wrong.'

Angie frowned. 'Adam?'

'They, whoever they are, don't exist. They are non-people. I don't see them or hear them, they never enter my mind and never will.'

'But you hate them,' Angie nodded, drinking, 'of course you do.'

Adam's head went to his knees. 'I hate myself.'

'Adam,' said Angie sternly, 'you hate the people who killed Zoe.'

Adam's face as he looked up at her was strangely empty.

'Very well, you don't hate them. Do you then forgive them?' Angie asked.

Adam closed his eyes.

'Adam. Look at me. Zoe demands more than this. She *demands* that you be outraged by the . . . foulness of whoever dared, who dared to take the most precious thing she had and toss it in the street like . . . like nothing!' Angie's fingertips cranked Adam's face to look at her. 'Look at me! You can't be indifferent. Adam! You *must* either hate them or forgive!'

'I'm finished.'

'You are not. I will not let you be.'

'I am nothing.'

'You are much more than nothing,' Angie said. 'Come and I will show you what you are.'

Making him drink the whiskey, Angie led Adam into her bedroom with the patchwork quilt and undressed him like an invalid. She lay beside his big body which was shivering in the June heat and with great resolve flowed her warmth into it. 'There,' she said and stroked his big face. 'Look how strong you are now, Adam.'

Although it was past midnight when he came home, Adam was drawn to his customary place beyond the kitchen. Angie's smell was on his hands; her words were in his head. In moonlight the garden had assumed a status impossible by day: scents from round and about had wafted in and mingled with the night light to give an impression of order and beauty. They had been proud of the garden, Zoe and he, had seen their desert as a rough jewel hidden deep in Sidcup's husbandry. The shrill of the telephone seemed like the distant revolutions of a night creature's wings.

'Adam?'

'Yes.'

'Adam, thank God, we've been trying to get you all evening. This is Ashby.'

Adam looked at the phone. 'Ashby.'

'Yes. Adam, we thought it best that you should hear this from us rather than read it in the morning.'

Adam shook his head. 'Read?'

'Adam, in Ireland, in Dublin this afternoon, the IRA bastard, Doyle, our extradition request was heard.'

To Adam Ashby's words had the partial clarity of a foreign language long neglected.

'I don't quite know how to tell you this,' Ashby said, 'but he walked from the court scot free. They said we'd spelt the name of their pissing country wrong, can you believe? Adam?'

'Yes.'

'There's going to be a bloody awful row, I can guarantee that,' Ashby said. 'It's obscene. It's as if they wait their moment. Everyone in here is most upset for you. The maximum pressures will be exerted, Anglo-Irish talks or not. I am sorry, we all are.'

Lurching back through the kitchen and out Adam gulped in sweet night and sat with a crash into his chair. Bit by bit the moon journeyed: Adam sat. He imagined himself rushing back inside to the understairs with its sweet smells of the past, flinging out magazines in bundles, suitcases still with airline tags, shoes that once had hiked the Chilterns, until lastly he fastened on the steel of a spade. He saw himself toiling nobly, spade clean between his hands, firm beneath his foot as he punched and stamped, levered and hefted, churning up the deep, ripe earth. Everything became possible that night. He saw all the foibles of his life, all his blind chargings and dumb attempts at reason laid out spoor-like behind him. He could fly. Over brown plateau and white, he soared. Towns nestled in the moulded indentation of down and dell. Twisting rivers, previously incoherent, suddenly flowed by way of softest marl in passages of utter rationality. Hate blossomed in the whisper of the jet-stream.

Through the blastproof windows of QAG, London simmered in its late August lassitude. Adam showed his pass and took the lift to the fifth floor, Division F4. He gained his office and inwards after him tramped faithful Rose.

'How blooms my Rose?'

'Gracefully, I hope. In a cottage in Devon with cool cider for the long weekend. And no television.'

'Then be gone.'

'I shall. Alison called.' Rose's mouth line showed a sturdy kinship. 'She asks, can you bring home something for your supper. She's going out.'

' 'Tis done. Now, Lady Rose, these lonely turrets flee! The days of summer shrink before th'equinox when rose's bloom shall wither on the vine.'

'We've become quite the gardener, haven't we?' Rose smiled. 'Have a nice weekend, Adam.'

Adam watched her away. As if nothing had ever happened he had the run of old. What was done was forgotten. Protests to Ireland over the failed extradition faded with the summer recess and Zoe's killers became as distant in the minds of those who managed policy as her fragrance had become to Adam. But in the sizzling weeks that had ended June and through wet, steamy July Counsell had resought his advantage.

'Purely in admiration I say this, but there are marriages that 'don't survive what you've been through, lad. Strain. Inability to communicate,' said Counsell.

'We talk – in ways we didn't before.'

'Never do, some people. Tragic,' Counsell said and poured tea. 'When you say you talk – I mean, that must be hard – do you go over the incident itself? Throw me out if I'm overstepping, it's just that I feel close to you in this, Adam.'

'We talk about the circumstances surrounding the bomb, yes. The perverse, millions to one chance of someone you love being a victim.'

'And the circumstances you talk about, operational details and so on . . .'

'Nothing ever goes out. You should know that, Robin.'

'Don't pick me up wrong, lad,' Counsell said, his jowls pallid and untinged. 'Helps to natter about these things.'

Work resumed as usual. Adam picked his way through delicate submissions; Ashby wallowed in Syrians and Serbs and Croatians and Palestinians, all of whom seem to have picked London as the great, international crossroad of disenfranchised dissent. Adam, no longer visible as a figure of bereavement, sank back thoroughly into the texture of everyday affairs as stones sink into grave-soil. Across at The Buckingham for the retirement drinks of a main hall plod, Adam was cornered by a grade 7 he barely knew. 'If I was you, with respect, I don't think I could contain myself, you know? Walking around free as air, the bastards are, I hear. Makes you lose your faith in justice, doesn't it?' Adam walked away, refusing to believe that Counsell would use such a crude, flanking movement; he still admired the system in a peculiar way – the way a schoolboy admired his alma mater.

London traffic rose in pitch and everywhere wristwatches began to chime and bells to toll. He regretted that he would have to leave his garden, veined with green hoses that carried water nightly to peaty soil, from whose fresh beds wafted tantalizing scents, up whose walls were rising on trellises the juvenile stemmings of camellia and pyracantha. Two evenings before when Alison had been taken driving – Adam never asked where – Becky had come to watch.

'This I don't believe.'

'You like it?'

'I see it and squirm at what's hidden behind my house.'

Adam put aside a rake and came to sit beside her. 'I've never thanked you properly, and Ricky, for what you did.'

'What? Forget it.'

'It was spontaneous.'

'Come on I said forget it.'

'Okay. But I couldn't have made it without you, alright?'

'Alright.' Becky lay back on tiny grass shoots, her feet poking tilled soil. She had on light jeans and a shirt that when she was a-lying parted to show the firm puddings of her belly. 'You've changed, haven't you, Adam? Like this garden. I don't know how exactly since I've nothing to compare either of you with before, but it's something I'm sure of.'

'We all change, all the time.'

'Not in the way I'm talking about. I didn't know Alison either – not that I know her now – but Alison hasn't changed, I'd bet.'

'Maybe you're right.'

Slowly she rolled over and looks up at him with clear eyes. 'You know something? I've changed too. People would laugh if I said it – but who are people? – who gives one shit? – but I know me and I know there's been a change.'

The same ferocious integrity had shone for Adam that night. 'Whatever happens, I hope you'll be happy,' he said softly.

'That's exactly it,' Becky nodded. 'I don't know how, but I think I have a shot at that now, somehow. In my life, you know, you have to be hard. But it doesn't go with being happy. You showed me how sweet softness can be.'

Adam had known her face forever. 'Can I ask you something?'

'Sure.'

'If anything happened to me, if I was run over by a bus or the like, do you think you could keep an eye on Alison? You know, help her over the hard bits?'

Sunlight made sparks on the fat tears that suddenly wanted out down Becky's cheeks, but she was too much the star to let them. 'Sure, Adam,' she had said, looking away. 'Sure.'

With whirring of revolving heads the weekend polishing began distantly. Adam rose from his desk. Nothing could be taken or touched that might speak of premeditation. Photographs, paper-

weights, tidy tubs, a favourite pen would soon all bear tags in their
limbo. With a final, almost fond, look, he made his way along the
corridor and into Counsell's office. Clinging smells of the man.
Adam's swift fingers spun the dials to clicking. Eight months. The
blue eyes had seen three seasons come and go. Adam squatted to
trundle out the bottom drawer. Surely . . . The floor cleaners
sawed and hummed in the shrinking distance. Box with steel lid.
Somewhere a telephone had begun to ring. Surely in Counsell's
convalescing mind there must have formed the first hatch of
suspicion. Adam's fingers rummaged, he closed on the report and
lifted it out. Why? Along its spine bound with white, plastic coil,
the buff cover of the report looked shabby. Three strides to the
copier in the adjoining office. He punched the button and it
groaned into life. Why? Why when he must have known? Surely
self-preservation alone. . . ? The machine sighed, 'Ready', Adam
tore back the top, slapped down the first, open page, hit 'Print'.
Vanity, it had to be, towering, arrogant vanity that had made
Counsell play God with these contents in the first place. Adam
peeled back the top, opened out the second page, slapped it down,
pressed 'Print'. Vanity that said you were first among men, that
righteousness would always prevail. Or an assumption that Adam
was on his side? Because Adam had known yet done nothing? The
unanswered phone rang on, persistent. Adam copied the third
page and saw with discomfort the thickness of what remained. Or
was this a sprung trap that Adam could never have resisted as
events had proved? Fourth page. The machine groaned and red
letters winked 'Paper Out'. The telephone rang on, expecting to
be answered. Adam folded double the report, shoved it inside his
jacket, scooped out the few printed pages and bundled them in
too, stabbed off the copier and crouching, shut the box, replaced
it, slammed shut the drawer, spun the lock, rose and strode out
looking neither way. In the lift thoughts bombarded him like
falling stars. He stepped out through the opening doors into the
main hall.
   'Mr Coleraine?'
   'Yes?'
   'One moment, if you would, sir.'
   As though mist a grey-haired constable approached.
   'Yes?'

'We won't be meeting again, sir.'

'I . . .'

'I didn't get an opportunity to say how very sorry I am. It may be out of place to say so, but I pray every night for your daughter, sir.'

Dimly Adam realised that he had attended this man's retirement presentation some weeks before. 'Thank you. Thank you very much.'

'I just thought if you knew that, then you mightn't feel quite so much alone.'

'You're very kind.'

The policeman looked around him wistfully. 'This is my last day. I'll miss the old place. It grows on you. But when your time comes, you must bow to it.'

'Yes,' Adam said, 'I know.'

'Goodbye, sir.'

He was let out into the mellow evening. All over England people were going home.

A Distinguished Career

Sir Trevor Tice brushed back an errant, blond lock of hair and looked wistfully at the sky through the high window of the room in Iveagh house. 'At the end of August last, Adam Coleraine disappeared.'

'Disappeared.'

'Disappeared, Detective Superintendent.' Tice smiled to show that he himself had not accepted the position easily. 'Literally.'

'Sounds like a person who might be dead,' I said.

Maguire looked at me and nodded as if this was a point he had already made; but Tice's head movements showed him not prepared to accept this as the sole possibility. 'In the absence of a body, death must always be in doubt,' he said. 'Coleraine's was not a suicidal character type and these things appear to run pretty much true to form.' Tice shifted his buttocks. 'On the other hand, a week after his disappearance we . . . came into good grounds for believing that he had . . . improperly obtained a copy of your report on Northern Ireland.'

'Outrageous, eh?' Maguire asked me with a shake of disbelief, although what exactly he considered outrageous was not clear since the choice was becoming extensive.

'And your conclusion, Sir Trevor?'

'Revenge must be the motive,' Tice indulged. 'But Coleraine is also, need I say, by definition, a repository of extremely valuable information on all aspects of British Government security policy.'

'You have made huge efforts to trace this man . . .' prompted Maguire.

'We have, insofar as we can without warning the IRA that there may be a walking Home Office encyclopaedia on the loose, done everything in our power to find him,' Tice said drily. 'But this is a man who won't easily be found, Detective Superintendent. A senior Home Office employee, as Coleraine was, has access to a wide range of documents, to passports, for example. He could easily have one *nom de guerre* – or ten.' Tice cleared his throat. 'He could easily be armed. We need help. Your report is his blueprint. With it we can find him.'

My first instinct was mirth and it was all the things that had not been said that I found so funny. Sir Trevor would wriggle but never would he actually admit to the abrupt resignation of Sir Robin Counsell, now abundantly clear, a resignation under a cloud of disgrace following the disappearance of a report that he should never have had in the first place. That Counsell had broken the Official Secrets Act by removing from Stormont to London a top secret report; that he had thus implicated himself as a prime suspect in an inquiry to which that report was central; that British Government assurances to us about the conveyance of such information had been meaningless, none of these matters would be given the flesh of words that day in Iveagh House, and I found that funny. Nor, reciprocally, would be mentioned the enlarging back into society on a pretext certain to grossly insult, the man wanted in connection with the bomb, never out of diplomatic nicety would that act of judicial pigheadedness be mentioned by our justice minister.

'Detective Superintendent Kilkenny, this is a matter of great importance and urgency to the British government, overspilling, as it does, into areas far outside those of just Northern Ireland.' Tice's long fingers floated in Minister Maguire's direction. 'The effect of the Irish government's acquiescence to our request in the matter cannot be overestimated.'

I struggled with my next instinct which was anger. It would be base of me to use my position to let Tice know exactly what I thought of him, of the people he worked for and their extraordinary incompetence; it would be stupid of me to take any personal satisfaction from the soothing noises that my anger would undoubtedly provoke.

'I would appreciate a moment alone,' I said, getting up.

'No, no!' Maguire was up before me. 'You stay here, Brian. Sir Trevor. . . ?'

'Of course,' said Tice dryly, unbending upright and allowing himself to be shooed out in front of Maguire whose attitude to dignity and office was becoming increasingly apparent.

Alone, several things assailed me, apart from the fact that what Tice had said seemed to have the ring of truth. The situation was extraordinarily untidy. A man loose, as it were, with my report, Irish republicans identified to him by name – not that that was guaranteed to find him what he sought, but I saw how easily he might imagine it could. I felt an unaccountable responsibility for the mess. Then there was the situation between the two countries: Maguire was an upstart whose earlier presumption that his political future might be in some way significant to me had consolidated my total indifference to him: but I had not spent the last fifteen years without forming an opinion as to the benefits to Ireland were Britain's army to get out. And finally, there was Adam Coleraine. If he was alive, not knowing him a whit more than a million other men whose only daughters have been taken, the utter agony of his situation ignited in me a reaction, and I made my mind up.

Maguire was talking to Janet, Tice to someone from the NIO, when I looked out. They came in and Maguire closed the door, carefully as a gun breech.

'I will not,' I said, 'give you the report.' I closed my eyes to shut Maguire off. 'But, if you wish, I will try to find him.'

You may wonder, Gilly, as I often do in the way of people with time for reflection, about the casting of each individual link in a chain of events. Vincent Ashe had come to me with a purpose; our chat at the Fianna had been anything but a chance encounter. By the time this had become clear it was largely irrelevant. If I noted the exact date after that first summer's evening that he called me up then I have long since lost the note.

'It's Vincent Ashe.'

I asked how he had been.

'The same as always. Wishing the good Lord had made days of more than twenty-four hours, too lazy to be up good and early to make use of the hours He gave us.'

I laughed.

'I'd like to chat about something.'

'Yes?'

'This evening?'

'Yes,' I said cautiously.

'Say seven. You know the first car park on Sandymount Strand after the Martello Tower, going out of town?'

'Yes, I do . . .'

'At seven, then.'

I stayed on until six-thirty in Harcourt Square, drove down to and across the Liffey, recrossed it after the Custom House and followed the cobbled quays. Under the gas silos and through Ringsend, my instinct as to what lay in store nagged me. My images of Sandymount that evening are of tide out, some families still playing in the slanting light, seagulls on the miles-out shore line. He came from right to left, hands in the pockets of ribbed slacks, the top half of him in a windcheater. As he came nearer, the grin in the skew-ways set of his jaw grew.

'My friend.'

His hand was as big as mine. He slammed the door.

'It's a poor sea as seas go,' he chuckled, 'but anything's better than a mass of still water.' The profile he presented to me was unblemished. He said, 'I'm probably offending a Roscommon man by saying that, you that have Lough Ree, water that you can swim in and fish in – and drink. You see, for us water was a magnificent god. He frothed and pounded every minute of the day and night at Miltown Malbay, a great, unsubdueable creature that ate bit by bit into our rock and to whom a million years was only a minute.'

It was only our second time of meeting, but to the match-like sailboarders over at Dun Laoire we must have looked ancient friends.

'Imagine a million years as a minute! Imagine our planet as a speck of sand on the great strand of God's universe! We may not be central to His plan but like the sand grain to the rest of the shore, we're an equal and vital part of it, of that I'm sure.'

As at our first meeting, I was learning that it was more profitable – and more pleasant – simply to listen.

'God made animals and He made man, but only to man did He give freedom of choice – which is also to say, the choice to be free! Imagine a gift from the hand of God ignored! Could there be a greater sin? How can we ever be free from sin if we do not rise above the station of animals and seize God's gifts?'

His voice rose and fell.

'Ireland is a beautiful woman. I'm sure you know infatuation, Brian. If you don't, let me tell you.

"My love consumes me.
I think of her and in the marrow of my bones
there springs an ooze.
I see her in chains and I feel myself rise.
All her smells are sweetness.
Wet, bedraggled, bloodied or bruised
Her beauty is unblemished."

I'm besotted with Ireland, Brian. If I could just fold myself into her and lie there close, she and me, I would happily die.'

He meant it, I think.

'But when someone you love is in chains, how can you die happy?' He splayed the fingertips of one hand on the windscreen glass. 'I am crushed by a dilemma, Brian. You see, from time to time I hear things.'

Over Dun Laoire they sky had begun to streak a little crimson. My nagging instinct had not let me down.

'Down here, up there. In New York as well. I'm welcome in certain circles. What I hear and see drags my heart in two directions.'

There was the feeling of being suddenly on the verge of something important.

'I read the papers and see things going off that I knew about three weeks ago. One part of me shouts, "God save Ireland!", but there's another part that's screaming, "God save Ireland from all of this!" Am I wrong to be telling you, Brian?'

'I don't think so.'

His breath came out, slow and rubbery. 'Thank God,' he said and made the sign of the cross.

So began a process of information transferral that, in the experience of the Dublin intelligence community, was unique. It outlasted by a distance the most optimistic predictions and was based on one rule only: that Vincent Ashe did not exist. Two months after Sandymount, two IRA suspects long sought in both countries were picked up in a bomb factory in East Tyrone with much fanfare and rejoicing. Two months later we intercepted mortars going aboard the Rosslare to Fishguard ferry. On my tip,

66

three Irishmen were arrested in Baden-Baden, brought home and subsequently convicted. My opinion was sought more. I rose. The picture in Dublin was increasingly painted by my flawless hand.

'I have no children, but I observe other people's – Tom's and Jim's, for example.'

A January night out at Dollymount with rain beating in from the Kish.

'For years they're a little clutch of tadpoles, all the same, their father's eyes, their mother's cheeks, and so on. You can't tell one from the other. They all smile up at me, their eyes full of gentle wonder and trust. Then lines begin to be crossed. One by one they go, each one different but all ultimately going in the same direction, and you realise that the transformation you are seeing is as inevitable for them as for the tadpole.'

I recall Dollymount particularly. The intermittent wiper cleared the water so I could see the wing mirrors.

'What is that inevitability based on? Nature? God? Are we not just copycat versions of the world that made us? Are we made in the world's image, or it in ours? What is a nation? It is the sovereign fusing of a people and a place in a process of evolution.

"My lover has no age.
She has died and re-greened,
Season upon season. Agelessly.
My lover can wait for me forever."

A nation may exist in infancy or in adolescence and it may even not be recognised by name. But like the child, with total inevitability, its maturity must eventually come.'

Later we drafted in over sixty men from as far south as Athlone. By way of Letterkenny and Milford we must have been stared at, Uzi-toting city slickers with our cut of having seen it all before. We sealed off the roads and the fishing port of Downings and at five in the morning when all men are meant to be lowest, we shot dead one man in his underwear and took into custody three more, every man jack of them lifers from both sides of the border.

I rose. But I was not alone in my rising. There were times when I might easily have broken the only rule – once with Arty, for example, when he was my Chief Superintendent and the mutual sharing of all our sources to protect the event of our own sudden demise was suddenly seen as critical and compelling – but I didn't. I played by the rules of my new partnership. I took out the targets Vincent gave us; I left untouched those Vincent said should be left untouched. I thought he was working for me but, equally at least, looking out over a wet Bailey in Spring or a windswept Portmarnock in autumn, listening to his never-quiescent mind in its ceaseless tussle with the paradox of the thing he loved, I was working for him.

They barter the future of the living.
The legacy of the dead behind closed doors.
What right have they to so deal?
I see a whole, complacent race led docile-like
And my gullet stales.
Rather a rat would eat into my heart.
We will blow complacency, into a million fragments
And watch it wither before storms of outrage.

I never wanted higher than super, which was just as well because four months after my famous report, the golden stream that had so long fed my ascent dried up. I could do nothing; it had always been his prerogative. There being no surer proof of performance than a lofty reputation, it took them six months up in the Park to twig that it was some time since I had actually delivered.

In such a context, going home from Harcourt Street with the file on Adam Coleraine, reading and rereading the information, realising with each passing minute just exactly how stupid the Brits had been but simultaneously grasping how we could help our-selves by helping them, it was with considerable misgivings as to my own circumspection that I lifted the phone and, for the only time in fifteen years, rang Vincent Ashe.

Vincent was not there. His secretary in Ashe Brothers was vague; he was out of the country, she thought; she would pass on the message when he got back.

In the fallow days that followed I had time to imprint on my mind everything Tice had seen fit to share with me about Adam Coleraine: his schools, his young life and marriage, his each promotion in the Home Office, all was there. I became aware of his extended family, out to Pom's widowed sister in Jackson, Oregon. They did not entirely dismiss the notion that he had been abducted and, in their early enquiries through Interpol, promoted that possibility. They knew about Angie, about her business. In early September, when she flew from London to San Francisco, she might have been momentarily flattered to know that a team of four Scotland Yard men hung every minute to her skirts. They knew about Adam's bank account, about the ten thousand pounds he withdrew over July and August. His credit cards, stockbroker, solicitor: all had been nitpicked, analysed and entered on a fold-out sheet that made him look like a tangled business organisation rather than an ordinary life.

Do you remember that last Christmas, Gilly? I do. I remember it now as a golden land that can never be regained. Nothing much was happening in the way of work. Janet had rung as the sky hung dead and heavy over Dublin. She sounded testy. 'How does it look?'

'I've put out a line,' I replied. 'Now I have to wait.'

'There's pressure the whole time from the other side,' Janet said. 'It's leading to impatience here.'

'Things have to take their course.'

'But the course is of your choosing, Brian.'

'The chances are, this man will be washed up tomorrow in the Thames.'

'From the Brits' point of view, better than being washed up in the Lagan,' said Janet tersely.

I could see how one would not want to get the wrong side of her. 'Coleraine's been missing since the summer's end,' I said, 'and even a standing army cannot find him. If he's up there, which I doubt very much, my way's the best hope.'

'So you keep saying,' Janet had remarked.

I thought about my last conversations in Iveagh House.

'I know you will understand me, Sir Trevor, when I say I want no help. No back up. No cover, however well intended. You'll have to trust me. If I find him, I'll let you know.'

'We do not propose to interfere,' Tice replied.

'In the course of this exercise it may be that other persons are . . . uncovered,' I went on. 'Such a situation, if arising, should not be taken advantage of by either side. And if Adam Coleraine is in possession of my report, then I think its proper place is in my hands.'

'The objective is clear,' Tice said stiffly. 'We are not interested in the extraneous.'

'We're all eye to eye on this one, Brian,' Cyril Maguire chimed.

'With respect, Sir Trevor,' I said, 'I would like to learn what your plans are for Adam Coleraine.'

Sir Trevor's icy sweep summed up what he thought of the workings of things this side of George's Channel. 'He will be repatriated, Detective Superintendent, with the full protection of the law,' he pronounced.

Having related the British undertakings in all their hollowness, it would be one-sided not to show how we matched them.

'Minister,' I said when the British entourage had been shepherded away, 'I'm sure you realise that any operations whatsoever by the force in Northern Ireland are expressly forbidden.'

'In cases where national security is at stake, exceptions arise,' Maguire nodded.

'Nonetheless . . .'

'The minister for justice has considerable powers for retroactive sanction.'

'From my point of view, sanction in advance would be better.'

'We wouldn't be in this position if you'd simply given them the fuckin' report, would we?' He smiled quickly to show that even friends quarrel. 'Ah look, of course I'll give you sanction in advance – what? – a letter, I suppose, I'll have to get advice from inside, privately, of course. I'll ask Dick Jennings to draw something up, something that'll be watertight from your point of view,' were his last words on the subject.

A routine description of Adam Coleraine went to our stations around the country, but this was done more in duty than in hope: if Tice with his great security apparatus, its tentacles slithering down through Kerry and Clare, could not find him, we had little chance.

We took off then, didn't we, Gilly? Away from the balloons and the bunting, we went to our cottage in Ballyroy that only the guillemot know. We sat on rocks, looking out on the cold sea that sat flat on a stony shore. We built a fire that we never let die, and lit tilly lamps, and went to bed in wool blankets laid out on wattles on the big, warm hearth. What I would give now to know that time again.

On the first grey Monday of January when the telephone rang I was sure it was Janet but the voice was Vincent Ashe's.

'Happy New Year.' He sounded as if we still did business monthly. 'I only get your message yesterday.'

'I need to chat.'

'Trouble?'

I hesitated. 'No, no, I wouldn't say that.'

'How about the place of our first date? Seven-thirty?'

I put the phone down slowly. It was the way he'd said 'trouble'. After a gap of over a year, it suddenly brought home to me that he saw us both as very much on the same side. I took the long, climbing curve over Dublin by way of Stepaside. The car park was empty. Looking out over Dun Laoire, over the sea in its glow of yellow winter, I realised I could never be on the same side as Vincent.

'Brian.'

He was at the other door in an Aran high-neck and a loose, corduroy jacket. We shook hands as he got in and arranged himself sideways, one leg tucked beneath him. He seemed not an inch different. 'Good to see you,' he said and the skew-ways grin lit up his long face.

'Long time.'

'I'm not down here as much as I used to be.'

'You haven't changed, Vincent.'

'Ahhh – ' He waved his hand. 'Does the sea change? Do the cliffs change? You'd say not, but everything changes. Everything. Changing even as we wonder. Time is the only constant, time never changes. When God and Nature and the whole lot of them are gone, time will be there, smiling like a sphinx at us.' He looked at me and smiled as if to say that he defied the laws he had just expounded. 'You wanted to chat.'

'I need a favour done.'

He nodded once.

'I need to find a man.'

He looked at me. 'Just a man?'

'He may be up north. We need him out.'

He sat back to study the night sea. 'Once there might have been a small part of me that thought there was a side to you, Brian, but I'm now sure that part would have been wrong. You are a man of honour. When you wrote out what they asked you, there were nights, I admit, when I wondered if you would tell them my name. But you never did.'

I could not help but smile in surprise. 'You . . . saw a copy of the report?'

' "The province of Northern Ireland is a jungle, not only in its extreme impenetrability but also in the multiplicity of dangers that exist for anyone venturing into its habitat," ' he said. 'You made our country sound like somewhere you had been on safari.'

I had fought before I wrote it, but I wouldn't tell him that.

' "Republican strongholds cover the entire province: from the border hills of Armagh in the south to the glens of Antrim in the north, from Derry in the west to Belfast in the east." '

'Okay,' I nodded, 'okay.'

He looked at me and slapped my shoulder. 'I love the part about a mass consciousness, the collective movement of a people who in the last election cast a hundred thousand votes for armed subversion. At least in some things you were a good student, Brian!'

'I regret that report,' I said quietly.

'Other people regretted it too,' Vincent shrugged as if to an inevitable force. 'People in Derry and Maghera, in Magherafelt and Ballymurphy and Augnacloy. But, in fairness, you kept back the names I asked you, Brian, and the ones you gave them, ach, I think they already knew.'

'I still regret it.'

'It marked the end of the road between us.'

'I regret innocent people may have died.'

'There was a great thinning,' he nodded. 'We caused much change, Brian, you and me. We shaped the universe those nights. We rose above the qualms of petty men and saw that blood at the birth of a nation is a thing of beauty.'

'I don't condone terror – by any name.'

He made a downturned mouth. 'What is terror? An erupting volcano? Did God worry about such things when He made the world?

"There was no smallness in creation.
He made the Alps, the Causeway of the Giants,
The River Nile
Without concern for pettiness."

When you create beauty, the concerns of midgets are forgotten, Brian.'

I asked coldly, 'Will you help me?'

'You want a man out, Brian,' he said slowly. 'I know you wouldn't ask me for something I couldn't give. You know our people up there, their hopes and dreams of which we've often spoken, so this man you want out couldn't be a weasel, could he? More a lost lamb he'd have to be, am I right? I'm sure I am.'

'He was bereaved,' I answered quietly. 'The bomb in Paddington. His only daughter.'

'Ahhh,' he sighed and shook his head.

'He's a Home Office employee. He took a copy of my report.'

Vincent looked over sharply. 'For what purpose?'

'Maybe he wants to get those who did it,' I said quietly.

Vincent's face showed disbelief.

'Grief drives men into places where reason would never take them,' I said.

'That report is over a year old,' Vincent said. 'It will tell him nothing.'

'James Pierce Doyle,' I said. 'Wanted in England for the bomb, a failed extradition. His name is in the report, for example.'

Vincent seemed impatient.

I said, 'Of course, Doyle could be dead, for all I know.'

'Doyle's is not a name that I'm familiar with.'

'Look, Vincent, I'm not asking something for nothing.'

'Friends can do that.'

'There are political developments. The dreams you often talked of could become realities.'

Our breaths spewed out in the silence and made mist on the window glass.

'Who is the man you're looking for?'

I told him; I gave him Adam's photograph. Vincent sat, his hands in his lap. 'I would most likely have come across him, but I have not.'

'He's undercover.'

Vincent shook his head impatiently. 'Not in West Belfast. Look, do you know he's in the North? That he's even alive?'

'No.'

'Why are you doing this?'

'Because I feel I should.'

'You're sure about the request made of you?'

'In what way?'

'That this man Coleraine exists?'

'You mean. . . ?'

'Never trust the Brits when it comes to Ireland, Brian,' he said quietly. 'God knows what they're setting you up for.'

I wasn't going to let him see from my face the doubts that he made rise inside me. 'This is for real,' I said firmly. 'This reaches to the top of both governments.'

'Nothing is for real, Brian. Nothing.' His hand went out. 'To all the years.' His funny grin was in its place. 'I'll call.'

He went down the sea wall and the night gathered him. I had expected a reaction from him at my mention of political dreams coming true. I began the drive back over the mountains. Why had he not reacted? Was it that if a dream came true it was then no longer a dream? At traffic lights, a car came at speed around the corner behind me and stood on its nose. Two men. A dirty number plate. On the green I went left instead of straight, up a steep road. I had not seen the car Vincent had come in. On a plateau I turned and killed the engine. No lights followed the course below me; no car's engine could be heard. I waited and watched for fifteen minutes but the night was empty of menace as the new year was of wisdom. I got home and sipped a whiskey and thought of the passage of time and the things he had said. I doubted Vincent then. I would not have been surprised if that night turned out to be our last. But four mornings later he called again.

'I may have something for you.'

I said, 'Good.'

'You know Butler's Bridge?'

'North of Cavan.'

'A pub called The Bridge on the Belturbet road. The car park.

Twelve-thirty. And Brian – drive the car you were in at Sandy-mount.'

The timing was off by a couple of weeks, that was all; had Vincent come back to me a week later, everything might have fallen very differently. I checked out of Harcourt Square on some pretext and drove up the Navan Road clear-headed. The venue spoke for success beyond expectation. He had no need to drag me up to the border were the news negative. Adam Coleraine was alive, he had been safely taken, we would produce him in Dublin to Tice and his lot; the last, loose end from a bad decision of two years ago would be tidied up on the borders of Cavan and Fermanagh.

Through Kells and Virginia the treeless hills rose more cluttered and together and little lakes appeared. In this scaled-down panorama a man could never walk out to his herding without his neighbour's knowledge. A low sun gave a bit of cheer to the stonework of the village bridge as I turned in the pub's car park and faced out, diagonally across from the turn to Clover Hill.

Twelve-thirty came and went. At ten to one the daylight was already past its best when two countrymen with the huddled look of endemic hardship drove up on the one tractor and went into the pub. Traffic was sporadic. A green van from the Irish postal service made for Belturbet; a yellow van from the Electricity Board pulled in beside me and four big men took out a Primus and put a kettle to boil. I was travelling light; my standard issue Uzi had stayed in Harcourt Street, as had the old Walther PP with which I'd trained my wrists even on the morning I'd gone to be married. At one o'clock the kettle boiled. A minute later, a squad car came slowly from the direction of Belturbet and passed without a glance. A school bus, empty, drew in beside the electricity men and its driver took out his foil-wrapped lunch. At ten past one, an old, white Fiesta nosed out from the Clover Hill road and hung for a minute. It flashed. The sweet smell of the van men's tobacco drifted over to me. The Fiesta flashed again, twice. I started up and we set off at a gentle pace in the direction of Belturbet.

I stayed forty yards back from the car which had two men in it. On a long, exposed stretch with grey lakes left and right they pulled in and I did likewise, engines running. No one got out.

Traffic went by for ten minutes. We resumed, unhurriedly and two miles short of Belturbet, with correct signals, we turned right, up a narrow road, past a sign saying 'Unapproved'.

I know fishermen who give their lives to these hill-fringed lakes and who joke when they get home as to which side of the border the trout came from. The road bent and switched and doubled back on itself and, where faint white crosses had been painted on the tarmac, the rule of England ended and the Irish Republic began. We turned up a narrower road and off it again, up a meandering boreen. In the half light the sight of smoke from the chimneys of cosy cottages made nonsense of terror and unrest. I still kept my distance from the Fiesta. We passed a woman in a paisley apron who paused from sweeping her step and cheerfully waved; more white marks were crossed; we crawled around another bend and I found myself looking up at a rifle.

'Out!'

A knitted face mask above the Kalashnikov.

'On to the cawr!'

'Car' is 'cawr' in West Belfast. I was too slow. He hauled me out and flung me over the back of the Fiesta. In four seconds he knew I was clean. I heard another engine somewhere behind.

'Hit the fuckin' floor! Faice doun!'

I was kicked into the car, my face rammed to pitted metal as the Fiesta screamed uphill. The driver kept shouting, 'Fuckin' basterds!' as he threw the car around bends. At every turn my head struck the seat mountings. In our swerving, swearing, lurching climb, each time the chassis scraped the collar of a pothole, the whole Cavan–Fermanagh border was engraved on my head. At last the urgency subsided. We continued to climb and dip, and we kept scraping the road, but 'Fuckin' basterds' was said more in derision than in alarm. Each time our driver thrashed through the gears exhaust belched up through the rusted floor and made my air poison. It was not the time to ask about Vincent Ashe, or where we were going. I tried to think of the cottages we were sure to be passing with their trim thatches and their comely women who would always help a man to a safe haven. I wondered about the fucking bawstards and I wondered about my own car. I was abruptly sick. The man with his feet on me swore and opened the windows. We lurched and bumped up a steep track and hit the lip of a cattle grid with a massive, clanging wallop that made every bone in my head and neck sing. We stopped. The doors opened and the weight on me eased. There were no voices or commands. I hauled out, shivering, and saw the inside contours of a shed. There were no hooded men, just Vincent, a few paces away.

'Brian.'

'Vincent.'

From within twenty yards came a burst of radio static.

'Come on in here a minute.'

I followed him into a room that was still used as a farm dairy: concrete floor and walls, a sink, a shore. One light bulb dangled. It was freezing and I had a massive headache.

'Why don't you clean yourself,' he said gently. 'There's a towel there.'

I slopped water on to my shirt front from the high tap and put my head under it for a full minute. I felt better when I turned around, drying myself, and found him looking cautiously at me.

'There's no, ah . . .' he half grinned '. . . no clever electronic toy on you, is there, Brian?'

'No, there's not. What's going on, Vincent?'

'You don't know, Brian?'

'Come on,' I said, 'you brought me up here.'

Vincent stuck his hands into the old windcheater. 'Then I've bad news for you.'

'What kind of bad news?'

'The kind that often gets worse.' He looked away so the light caught his eye. 'I passed your request on, you know? The people I have contact with, they don't know this man you're looking for. There's no one to fit the description. But you believe he exists, Brian. You think there's someone on the loose called Adam Coleraine and you believe that in finding him we might all be helping Ireland. I'm sure you do.'

I could hear cars outside. He was between me and the door.

'What do you mean?'

'You've been set up like I said you would be. They've used you, Brian, to try and destroy us.'

'You're wrong.'

'Am I? After that night in Sandymount, I thought it was the Dublin crowd. I didn't think the Brits would have the brains.'

'You're wrong!' I heard swelling shouts. There was a sudden change in the air. 'You're wrong, Vincent!'

'Am I? You've grown dull, Brian. You take everything for granted. We have our wits about us because we have something precious to fight for, but you and your likes are sleepwalking through history.'

The door came in. For a moment I thought the team of seething men had a weight between them, then I saw they were fighting for something at their centre. Crashing across the dairy they laboured. As they spilled back, I saw mouths open but wordless. A big, bald man lunged over heads with the barrel of a revolver. His face was twisted into an old root.

'*SAS . . . bawstard . . .*'

At their centre I glimpsed reddish hair and a bushy, red moustache. The scrum reeled and plunged. A boy with a white face threw himself in a vigorous leap over the top, grabbed two fistfuls of the red hair and brought the lot of them sprawling.

'*SAS bawstard!*'

'I swear to . . .'

'*Murderin' fucker!*'

I suddenly saw him clearly. He seemed frail and all red, hair and skin. I saw him try to crawl away. There was a big fellow with a black complexion who leapt on him and flung him backwards at the wall and grasped him about the nose and mouth the way you'd catch a beast, and pounded down the head as if it were a lump for breaking concrete. The white boy, deprived, stood shakily and began a desperate kicking. The red man's shirt had come away and I saw his freckled chest. Another lad burst away the big fellow's head grip with thick, tattooed forearms and began to punch down methodically. Someone grasped at the waistband of the trousers and dragged them down off the hips and set about the privates. Fresh men tumbled those in possession. In the brief space the bald man appeared on one knee. He plunged the nose of his gun into the red man's right eye and the explosion suspended everything. Egg-like white fluffed out through the red, red hair.

They all lay panting up at nothing. The only sounds were of breath gulped and radio static. The bald man got slowly to his feet, wiped his gun and tucked it into the band of his trousers: his face was smooth and regular as his head. My headache came back with

78

a surge. I had forgotten it; I had forgotten Vincent. I whirled around but he was nowhere in the dairy.

One by one they began to disentangle as players do after a maul. Some shook themselves and ambled out. A small-sized youth built like a ploughman paused at the body, leant down and carefully spat in the face. Even then, with a death on the floor as proof of broken promises, I still did not believe I had been set up. Even in the midst of such horror, Adam Coleraine appeared far too real to be the product of a civil servant's imagination.

'He was the dawg, yewr the rabbit.' The big, dark fellow addressed me. He was last up. His beard was several days rough but his eyes were clean.

'I want to see Vincent Ashe,' I said.

'Do ye nigh, indeed?'

To one side the white-faced boy was staring at me. Of the others only the bald man remained: he had found a water hose and was sluicing blood down a shore.

'Do ye indeed?' The big fellow brought over a stool and put it down. 'Put yer arse on that, Mr Dublin.'

'I'll stand, thanks.'

The boy came from nowhere. 'Put yer fuckin' arse on it!' he shouted. He stabbed his thumb over his shoulder. 'He got off light, y'understawn'?'

The bald man carefully hosed the wall. I sat.

'Ye'r going to teyll us thengs, Mr Dublin,' the big fellow said. 'Ye'r going to teyll us avir'thin'.'

'I'll tell you what I can.'

'Ye'll teyll us what yer fuckin' asked, pal!' The boy seemed to have taken a massive aversion to me.

'Take it easy, he den' say he wun'. What's yer neyem?'

'Brian Kilkenny.'

'What d'y'do?'

'I'm a detective superintendent with the Garda Siochana.'

'Ye'r goin' to cooperate, aren't ye, Brian?'

'I'll do my best.'

'Ther.' My questioner turned to his young companion. 'He's goin' t'coopereat, so there's no prawblm.'

'I'd like to ask a question,' I said.

'Be all means, Brian, we're in no hurry.'

'Where is Vincent? Why isn't he here?'

'Don't ye worry abowt Vincent, Brian. Ye'v enough to worry about, let me tell ye.'

'Has Vincent explained to you why I'm here?'

'Brian, take my advice, ye ferget abowt Vincent. He doesn' exest, a'right? The only thing that matters nigh in yer leyfe is the next few menets. Nothin' that's ever happen' to ye before'll be so importan'.'

I could hear the cleansing hose, but all I could see were his clear eyes.

'Who's the mon, Brian?'

'The. . . ?'

'The mon, Brian, the wee mon beheyn me here?'

The boy gave a snigger.

'I don't know.'

'Ye don't *know*? Jesus Christ, Brian, we thought he was havin' it off with yer missas.'

The boy laughed outright.

'I don't know him – and you know that.'

'I don't know nothin', Brian. He's been livin' with yez. Yez go for a wee dreyve and he's beheyn yez. Ye take the missas for a drink an' him an' a mate, they're watchin' yez. Don't tell me ye don't *know* him, Brian.'

'I don't know him,' I said, my anger all against Tice. 'I came here because Vincent asked me to. I never knew I was being followed.'

The big fellow shook his head. 'They were behind ye from Nawvan. Two cawrs. Fieve mile swop-ovir. Two more of'm awn a trackter in Butler's Bridge – a fuckin' trackter!'

'I didn't know.'

'He's full o' shet!' The boy was upset again. 'Ye'r a copper. Unless ye'r a fuckin' fool ye knew. Of course ye knew. How many more of'm are there that we missed, hey? Wha'd be the story if we hadn't done a divershin?'

'I didn't know and I don't know.'

'Full o' shet!'

'What's the plawn, Brian? What can we expect nigh?'

'An important British civil servant is missing,' I said evenly. 'I said I'd try to find him.'

80

'Ach, Brian, ye don't believe that. There's no cevel servan', it's a chile's story. A sat-up.'

'I don't believe it is.'

'They put the frightners on ye, Brian. Ye agreed t'ever'thin'. Admit it, nigh. Ye'r goin' to teyll us in the eynd.'

'He's full o' shet – smell him.'

'What's the story, Brian?'

'I told Vincent everything I know. The man's name is Adam Coleraine. I gave Vincent his photograph.'

The bald man came over, drying his hands. 'No such mon.'

'Brian.' My questioner smiled reasonably. 'We know all about ye. Ye'r a decent mon that loves his country as much as all of us. Ye'v helped us over the yers, we know that.'

So did I, too well.

'But teymes cheyenge. People cheyenge. They made ye part of one last big push and said ye'd be looked awfter. Ye lost the faith, Brian.'

'That is not true.'

'Full – o' – shet!'

'Ye know in your hawrt this whole theng about a Home Office Bret in Ulster is an invantion.'

'I don't believe it is an invention.'

'Shet!'

'Yer tryin' ar patience, Brian.'

'I believe Adam Coleraine exists,' I repeated. 'I believe the Brits in this case.'

The boy thrust his head in. 'So ye believe them, not us, is that it?'

I said, 'Stay here forever if you like, but I can only tell you the truth.'

'If we like? If we like?' The boy looked at me incredulously. 'Ye'r tellin' us what we can do, are ye? Ye'r a cheeky fucker, no doubt. Ye'd tell the Pope high to say mass, wudn' ye? Weyll I'll tell ye something', we don' have teyme to set here foraver.' He was shaking as he walked to the bald man and snatched out the revolver from his belt. 'Yer freyn beheyn me takin' his reyst on the floor has forever, but we don'! Ye'r shortly goin' to have forever unless ye find your fuckin' tongue!'

'Take it easy, Sean . . .'

'Shut yer mowth!' He shoved the barrel hard into my cheek. 'Forever and ever, ameyn! Now ye'v got as long as it takes to put yer mouth around a word to tell us what's really goin' on – and please God, please! please! say ye don't know because I hate yer fuckin' feyce and I want to spread it all over the fuckin' wall beheyn ye!'

I watched his mad, young eyes and I can tell you without shame that my only prayer was that it wouldn't hurt.

'I – don't – know – '

He pulled the trigger and I stiffened as the hammer struck the empty chamber. In the room reeling I could hear soft laughter.

'Ye'r a naughty lad, Brian,' said the one with black hair. 'Ye'v wet yer pawnts.'

Looking back, Gilly, I find my brain has filed that day in the compartment it reserves for ugly dreams. Men didn't allow themselves to become creatures of the hate I had witnessed; it was too extreme. But I didn't dream the plastic tape that cut the circulation from my feet and hands and bound the wad into my mouth; nor did I dream that I was trussed double and dropped into a car boot. Whenever my mind tries to persuade me the day was a dream, I remind myself of how it felt to be in the cold lap of the red-haired man whom they'd bent in before me.

There were long stops on that journey, long periods of night silence, when the only persistent reality was the magnitude of my own failure. I had been betrayed by Tice, by our own side; they had not considered me worthy of their loyalty. The cold from my companion's body sparked off a fever in my own. I drifted into a disembodied series of imaginings in which hours and minutes became freely interchangeable. The light growing in a hole six inches or six miles from my eyes was Vincent's eye and through it I swam to the sound of his laughter. I longed to straighten my spine and stand upright. I passed out and was woken by voices, by vehicle noises and the smell of petrol. Where I should have felt relief at being alive, I was eaten by foreboding. I was only being set free for a reason greater than the value of my own life; a bit of me died on that journey, Gilly.

It was silence, eventually, not noise that woke me. We were stopped. Traffic had become a constant. There was water noise and voices and the screech of bus brakes. Then loudhailers. People ordered back, back. The hee-haw of patrol cars and of ambulances. Water. The squeak of a solitary, rubber sole. Every pouch of what I'd left went into the one effort.

'Hmmmmmmmmmmmmmm . . .'

'Jesus Christ! There's a person in the boot!'

Some occasions go by leaving no more than the faintest imprint. I have tried to reproduce from my own resources all that happened in those next few hours but I have been forced back on the videos and papers that the children had the foresight to keep. A switchboard girl at the *Independent* took a call suggesting that a Northern Ireland car in O'Connell Street might be worth a look; she informed her duty editor; he verified the presence of the car and called the Bomb Squad. When the entire district at the core of the modern Ireland State was evacuated and when on television a bound and gagged garda officer whom no one had ever heard of was produced, and a corpse, it had been plain the ensuing cafuffle would not go away. Thoughts free and clear swam up through my sleeping brain fat. Vincent's voice, as never heard before: 'We caused much change, Brian, you and me. We shaped the universe those nights.' Fact, I knew in wonder, not a shaping metaphysical. Lazy speculation swung to a crash in bed sweat.

'Brian? Are you awake?'

In seductive semidarkness; arm strapped somehow. Light framed in the middle distance took time to resolve itself as the inspection window in a door.

'Gilly?'

'Ah, dere now, Brian, lie still, good lad.'

'Where's Gilly?' It seemed normal that Arty Gunn should be by my bedside.

'Brian, don't worry, she'll be here in a minute,' Arty said reassuringly.

'Arty?'

'You're alright, you're alright. By Jasus you had some eshcape, dough.'

'I had . . . what's. . . ?' I couldn't sit up and my arm stung.

'Lie still, lie still,' Arty whispered. 'You're on a dthrip, you're dehydthrated, boy.' His paw flesh pressed my forehead. 'You're roarin' hot still, but you're alright, that's the main thing.'

'Where. . . ?'

'Mount Carmel.'

'Jesus Christ, Arty . . .'

'I'm on your side, boy.'

'On my . . . side?'

Arty's big, round head was like an old school picture we used to have of Mr World. 'There's the commotion of a fuckin' lifetime goin' on,' he whispered. 'It's the end of the time for secrets between us, Brian.'

'What do you mean?' I asked hollowly.

'Me fein,' Aty said urgently, 'you look after me fein, boyo, because nobody else will. I'll thry and help you get away with this one besht I can.'

'Get away with what, Arty?'

'Brian, Brian, you were up where you should never have been,' said Arty sorrowfully. 'Dere's things you can do and things you can't do. This is serious, boyo. The papers are goin' mad. This could sink a government.'

'Wait!' I cried, sitting up and a needle jumped out of my arm. 'This wasn't some fegary! Maguire knew what I was doing. He sanctioned it as minister for justice! Has he told the papers about Adam Coleraine?'

Arty closed tight both his eyes as if to seal away what I'd said in deep catacombs. 'Brian, Brian, I don't want to hear talk about someone who doesn't exisht. We'll give them gobshites in the media deir pounda flesh but not the way they think. Tell me now the name of the bashtard who gulled you and what happened today'll be forgotten be dinner tomorra.'

I knew then he was a liar, because I knew a dead SAS man would not be forgotten.

'The name, Brian, the name of your man in the Provos.'

I thought of Vincent and his surging poetry; I looked at Arty's avaricious face and thought of my dwindling assets. 'How is Maguire explaining the dead Brit?' I asked.

'Leave all that to us,' said Arty impatiently, adding, 'God resht his soul. But we need the name, Brian, Maguire needs the name to take away all the attention from your calamity.'

'I can't give you the name.'

'Now, Brian,' Arty chuckled as if enforcing the rules at musical chairs. 'You're not thinkin' shtraight. He's no good to you or to anyone anymore. Think of yourself, your family.'

'Tice had me followed,' I panted. '*His* man is dead. Ask Tice and Maguire to come up with something.'

'D'ye want it shtraight, so?' asked Arty, suddenly rough. 'You haven't many frinds, boyo.'

'The minister . . .'

'This mornin's changed ever'tin,' Arty snarled, one big fist bunched. 'Give me the name now and act like a man, not a fuckin' weasel.'

'I want to see my wife.'

'You can see anyone you want when you shtart cooperatin',' Arty hissed.

I believe if he thought violence would have worked he would have used it.

'Arty,' I said, 'I want to see my wife.'

I could see him look for a last way around me, then he stood up as if suddenly he wanted to be out of there. I put out my hand. 'Let's not end it like this, Arty. Let's shake and end it remembering all the decent times between us.'

He nearly did, but the cute boy in him took over and he buttoned his jacket and knocked on the door to be let out. A nurse came in after that and then you, my Gilly. I could see the black daubs of exhaustion around your eyes.

'I'm okay,' I said.

You were in shreds. You began, 'I tried . . .'

'Don't worry,' I said as you put your arms around me.

'Oh Brian!' you gasped. 'It's horrible the things they're saying about you!'

A doctor was telling me how foolish I was to insist on discharging myself; you were sitting there, telling me of the circus outside the hospital. All I heard was Vincent's voice: My love consumes me. He had chosen well in me that June night long ago. He had moulded me into a vessel of his own making where he was the font beyond which I never had to drink for my filling: 'There was no smallness in creation./ He made the Alps, the Causeway of the

Giants./ The river Nile'. It may have been the drugs but I laughed outright.

'Are you going to be alright?' the nurse frowned in the lift. 'There's a right lot of them out there, you know.'

'I'll be fine,' I said. I had dressed in the clothes you had brought me; all I wanted was home and a lot of time. I remember wondering as I paid the bill if I would be refunded. Picking up my bag, my arm around you, we walked for the doors. The inward surge was tremendous. We steadied each other under a burst of light. Will we ever forget it?

'Brian! This way!'

'Brian! Brian!'

'Who's the dead Brit, Brian?'

'Brian, what were you doing in Northern Ireland?'

We stood, dazed, the way the world would see us. Arty must have known exactly what would happen.

'Oh, God!' you cried.

'Where's the car?' I shouted.

'Brian! Give your wife a kiss!'

I made straight into them. They made no attempt to part.

'Hey! Watch out!'

I put my shoulder into it. One of them tried to bar our way but when I kneed him hard he pushed over. A microphone blocked my vision until eventually I had to drive it and its handler to the ground. Jostled and grabbed at, I fought. When one of them grabbed my collar I gave his wrist a twist he wouldn't forget. I saw the mob near Butler's Bridge. I heard Vincent. From the pictures, later, I was savage. At your car they jammed us tight to the doors. Up on the bonnet they got and on to the roof.

'Brian! Brian!'

Then a camera exploded at your face and you screamed. I thrashed the bag in an arc, spinning cameras and microphones. We bundled in and I went for Orwell Road as men with cameras on shoulder ran either side and men and women held on to the door handles and screamed in through the windows.

'Not one person there to help us!' I cried as we bumped out.

You were sobbing. I raced for the Dodder and some of the shouted questions began to filter through. 'Tell me exactly what is being said?' I asked.

'I don't know,' you said. 'Nothing and everything. They make it sound like you're some kind . . . of a thief!'

We took the bypass and got off for Palmerstown short of the toll bridge. Coming up our road I saw crowds of people. Cameras on tripods were set up on the back of pick-up trucks and, down the length of three houses, was parked an outside broadcast unit.

'I don't believe this,' I said, and I didn't. People were packed so tight around the car that I had to stop. Lights burst around us. Faces pressed up against every window, all shouting. Men with cameras fought men with microphones and women speaking into portable telephones. For a moment I thought they must have got the wrong car, then we were rocked by a vigorous scuffling and Cormac, our eldest boy, and two friends of his, all big, strong lads, claimed an area of ground around my door.

'What in God's name. . . ?' I shouted.

Cormac shouted. 'Mam! Get out!'

As I scrambled out and the lads made a circle around you, we burst for the house.

'Brian!'

'Who was the brit, Brian?'

Cormac and I skittled a few of them. They seemed enraged that I wouldn't give them a word. We made the front gate and Cormac made a run at a photographer who had set up in the garden. When I got in I knew it was nine o'clock because the television news jangle was playing and you were all staring at it. Simon came over and held my hand.

'A senior garda officer has been suspended pending an inquiry into dramatic events in Dublin today. Detective Superintendent Brian Kilkenny, described by senior Garda sources as having enjoyed a distinguished career . . .'

You turned it off. None of the children knew where to look.

Situations come, you deal with them, what more is there to say? You know the facts of those awful January days as well as I do. You functioned through them with me, so you must forgive my indulgence in bringing them all up again, but I feel I must. We tried to ignore the picture being painted with the brush and paint of innuendo supplied by Maguire's Department of Justice. The sight of my own face in the papers and on television became

87

common to us. Maverick. Rogue. The flirting promises of much worse to come. My statement through solicitors – asserting my willingness to cooperate fully with the minister's inquiry and pleading for our privacy to be respected – was issued during a week passed under seige. The dead man was the subject of intense speculation and each fresh tidbit on him was followed by fresh assaults on our bewildered ramparts as governments both sides of the Irish Sea sat in stony silence. Then one morning we looked out of the window and saw an empty street. They had gone as swallows go. Perhaps an aircraft had crashed in Dublin, or an election had been threatened, we never heard, did we?

I can think of no life left in those grey days of early February, no sign of hope. I went right down, I know. After all the action, I had anticipated the cut and thrust of an inquiry where I would be fighting for my reputation and my life, relishing the opportunity to clear my name; I was not prepared for the void. Nothing. No date for hearings, no statement from Maguire. I found it hard. I faltered. I was beyond the small talk of the friends you brought in to cheer me up by papering over the chasms; and to discuss the details of what I had been through with anyone was contrary to what I believed to be proper. I was staggering. I would fall and never get up. You all must have wondered that if something you had held so constant could so quickly change, perhaps everything you read and heard might in fact be true.

I did try to address the facts of my position. I met the Labour Party representative for our constituency, not because he had got my vote in the last election, but because he was known for rooting up matters that governments might prefer left interred. He believed my story, I think. The Dail question he put down for Cyril Maguire asked if 'the imperative for the government to find a missing, high-ranking British civil servant' was not the reason for my being in Northern Ireland. The man who had put his political future so trustingly in my hands replied: 'I do not propose to comment on the wild notions in the question except to say that I have every confidence in the judgement of the garda commissioner.'

The story died. One paper did a piece saying Joe O'Keeffe was for the chop and profiled his possible successors, with Arty smiling out benignly from near the top of the pile. There were rumours of trouble in Justice and I wondered what Janet thought of me now, or if she thought of me at all. She had once gone so far as to hope that we would always be friends, but friends are the happy constants in life, the people who ring when you expect them least but need them most; Janet Moriariaty never rang.

Days dragged with awful slowness and I realised that the most appalling sentence of all is to be forgotten. The children became used to the sight of me around the house. I went for walks alone. There was tension between you are me, Gilly, where none had ever existed. Although you never complained, I found you crying one night, cold tears of bewildered disappointment. It was tearing us apart. I was obsessed with two men; Adam Coleraine whose existence was now denied as a matter of course and Vincent Ashe whose career I had promoted.

'We will blow complacency into a million fragments
And watch it wither before storms of outrage.'

I shuddered at what was becoming increasingly obvious to me, but yet, to my shame, there were parts of me that were still under his spell.

'My lover has no age.
She has died and re-greened, season upon season.
Agelessly.
My lover can wait for me forever.

I was going to die, I knew, old and bitter, friendless, harbouring within me a time's speck of events that to everyone else was already a piece of history. I panicked. I *would* die. I *was* forgotten. I rang Arty's phone one morning but when I heard his voice I hung up. I was cracking. I could make a decision like that, call someone and then not have the courage to speak. I saw a different face in the shaving mirror. I heard voices when the house and myself had only each other for company, when the rest of the world was going about its business. It took many weeks to realise that this was us, not other people that you read about, shake your head and pity.

Then that late afternoon in the second week of February, someone pushed an evening paper through our letter box. Who did it, I never learned. The front page header hissed: 'Anglo-Irish Row'; the banner beneath it screamed: 'SUICIDE'.

I devoured the words. Robin Counsell. Found in Southampton. In a boat. Cooking gas. A Yorkshire newspaper had received Counsell's bitter justification and had managed to print it before the Home office had paralysed the media with injunctions. Northern Ireland! Poor Counsell! He had confessed, wept, agonised. He had told them of a missing person called Adam Coleraine.

Jubilation! All the instruments of my persecution were froth, everything was still there to be fought for, honour and self respect. Adam Coleraine existed! Or to be exact, he had existed up to August. As surely as everything had changed that day in O'Connell Street, now it had changed again. Two calls came from the media but they were perfunctory, something else was on the go of more interest, I was no longer the value I had once appeared. Next morning, despite the curt, Home Office dismissal of Counsell as 'sadly unbalanced', my elation was undiminished when I answered the telephone and Janet said, 'Hello, Brian.'

'Janet.'

'You've seen the papers?'

'Yes.'

'We should talk.'

Not 'how are you?', or 'I'm so sorry the way things turned out'; in a couple of months I had forgotten Janet.

' "We" being who?'

'You and me.'

Counsell's revelations had been to me like new blood, but to Janet's peers I reckoned the dead man's words must have been as sirens. Six hours after taking Janet's call, I'd crossed Ireland, slipped through grey Galway and was breasting the misty widths of Connemara. Majestic, bare mountain and sweeping, valley wilderness made Cavan and Fermanagh look like allotments. Janet was being sent over to do a quiet deal with me, I thought as I came into a boarded-up Clifden. I craved something other than the long nightmare my life had become, but I now saw Janet in the cold light of her own ambition and I was damned if I would deal.

She was parked outside a petrol station as she had said, and led the way in failing light down through the empty town and out a winding road with churning sea on one side and on the other, stone walls and donkeys. Road became lane, then track. Sea and wind raged up in demons. We spun our way up a path of smooth, wet boulder and around a bluff, stopping up short at a cottage. Janet took a key from a flowerpot and opened the door. When I followed in, she was adding peats to a glowing fire; rain clung in tiny, shining pom-poms to her tweed jacket and to her hair. It took me a moment to tumble that the glasses had gone and in place of the big eyes that missed nothing were eyes of normal size making her face altogether different.

'Hello, Brian,' she said, straightening up, bringing her big hands together.

'Nice view,' I said.

'Morning is best,' she said, looking suddenly angular and uncomfortable. 'It's been hard for you.'

'You take life as it comes.'

'Yes, but it's been hard.' She cleared her throat. 'I wanted to ring.'

I didn't react; I didn't see why I should help her. I saw her cheekbones for the first time, and the way she held her head.

'Everyone ran for cover,' she said, talking to the sea. 'Foreign Affairs went berserk and Maguire was ordered down to Leinster House. He came back ten years older.'

'A shame.'

She closed her eyes. 'I wanted to ring you but I knew I couldn't. I have some idea what you and your family went through and I despise what was done.' She looked at me. 'It was chaos. The Brits washed their hands of everything, a complete turnaround. Tice even intimated that the entire escapade was our fault and that in future His Majesty's Government would solve its own problems.' Janet's mouth was clamped tight. 'From then on it was naked self-preservation and you were the softest target, Brian. I'm sorry to be so blunt, but it happened that way.'

'I'm sorry too.'

'I knew you would have the strength.'

'I can handle a thousand Joe O'Keeffes and Cyril Maguires,' I said, 'but soft targets have wives and children who cannot.'

'I know,' Janet said. I could see her taking me in again. 'Would you like a drink?'

'Scotch, please.'

Bottles with fire's glow stood on a table by the big window

through which you could still just about see, but not hear, the sea. I watched her pour.

'I want to help you,' she said.

'How kind.'

'No one knows about this meeting,' she said quietly. 'I have told no one.'

'Just a spur of the moment thing.'

We drank silently at the fire, whisky warming to peat, and I saw Janet close her eyes again as if this was all more of an effort than she had been prepared for.

'You may choose not to believe this, Brian, but I do want to help you. I also want to help myself.'

I could have said, 'How unusual', but I bit my tongue.

'Counsell has made both things possible.' Janet took off her jacket and sat in one of those puffed, pigskin chairs from suites that cost more than a holiday. 'Maguire is in terminal trouble,' she said. 'He knows that nothing short of Lourdes is going to save him.'

'Why hasn't he passed mercifully on?'

'Because there's more talent in Jury's cabaret than there is in the government,' Janet said.

'Can he be cured?'

'By spectacular success.'

'Unlikely in his case.'

'Happy the minister for justice who dents the Provos and proves his party serious on terror in an election year,' Janet declared.

I thought of Arty's efforts in the hospital and I wondered if he had been sent in or if it had been a personal initiative.

'Happy the person who delivers his or her minister such an opportunity,' I observed.

'Quite,' said Janet sparely as if her ambition did not become her.

I was so tired suddenly, the result of all the bad weeks. I had forgotten how things worked. I was no longer able for the game. 'I'm just interested in getting my job back,' I said wearily. 'In clearing my name. Nothing more.'

'That's possible,' said Janet. 'If you can produce Coleraine, I believe Maguire will have to reinstate you.'

'How "produce" him? From where?'

'Look,' Janet said, 'since your experience, we've been seeing unexplained activity up north. Counsell's death and confession suddenly explain it – the Brits are still looking for Coleraine.'

I shrugged; I had no way of knowing the quality of Janet's information nor the true extent of her sincerity.

'Assume he is up there somewhere,' Janet said. 'He stole your report from the British Home Office. Your report contains, inter alia, the names of active nationalist subversives in Belfast. Coleraine thinks your report is the way to find those who killed his daughter. The Brits knew the report was the shortcut to finding him.'

It was black night out the window. In the firelight Janet looked anything but a manipulative woman and I found myself wondering why a person of her ability would be bothered to advance her career with people who would smear a father before his family.

'It's hard when you're a lifetime believing in the law to discover it means nothing when you most need it,' I said, regretting the bitterness that must have come across in my voice.

'Your report, Brian,' pressed Janet, whipper-in for years of wavering agendas.

'Yes,' I replied, for there didn't seem to be anything else to talk of and the long drive home across Ireland was nothing to hurry at. 'It no longer exists. I destroyed it with pleasure when all the shoot-to-kill rumpus started. But, yes, I can remember most of it and I cannot fathom what there might be in it for Coleraine that is not already known to British Intelligence.'

Janet frowned. 'No angle they might have missed?'

I shook my head. 'That's why last month I took the, call it, direct route.'

'Then everyone has overlooked something.' Janet went to the window and pulled the curtains and came slowly back with the bottle. 'Adam Coleraine has seen something in that report that he can use to his advantage. He's in Belfast. Has to be.'

'The IRA don't agree,' I said.

'That points to two possibilities,' Janet replied. 'Either they found him and then, having extracted what they could, killed him – but they would normally announce such an execution. Alternatively, when they went looking for him in response to your request he hadn't yet arrived in Belfast.'

She didn't seem to have grasped that my only lifeline into Ulster no longer existed. 'He may well be in Belfast,' I said, 'but if he is, he's beyond my reach.'

'You're wrong,' said Janet. 'There is someone who can help you up there.'

'Who?' I asked.

'Me,' Janet replied.

Gilly, before ever I embarked on my recounting I realised that the truth would bring you pain, but I believe it is only from the truth that you and I may yet salvage something. Janet had nudged off her shoes and sat with her legs stretched out to the fire and the whisky in her lap; she was too warm and comfortable to be leading me where I thought she was, but then I thought of her Northern proficiency that I, and I'm sure everyone else, had long taken for granted, and then I realised that Janet Moriarity was simply a flag of convenience and that I was being invited into a part of her life that she kept as a sanctuary. I could have stayed out, of course, but a return, empty-handed, to my personal desert in Dublin was not something I wanted to contemplate.

'Not the Falls,' I said with quiet intuition, although 'Janet' as a name was neutral.

'Tribes are extraordinary, aren't they?' she said. 'Modern societies have no need for all the old apparatus that is still used in places like Belfast, but beneath the surface we're still dogs sniffing for the coded smell.' She smiled. 'Not the Falls.'

I thought of all the meetings she must have attended over the years when Belfast Protestants would have been discussed by Irish governments in the manner of zoologists discussing a dangerous species, and my admiration for her increased. 'It's not known,' I said.

'It's not even vaguely an issue,' Janet said. 'At best it gives me keen insights, at worst it makes me ashamed. But I keep in touch. I have a mother and a brother. There are still family things that need doing.'

I was in a different league to this woman when it came to ruthless determination, but she fascinated me nonetheless. 'Say I was interested – which I'm not,' I said, 'but say I was, how would you see it working?'

'You're out with the Provos, Brian,' she said, leaning forward. 'You're out with everyone in Dublin. You're out with the Brits. The only people who can find this man for you are the Prods.'

Although you could throw a stone from parts of the Falls into the Shankill, the idea of going in there myself had always been beyond reasonable consideration. 'I think you're trying to rob me of my retirement,' I said.

'Brian, I can ask for a thing to be done. If he's there, they'll find him for you.'

'Assume I accepted,' I said, wondering how far I could press her, 'what would the deal be?'

'Your source,' Janet said simply.

I had come up through the ranks in an organisation where hard work and a little above average intelligence guaranteed promotion. Janet's ascent had required superior skills: the ability to trade in a political environment and a refusal to compromise her own aspirations. And so, although my first reaction was to be loyal to old promises, I realised too that what I was being loyal to was my own pride which refused to let me admit failure, and that this woman, for selfish reasons which she did not try to disguise, was offering me a way forward. In a way Janet had demonstrated her courage and was inviting me to do the same. She also understood my position; the easy ambivalence between the hunter and the hunted when both are Catholic and the forest is full of black, Protestant eyes. She was advancing her own career but she was also offering me a choice between continuing to protect the creature of my creation and of exciting the ghosts of my race. I told her Vincent's name.

'The one with. . . ?' Janet touched the left side of her face.

I nodded. 'Spends a lot of time in Belfast. They have a business there.'

'I see,' she said thoughtfully. 'Republican fringe, backhanders, a way around construction tenders when the right government is in, financially successful, American connections, Noraid perhaps, but . . . the whole way?'

'Yes.'

'I saw him three nights ago, at a ballet. He was on his own,' she remarked.

I felt a traitor, despite all I knew – and the fact that I was aware of how inappropriate my feelings were only made them worse. Janet could see my pain.

'This is hard for you, isn't it?'

'Why should it be?' I asked.

'You worked with him for how long? Ten years? He and you have the same blood. You made a pact, otherwise you could never have worked for so long. Have you ever told anyone his name?'

I shook my head. 'Not in fifteen years.'

She got up and came over and sat on her heels in front of me. 'It is possible to be carried along,' she said gently. 'We're all human. We're all fighting the sins of the past.'

'I admire his intellect and his passion,' I said, 'and in a funny way I respect the way he outwitted me. But for everything else, I despise him.'

'Tell me about his passion,' said Janet quietly.

' "My love consumes me.
I think of her and in the marrow of my bones there springs an ooze.
I see her in chains and I feel myself rise." '

Janet nodded slowly.

'Ireland is his woman, his lover. Ireland is central to a whole cycle of birth, passionate love, and death.

"I will bathe in the sweet, warm blood that floods between her thighs
As out of her poor, ravaged body comes something beautiful and whole."

He thinks himself a warrior as old as Cuchulain. Everything warm has been sucked out of him and has gone into the myth he has made. He is cold as clay.'

'A true professional,' said Janet quietly. 'I don't suppose he has left anything for us to get him on?'

I shook my head.

Janet reached out for my hand and pressed it in hers. 'Do you know what I think?' she said. 'I think that you should be given the biggest medal in Ireland for carrying this around in you for fifteen years.'

'I did it for myself,' I said.

96

'You mustn't blame yourself,' Janet said and her voice went suddenly husky. 'Passion recognises its own name.'

I looked at the fire and, even that late in the game, I felt perverse respect for him.

' "Rapture! Brave son!
Your only crime was birth to a mother chained.
Rapture! I see it in the way our young men wear their pride.
I see it on the Shankill, faces worried after four hundred years about their way home." '

'Four hundred years,' said Janet grimly. 'I was brought up on it. My brother still lives it every day.' She smiled sadly at me. 'The Brits made a big mistake when they sent us across that strip of flat sea.'

We were both victims in our own ways, both vulnerable. The huge risk that had earlier seemed to overhang us now looked insignificant as we sat there in the warmth, the needs of our flesh outranking ambition.

'It's a story as old as Ireland herself,' Janet whispered. 'Tone and McCorley and O'Donovan Rossa. Sands and Farrell and Savage and McCann. You all want that mythical woman, that infatuating dream. She can do no wrong, and when you hurt her you poison your own blood.'

We were surrounded by cold sea with only one another to turn to. I bent and kissed her and I could taste the whisky off her mouth even though I had been drinking it myself. I knelt beside her and opened her blouse and eased it off her shoulders. I reached back and opened her bra and brought my head down to her breasts. We made our love there at the fire and, later, in a bedroom by an open window over roaring sea. She would not let me sleep. There was a warm hunger to her that made me think of all the cold years spent shaping her career and made me ask myself if it had been worth it. At last we spun an exhausted tenderness that was as pure and ephemeral as the slow first light creeping over winter Connemara.

I drove home late the next day. There was peace inside me, running with every cup of blood, charging out to make quiver delightfully all the parts of me I had assumed dead. The wheel between my hands was weightless; we had touched innocence that neither of us might know again and, in making me confront the evil of Vincent, Janet had given me back myself to believe in. She would never again ask about Vincent's passion, or want to hear raging poems about blood and death. Janet had business from which she would not be deflected, but we both had memories of a night and a morning, of a low, inclining sun boring into manes rushing fantastically below us and making old gold of them. I wondered then about men who dreamt with passion and about dreamers and love and I wondered if the dreamer in me had been jilted that day in South Fermanagh and if what I had done had been for spite. Guilt was such a central part of our equation. Even when we had shed another thousand skins and stood proudly upright like little trees that had battled so long, would we still feel guilty about our own existence?

That damp afternoon, Dublin's lights glowed in the sky from as far out as Kinnegad. I was coming home better. I had chosen to risk death rather than live with the mockery of silent voices. You must have seen the change in me because you looked happy, the way you had in the old days when you had never known and would never ask where I had been. 'Supper is hot and waiting,' you smiled.

As I sat down, the phone rang and you answered it.

'Someone who won't give their name,' you said.

'Brian Kilkenny,' I said, taking the phone.

'This is Angie,' said a woman with a commanding voice.

I hadn't a clue. 'Angie?'

'Adam's friend.'

I remembered. 'Oh, yes.'

'Adam is alive,' she said.

*

The Residencia di San Paolo, the mother house of the Order of Friends of Paschal of Baylon, is set back far from busy sites of antiquity and tourist tramped piazzas in the Roman hills of Prenestini. It is a place of ochre *tegoli* and courtyards, of cool *terrazzis*, of lawns and gardens.

'Avanti.'

Padro Baptisto was writing in September's morning light. At fifty-three his hair was still lush black; women thought him far too handsome for a priest, San Paolo's novice master.

'Padre, buon giorno.'

'Signor Adam.' The priest rose and connected the tips of all fingers. 'Let us sit over here.' Leather chairs were placed for the aspect as Master Baptisto sat and reached under. 'Cioccolata, Signor Adam? From the Piazza Venezia.'

'Grazie.' Adam selected a dark whorl. Two weeks had passed for San Paolo's newest postulant. He had come, as Tice predicted, with a *nom de guerre*, a passport in the name of Cardew: as all eyes had searched for him to the west, he had gone south. He had read my report.

Master Baptisto asked softly. 'You know the function of the master of the novices, Signor Adam?'

'To do – ' Adam swallowed 'God's work in the choosing of men worthy of His calling to the Order. It cannot be a burden lightly carried, Padre.'

'My shoulders are very broad, Signor Adam.' Master Baptisto pressed out a smile. 'Yes, a work of choosing. An assessing of suitability for admission. Many men, however well intentioned, find the vows too much.' Padre Baptisto's hands floated upwards. 'That is no great crime. The way to heaven is never easy.'

Animal prowled in Master Baptisto.

'I am something of God's sentry,' said the priest and showed all his perfect, top teeth. 'I must admit only those of warm and open heart; be on my guard against the interloper, against men who would use us as a place to hide, whose motives are crooked or impure.'

Cat, Adam thought, the patience of, and the teeth.

'Neither must I be flattered by the attentions, or by the money' –the priest paused to let the dubious importance of this word be known – 'of those who might pretend to justify to us our own existence. Truth of purpose, openness in all things, past and present, and a love of Our Lord Jesus Christ, these are the only diplomatic papers I require. But they are essential ones, Signor Adam.' The priest smiled on, opening with the fingers of his left hand a notebook. He turned his shoulders to Adam. 'So . . .' He made a grave mouth. 'You are a man bereaved.'

'Yes, Padre.'

'Adam Carr-dev,' the priest said to show that even English was no obstacle to the truth. 'Ah, God help you, but God has strange ways, revealed to us only in prayer. Your daughter.'

'My daughter, yes.'

'An accident on the road . . .'

'Yes.'

'Instantaneous . . .'

'Yes.'

'God help you, but perhaps you can thank God that her death was instant, not a slow wasting of her young body. You loved her very much.'

The word 'love' held a different meaning for Baptisto. 'Love cannot describe it.'

'God save us love, but He also gave us His Son who is love.'

'She was everything to me.'

'Everything, yes, and so through her, then, dead, you heard the voice of Our Lord. No other children?'

'None.'

'But you have a wife.'

'We divorced.'

'Ah.'

'Some years ago. She lives in the United States. I have the papers.'

'I have seen all your papers,' said Baptisto the Cat through drowsy half eyes sideways. 'They are in perfect order the papers of Adam Carr-dev.'

'Yes, Padre.'

'You were a man of business,' said Master Baptisto as if the subject of Adam's family had been bled of profit.

'Yes, Padre.'

'Successful, yet . . . you walked away.'

'My partners agreed that the bulk of my money be paid to me over a number of years. In that way they were placed under no strain and I was relieved of the burden of having to deal with a large sum at a time when I was least equipped to.'

'Yesssss,' exhaled Baptisto and coiled his tongue, 'and you have already brought our Father Founder a gift of money.' He paused again on money, weighing it up briefly against probity, then moved on as if the exercise had been unworthy. 'But why did you choose our Order? You know that Paschal Baylon was just a simple confessor to men? To all men, no matter how vile their sin?'

'I know,' Adam replied. Having read my report, of course he knew, even if I had forgotten.

Adam slapped soap to chest and neck and double-cupped shimmering parabolas over head. Drying himself he took from its peg behind the door his habit and hefted it on, and prodded his toes into cool sandals. By the cloister fountains a novice, Fratello Francisco waved. High in San Paolo a bird insisted, 'cip! cip! cip!' It reminded him of Zoe's voice – but then, so did everything.

Signorina Brompton was fifty, or perhaps more. Her bushy hair was black and grey and it tumbled around her neck, firm and brown. Other details appertaining to Signorina Brompton were, strong legs, flat shoes and gay, billowing dresses.

'Mr Cardew.' She smiled as Adam sat on his usual chair, placed as was hers, in the shade of an almond tree.

'Miss Brompton.'

'How are you, Mr Cardew?'

'I am well, thank you, Miss Brompton,' Adam replied with formality. 'And you?'

'Very well, Mr Cardew, very well,' smiled Signorina Brompton, opening her file. 'Well, now.' She looked up with determined bonhomie. 'Is there anything you wish to tell me, anything at all that may have occurred to you since we last met?'

Signorina Brompton always made the same offer at the outset, so the stratagem must have contained a precedent of success.

'I don't think so,' Adam replied. He had come, in a way, to enjoy these sessions set up by Baptisto; Signorina Brompton was the only person with whom he could discuss his past, however obliquely.

Signorina Brompton peeked at her file. 'Your wife, Alice, Mr Cardew, if I may continue to so refer to her. In your sexual relationship, would you say you led Alice more than she led you, or the other way around?'

There has been the good times. Once on the beach in a place called Xlendi, their feet in the night surf, Oh! Adam!, if anyone should . . . 'Alice was attracted to me because . . . because I dominated her, physically as well as taking all the decisions. The fact that my strength, if you like, turned her on also turned me on. It lasted quite a long time.'

'But later?'

Unfortunately most of life came under 'later'. 'Later, I tired of the roles.' After Zoe, everything changed, her shape, her face, the tone of her skin, the way she walked and stood. The juicy Alison who, when she swam, flowed, water rippling down her back; who liked drinks with fruit in high glasses; who liked to be on top as often as below and came in hotel bedrooms better than in their own, she had slowly disappeared and into focus came a woman of little details: tense furrows at her mouth as she smoked a cigarette, a pinpoint in the filter for the smoke, a tiny prick, everything reduced in size, shrinking, dry, a trickle, life itself hurtling inwards with her in reductio. 'Alice seemed less . . . interested in me, later.'

'You have mentioned another woman, Audrey, who lived in Victoria.' Signorina Brompton had collected so much in her file. 'Was your sexual relationship with Audrey more satisfactory than that with Alice?'

Strong to weak. Angie to Alison. 'Yes.'

'Do you not feel guilty in taking this step and leaving Audrey? Might she not have expected to help you over this difficult time?'

Adam thought of Alison, bewildered; but he could never think of Angie like that. 'We discussed it. She accepted my decision.'

'Audrey seems like a woman of uncommon resolve,' observed Signorina Brompton.

'She is.'

'How often do you masturbate, Mr Cardew?'

'Ah . . . as often as the next,' replied Adam and looked at Signorina Brompton's strong, brown legs and laughed outright.

'Come, come, Mr Cardew, you know that in my field of work I must ask such a question. You are a man of the world, suddenly self-imprisoned here. How often?'

'Perhaps once a fortnight,' Adam answered.

'Very good.' Signorina Brompton brought the pen to her lips. 'The last time this occurred, who was mostly in your mind, Mr Cardew?'

'That is a most difficult question.'

'Nonetheless, one to which I require an answer.'

'You were, Miss Brompton.'

'How very gratifying,' Signorina Brompton said and made a

note in her file. 'Mother and father,' she said and looked up at Adam as if in concern for his parents' whereabouts. 'The very early years, Mr Cardew. Happy together, were they, your parents?'

Pom was ever one for tea. Used to make it happily whilst she stood at her tapestry frame even though he had been out working all day. Pom-pom! 'Yes.'

'A quiet house, was it?'

'In what way?'

'Did it bustle with people, much? Did mother's and father's friends call in?' asked Signorina Brompton.

'My father went to work every day, but yes, I do remember people in the house,' Adam replied.

'Men or women?'

'Oh, women if I remember.'

'What comes to mind?'

A smell came to Adam's mind. 'Perfume.' A feel came to Adam's mind. 'Fur. They wore fur coats in those days. Collars, stoles, dead things with heads still on.'

'And cuddled you to them no doubt, Mr Cardew. Very good,' Signorina Brompton wrote. 'You've just kicked a football and shattered a window. Who's going to give you hell to pay?'

'Father. He'd thrash me. Mother didn't worry about things like that.'

'Sound man. What about hols?'

'We took them,' Adam said. 'Historic towns. Bath, Edinburgh. Mother liked architecture.'

'Was she always the dominant one?'

'Yes and no.' Adam paused. 'She was an artist. It absorbed her . . . more than the usual household things.'

Signorina Brompton's little eyes flashed their comprehension. 'Absorbed her? More than her child, for example?'

'Could be.'

'Which is also probably, would you say, why she wouldn't have another?'

'Yes, I suppose so.'

'Did she ignore you, Mr Cardew?'

'More . . . indifference. She loved me, I'm sure.'

'So am I,' said Signorina Brompton, 'but she also loved her art. You had to compete.'

'Sorry?'

'Did she love you enough? You see, you competed with her art for her attention, did you not? She was absorbed, you were left there with nothing to do but fight. How precisely did you get her attention, Mr Cardew?'

'I believe I amused her.'

'Ah. . . ?'

'Acts. Different parts. Voices from the radio, that sort of thing.' Dan Dare, Pilot of the . . . Mrs Dale and ooold Waaalter Gaabriel. Then she would laugh and clap. Clever boy!

'You still play parts, don't you?' asked quietly, Signorina Brompton.

'Do I?'

'I'm not worried,' the woman said and smiled professionally, 'but it can cause a problem if oneself is always submerged to a part, so to speak. You see, sexually, you want your mother, Mr Cardew. You want to be dominated by a woman the way she dominated you. Your first sexual experiences, long forgotten in your conscious, are of her. Thus, your relationship with Alice suffered – she was the reverse of your requirement – whilst that with Audrey – a strong, mother figure – flourished.'

'I see.'

'Very good.' More gently, Signorina Brompton asked, 'How are you coping with your loss, Mr Cardew?'

She was the only person there who understood. 'Six months have gone but it's as if she died an hour ago,' Adam said quietly. 'If I wake with joy in my heart, the joy withers as soon as I wake. I try to cry out but something drags down my tongue by its roots. I look at trees and birds and I envy their existence. I see old people with exasperation. I look at myself and I wonder what death must mean. I spend all my waking day reconstructing hopeless options in which everything but history happens. I ask myself why I was unlucky enough ever to be born.' Adam looked at the analyst, at her narrowed eyes, at her quiet pen. 'I'd rather you forgot all that,' he said.

Signorina Brompton closed her eyes. 'God help you,' she said softly. With a deep breath she came to. 'Well, there it is,' she said brightly, closing her file, clipping away her pen, hiking her bag to her shoulder and allowing Adam to pull out the table. 'We probably shan't meet agin. Goodbye, Mr Cardew.'

'Goodbye, Miss Brompton.'

Adam had changed. Without his beard, the San Paolo regime had brought a hollowness to his cheek and a sharpness to his chin. Where before his flesh had corrugated, now it ran firm and smooth. Slumped in San Paolo's cool church, he could hear Zoe's footsteps in his head. He clung as if to life to the gem he had espied in my report.

'Avanti.'

Baptisto the Cat shared his stone tower with songbirds, safely but sadly in their cage.

'Padre.'

The priest sat briskly up, one elbow on the arm of his chair. 'Your confession.'

Adam knelt. 'Bless me, Padre, for I have sinned.'

'How have you sinned, Adam?'

'I have had doubts in the goodness of God, Padre.'

'God is infinitely good, Adam, all He asks of us is faith in His goodness. How have you doubted Him?'

'In asking myself, how could a good God countenance the misery of His own making?'

'That is a normal doubt. It is enough to trust in God's wisdom and to realise that His plan is beyond our comprehension. How else have you sinned, Adam?'

'In my mind.'

'Your thoughts.'

'Yes. I have sought in my mind harm to those whose actions caused the death of the one I loved.'

'That is normal. You must pray for their salvation. In what other thoughts have you sinned?'

'Those against purity.'

'With whom?'

'With women.'

'With women it is natural and normal. You must pray for strength to withstand such thoughts. You must mortify yourself in the knowledge that the joy of conquering lust far exceeds any animal climax. Perhaps there are your other sins, Adam, old sins that trouble your soul at night.'

'Those are my sins, Padre.'

Master Baptisto stroked his chin. 'The sacrament of penance is one of Christ's greatest gifts,' he purred. 'Within its code of solemn secrecy the penitent may divulge not alone his sins but also, in a manner that is childlike and innocent, all the aspects of his life that might otherwise remain troubled and hidden. We are two souls, Adam, interchangeable and indivisible in our love of Christ. Hide not from me your soul.'

Baptisto the Cat, seducer of souls: he would wait and wait until a man's soul was laid out in fillets.

'I hide nothing, Padre.'

'Mmm,' the priest hummed. 'We have a sub-house in Napoli, in the Quartiere Spagnolo, where but for God's hand the jaws of despair would never open and let go. Fratello Francisco has already gone there. You will find Padre Patrizio an interesting penance. Until Christmas, then.'

'Grazie, Padre.'

November was marked only by the shorter evenings, not by the sudden frosts and snows that were sweeping England. Italian papers and television dealt with matters English fleetingly; Adam yearned to ring someone and ask: how is Alison faring? And Angie? What are they thinking in QAG? Have they forgotten me? Have they discovered what I took with me? How is Counsell?

'Of course, St Patrick was an Englishman,' said Father Patrick, adding, 'like yourself, Mr Adam, I am right?' Despite the Neapolitan nut of his old face, Father Patrick spoke with the whining burr of the Falls. They walked through ancient tenements, pinned by a web of scaffolding against collapse: Adam, Father Patrick and raven-haired Fratello Francisco from Palermo.

'Bit of a mystery man, St Pat, you know,' said Father Patrick slyly. 'Shelves of books, wondering who he was, where he came from. Popped up in Ireland out of the blue. A bit like yourself in Rome.' The old priest suddenly ignited:

' "Hail glorious Saint Patrick, dear saint of our isle,
On us thy poor children bestow a sweet smile . . ." '

'Salve Padre Patrizio!'

' ". . . And now thou art high in the mansions above . . ." '

Leaning out warmly to observe from a first-floor window was a girl of sixteen. The sun spanked off Francisco's upraised smile.

' ". . . On Eireann's green valleys look down in thy love!" '

'Evviva, Padre Patrizio!'

'Grazie, grazie, cara signorina.'

'You have quite a following, Father.'

'I was the Gigli of our house in West Belfast, didn't you know?' Father Patrick forged into a courtyard where, among steel uprights, stools and crates were set. 'Papa Cecilio! Tre espressi, per favore!' The old priest winked to Adam. 'Papa Cecilio's devotion to Our Lord means coffee for His servants.' He had very pale blue eyes; and once he had red hair some of which still sprouted from his eyebrows, though his head was bare as Papa Cecilio's doorstep. All around was hung with washing through which morning sunlight glanced. Father Patrick produced, one by one, three cigarettes. 'A rare instance where the expressly forbidden may be ignored without the incurring of sin.'

'Il cuore del Padre,' said Francisco cheerfully as Father Patrick cupped light for all of them from a cheap lighter.

'One cigarette a day couldn't kill a man,' Father Patrick scoffed. 'Ah, Papa, grazie.'

'Ecco Padre, Fratelli.' Papa Cecilio, ripe pepperoni. Fat thumb and finger transferred steadily three viscous jewels. 'Prego.'

Father Patrick drew down smoke in one terrific gulp and leant back as fumes seeped ecstatically out his nostrils. 'Ah, this is the life,' he said. 'Isn't this the life, Francisco?'

'Life is good!' smiled swarthy Francisco and flicked his coffee down in one.

'You find happiness where you expect misery,' sighed Father Patrick happily. 'Nothing is as it seems, not even hope. But maybe that's not your experience, Mr Adam?'

'We manufacture hope,' Adam said, and then feeling suddenly reckless added, 'in the same way as we manufacture God.'

'Black heresy, He's meant to have manufactured us, but I'll overlook it,' Father Patrick said. He suddenly looked and saw Francisco at the neck of the alleyway. 'Hey, where's that young fellow off to? Francisco! We have work to do!'

'Torno subito!' Francisco waved.

Father Patrick shook his head, inhaled his cigarette. 'So, tell us, where did you say you came from, Mr Adam?'

'I didn't,' Adam smiled, 'but I lived in London.'

'You'll have to forgive my curiosity,' the priest said. 'Born with it, you know. At least it means my head still works. Tell us, what hope can be manufactured from grief?'

'Little,' Adam replied, on his guard.

'That is what I would imagine,' Father Patrick nodded. 'A celibate can never know the joy you once knew, but equally I am spared the grief.'

'You may be the luckier.'

'Tell me about the love for a child, Mr Adam.'

'Whatever it is, there is no recovering from it.'

'Then I think you are the luckier.'

'You have the love of God, Father.'

'Ach!' Father Patrick shook his head. 'Love of God is an acquired state of mind. It shouldn't be called love at all, more like respect, or recognition of your place in the run of things.'

'Is it still that difficult?'

'Anything alive always has problems. I comfort myself as being answerable ultimately to some random yet benign force.'

'Random?'

'Little children die of AIDS,' Father Patrick said. 'They are totally innocent and good – how could they be otherwise? God, we believe, is just and fair. He is also meant to be all-powerful. If God is all-powerful *and* just and fair, how can he allow little children to die of AIDS? Is it that they deserve to die in this way? Surely not. Is it part of God's hidden plan? That's a lot of baloney to the mind of a modern man. Is it that God is *not* good? To be not good is to be evil, and since evil wouldn't be identifiable without the existence of good, then if God is evil, good exists by some other name than God. Is it not, Mr Adam, that God is good and the little children don't deserve to die, but that God can't do anything about it because He is not all-powerful?'

'God is meant to have created the universe,' Adam said.

'Just because you create something, Mr Adam, doesn't mean you're all-powerful. Parents create a child, but they can't control it. An artist creates a painting or a piece of music, but can't control the effect it may have on millions. God may be more human than we give Him credit for. That's a personal view, mind.' Father Patrick peered at the mouth of the alleyway. 'There are few things more random than Fratello Francisco. Heaven help me, but I'm taking him home to Belfast with me in January.'

'I'd like to go there some day.'

The old priest cocked a foxy eyebrow. 'Are you sure you're not a spy from MI5?' he asked solemnly.

Adam carried everywhere images of Zoe: in all her ages, dead from a distance, in his arms as a child, in Giorgio's as a woman. He could never believe afresh that she was dead; each time he took the punch as if it was the first; each time he blamed himself anew. Seeing life in full flow and himself peering in was too much. One November day, with the clatter of Naples all around him, he rang Angie.

'Hello?'

Adam imagined the room, sunny even in November; the cat; the rugs and whitewashed walls.

'Hello? Who is this?'

He could not speak. Behind him, Papa Cecilio bellowed from his courtyard to his kitchen.

'It's you, Adam, isn't it?' came Angie's voice with its hint of scolding into dusty Naples.

Adam could only think of the cruelty of life's illusions.

'Adam, if it's you, I do love you,' Angie said.

Adam replaced the phone as curious, huge-eyed children in bare feet stared. Loneliness reached an exquisite perfection that day in Naples.

At the year's turn, the gardens of San Paolo were cold and empty after Naples: the thing had almost run its course and still lay in the balance, undecided. Back for his last mass came old Padre Patrizio, but without Fratello Francisco. The young raven of Palermo had taken off with a girl from the Quartiere Spagnolo. The defection drove Master Baptisto's sense of betrayal to new heights.

'Each year's crop of novices is like a wine harvest,' he said softly. 'Some years, a rich vintage. Other years the vines breed . . . rot.'

Adam was desperate for something to give this hateful man.

'Rot, Adam.'

'If I have fallen in any sin . . .'

'Want of charity, Adam!'

'Padre?'

'Towards me, Adam!' Master Baptisto's hands clutched at his chest, flowered. 'Lack of charity towards me! You came as a stranger. I took you into San Paolo with openness and trust. Sent you to Naples. Now there is talk of your going to Belfast with Padre Patrizio. I will not let you go! I do not lock my doors at night; neither do I lock my heart or mind. A thief locks his door because he sees all men as he is.'

What had driven Baptisto in here all those years ago, Adam struggled to wonder? What had the man suffered? Or run from himself? Or given up?

'The Lamb of God must defend Himself from betrayers!' hissed Master Baptisto.

' "Betrayers", Padre?'

'You say my words to make it seem it is you that is under attack!' cried the priest in consternation.

A need aching to be satisfied – but what? 'My future is in your hands, Padre.'

'This is a time for birth and rebirth!' Baptisto hit down his fist as if to bludgeon the frustration that was engulfing him. 'Rebirth, now or never, Adam! Now or never!' He adjusted himself sideways. 'Your confession.'

'Bless me, Padre,' said Adam kneeling, 'for I have sinned.'

'How have you sinned?'

'There were other women,' Adam said and covertly watched the priest's side face.

'You are brave, Adam,' whispered Master Baptisto. 'You have come to march in Christ's army.'

'I loved another woman in particular.'

'Poor flesh!'

'That is the life I have left behind.'

'Men do not run from mere adultery. You come suddenly to a foreign land to seek the life in Christ in His Order of Friends. Why?'

'In my grief I seek my salvation.'

'Grief is a transient condition. I understand grief. You have other reasons.'

'I have no other reasons.'

'You are a false man!' Master Baptisto cried, turned eyes burning. 'You come here for a hidden secret!'

'Please, Padre.'

'Tell me now or never!'

'I have.'

'There is more!' The priest tapped his nose. 'Has this been wrong for twenty years? Believe me when I tell you, I can smell the guilt in a man's soul.'

'What would you have me say?'

'The truth!'

'I have.'

'You lie! You hide! There is no place for you here, dissembler!'

'Damn it!' Adam shouted up. 'What do you want me to do?'

'Expurgate your pride!'

'My only pride was in those I loved!'

'Yet even as you pretended to love them you sneered at their innocence and swelled other vessels with your sin!'

'You . . . swine!'

'There! That is why I say you are a false man!' cried Master Baptisto in triumph. 'You take love for granted. I will not allow you to take for granted the love of our Order, to turn it to your own ends, whatever they may be! Tell me otherwise!'

In the priest's nostrils, in the hot coals of his eyes, prurience boiled and in a white hot second of revulsion Adam realised what would satisfy the man. That was the moment when with a word Adam might have squandered the treasure he had culled from my report, but he held. Master Baptisto had crossed with busy breath to a cupboard and was returning, one hand by his side.

'Come with me,' he said, allowing Adam to precede him to his bathroom. 'Remove your habit, Adam.'

'Remove. . . ?'

'Your habit,' repeated Master Baptisto.

Adam lifted up and off his habit and stood gingerly in shorts and halter six inches taller than the master of novices whose eyes were cast in a slant of avoidance.

'Take the discipline.'

111

A handle of well-polished wood had bound to it short lengths of fishing cord with tips of tiny razor fragments.

'Stand in the bath.'

Three sides were white tiled. Across the front ran a curtain rail.

'Draw the curtain.'

Adam's head was level with the rail as he drew the white plastic. On the floor outside he could see handsome Master Baptisto kneel and touch all four points in a wide cross.

'Adam, God allowed His Son to be scourged. Your penance for all the past sins of your life is to mortify your flesh. In that mortifying you will also drive out the pride that has seized you and so open your soul to me. Apply the discipline bravely, Adam, and show me that you are worthy of Christ's calling.'

Adam felt himself in the grip of an obscene seduction that, even as he stood there, caused his penis to fill. The first over-shoulder lash sent through him stinging a chorus of raw screams. 'Ah!' Around his belly he wound into the small of his back the teeth and felt his skin puncture. 'Ah!' He transferred hands and flogged his shoulders and opened his eyes to see a coin of his own flesh sliding lazily down a tile. 'Oh, Jesus Christ.'

'Call to Christ, call out to Him, Adam!'

Adam swung the dripping heads. 'Oh Jesus!' Sticky blood began a dribble through his groin and down his thighs to make his feet glue. 'Jesus!'

'Kneel and continue the discipline.'

Adam smeared the bath's smooth sides. 'Ah!'

'You feel a cleansing, Adam?'

Adam's heavy hand guided the flails and he screamed out long, 'Ohhhh Jeeesus!' Flaccid.

'Tell me everything of your sin, Adam!'

He still could not give words to the lie. 'Oh, Christ, I have.'

'You hide from Christ's love!'

'God help me, I do not.'

'Why have you come to San Paolo, Adam?' the priest asked, not inches away. 'Apply the discipline and speak the truth. What is your secret?'

'Ah, ah . . . I can't do this anymore . . .'

'You feel a cleansing rising within you like a young bride feels

112

the first joyful kick in her womb, Adam! Tell me your secret! Apply the discipline!'

'Oh my God . . , the blood . . . I have . . .'

'Yes!'

'Sinned.'

'Yes! Apply the discipline! You have sinned!'

'Ah! Yes!'

'Against God and Nature?'

'Yes!'

'Tell me, Adam, then you may cease to apply the discipline. Tell me!'

Blood everywhere, and tears. But, despite them, victory was near at hand. 'I – loved – a – young – girl.'

'God forgives you, Adam, He forgives you! Go on!'

'I loved her – more than her mother.'

'She was . . . your daughter?'

'Yes!' Adam cried and bared his teeth and buried between his spattered knees his face.

'Do you hate yourself, Adam, more than you have ever loved?'

'Yes. Yes. Yes. Yes. Yes.'

A slow, shuddering exhalation came from the other side of the curtain and all the friction that had charged the air melted. 'God trembles, but He forgives you, Adam,' sighed Master Baptisto. 'I know now from what you hide.'

Zoe, forgive me for feeding your beautiful body to this monster's imagination.

'God abhors your dreadful sin, Adam, but in the expunging of your pride and the sharing with me of your dark soul, it is forgiven. You have taken a huge step on the road to Christ. Brother Adam, you are welcome into our midst.'

Citlet Pretty

I should, of course, have remembered Angie. Her house and business in Victoria, her relationship with Adam and her following to San Francisco had all been treated in great detail in Sir Trevor Tice's file. Two days after Angie's call I drove to a hotel on Dublin's north side used mainly by American tourists and half empty in March. Although I was uncomfortable that Angie was seeing fit to come and tell me rather than the police in the UK what she knew, and that consequently my new status (or non-status) may have give her the wrong impression, I was equally full of the high hopes that come with the unexpected appearance of a short cut. On the far side of the otherwise unoccupied hotel lounge sat a fair-haired woman of forty with a square, determined face.

'You had a pleasant trip, I hope,' I said as we shook hands.

'Under the circumstances,' said Angie.

I sat and observed her taking the measure of me. If a last-minute decision on her part was required before deciding to trust me, that was fine. Angie had long, capable fingers and white, pointed fingernails. She wore no jewellery. 'I've never been to Ireland before,' she remarked, looking around. 'Dublin is somehow bigger than I had imagined.'

I mentioned something about modern cities and the times we live in, and ordered tea.

'Superintendent, may I enquire what obligations your position puts you under in respect of anything I may tell you?'

There was a taut brightness about her that put me in mind of an evangelist. 'What is your information about my position?'

'You went to Ulster to find Adam. You were implicated in the death of an SAS officer. You have been suspended. At least that is what the newspapers said.'

'They were right.'

'Then we can talk unofficially.'

'I can listen unofficially.'

'May I then ask, what were your intentions, had you found Adam, Superintendent?'

She was the sort of woman whom a man hates to cross and will avoid dealing with in order not to risk doing so. 'At the time, to bring him back to Dublin and see him safely home,' I replied carefully.

'And now?'

'That's a hypothetical question.'

'Hypothetically, then.'

'To bring him back to Dublin,' I replied, 'but rather than talk in such hypotheses, Angie, it may be better not to talk at all.'

'Adam has gone outside the system,' said Angie, undeterred. 'He's now an embarrassment to the people he once worked with. They don't like being embarrassed. I need someone to talk to, Superintendent.'

'I suggest you call me Brian.'

'Brian,' Angie said firmly.

'Why don't you tell me about Adam, Angie,' I said reassuringly. 'I think we both now have a reasonable picture of each other.'

She summed me up by whatever yardstick she was using. 'I feel . . . accountable, Brian. Adam and I, you may know, we have had a relationship . . .'

I nodded to spare her the burden of the details.

'I went overboard on Adam, I now see. To me he seemed to just . . . accept the fact that a suspect had been set free from a court over here and that that was that. I could not accept it. I wanted him to use his position to bring pressure to bear, to fight, fight, not to lie down, but not to . . . do what he appears to have done.'

'Which is what, Angie?'

She looked at me defiantly. 'I believe he's on a revenge mission.'

Tea was brought to us across the lounge by trolley and served in sturdy cups with gilt rims. 'Did Adam ever mention a plan?' I asked and poured.

'No, not at all.'

'Did he mention Sir Robin Counsell?'

'Never.'

'Or a secret report on the IRA?'

'No.'

'Did you get the impression, after you went overboard on him, as you put it, that Adam was out to avenge Zoe's death?'

Angie's eyes flashed a salvo at me. 'To the contrary,' she said coolly, 'he seemed suddenly to recover.'

'You say you know that Adam's alive, Angie.'

'Yes. He rang me.'

'When?'

'Mid-November.'

'Mid-November?'

'I know it sounds an impossibly long time ago.'

It did. But at least if he was alive in November it ruled out suicide. You don't go away and wait two months before doing it. 'Who did you tell about this call?'

Angie looked at me as if I almost amused her. 'When first Adam disapeared I rang the police every day. Then my telephone began making peculiar noises. I went to San Francisco on business in September and I was followed, all the way to San Francisco. I suppose you can understand that.'

I said it was difficult sometimes to understand anything.

'I nearly rang them to tell them Adam had contacted me, then I stopped to think. For them he's obviously a criminal, but for me he's done nothing wrong. It's his safety I'm concerned about and, in that respect, his so-called colleagues couldn't care less. To whom could I turn?' Angie asked, looking at me deeply. 'In January I read your name in the newspapers, Brian. If I may say so, I thought, anyone whom the system so vilifies may, for reasons that are beyond me, be on Adam's side. I nearly rang you then, but I hadn't the courage. Then last week I read about Sir Robin Counsell's suicide.'

Counsell again. Had ever one man's lonely death brought about such prospects of redemption?

'I could see the whole thing was rotten to the core,' said Angie grimly. 'Just as I told Adam that Zoe deserves more, I told myself that Adam deserves more. He mustn't go the way of Counsell. He must be found. He must be persuaded to abandon whatever madness he has set out on.' Angie made a little shrug that was a suddenly soft gesture in her otherwse determined facade. 'I have found the courage.'

116

It had crossed my mind that this woman might have been turned by Tice; but having met her I knew that whatever else she might be, at least duplicity in her was not an issue. 'So where was he ringing from, Angie?'

'I don't know.'

I looked at her. 'What did he say?'

'Nothing.'

'I see,' I said, as my short cut ran out.

'There was just background noise,' said Angie. 'But it was Adam. I know.'

'This was around the time your phone was being tapped,' I remarked.

'This wasn't some ham-fisted effort to tap my phone,' said Angie impatiently. 'This was Adam. I know. He was still alive. He is. I know he is.'

Life stirred as lunchtime got underway. From the upper deck of a bus squealing past, white faces looked in at us. Adam Coleraine may or may not have been drifting about in the ether last November, four months before. It didn't bolster confidence.

'What I really want to say,' said Angie quietly, 'is that if you find him, then I can help you. That's why I'm here. I want him home alive. Adam will listen to me.'

'Thank you,' I said, reluctant to give her any indication as to my intentions.

'You don' believe me, do you?' Angie asked. 'You think the last thing in the world you would want is to involve me, a woman, I know. But Adam doesn't know you, Superintendent. He may react violently. He would not so react were I there. I could persuade him.'

I could see how she might. 'Trust me,' I said. 'If I genuinely think I need you, then I will ring you.'

'Do you promise that?' Angie asked with a look that dared promises to be broken.

'Yes,' I replied, only because I could never visualise the circumstances arising. 'Try not to worry.'

We walked out together through the front door of the hotel as if to poke our meeting in the eye of whoever might be watching.

'I know logic points to Adam's being in Ulster, Brian,' Angie

117

said and looked suddenly uncomfortable. 'I don't want to say this, but I feel I must.'

It seemed impossible to me that anyone could hold such strong beliefs in the midst of so many uncertainties. 'Yes?' I said.

'I'm *sure* it was Adam on the phone. But equally I'm sure the call was made from a foreign country. Spain or Italy perhaps. There were background noises.'

'Spain or Italy,' I repeated. I had never met someone quite like Angie before.

'It doesn't help, does it?' Angie sighed. 'I'm sorry, but you had to know.'

I put her into a taxi for the airport and began the drive back across town. The best way to deal with the meeting I had just had, I reckoned, was to forget it.

*

Belfast to Adam that January had been a little city all rushed up the neck of a pretty valley to cling to the last fair ground before the sea: a nucleus of stern buildings put up a century ago to make fast the stanchions of empire; great, ship-building cranes that reared from the very heartland to show why the city had survived; a grid-like centre that mimicked places such as New York, a borrowed sense of importance created by canyons, bustle, a telescoping vista of many blocks full with the echo of traffic and ending with distant mountains. A little city, Belfast was for him, but pretty; a citlet pretty.

Saint Paschal's Belfast residence was once the home of a man who shipped flax and wanted to live in the country. High on the western Valley Road between city and mountain, it stood like a mother over all the ranks of little roofs marching down the glen. From a high sitting room overlooking a garden, Adam looked down on the mesh of streets below him, the Craigs and Torneroy, the hill of Hannahstown, the Ionans that crept like fingers up out of Ballymurphy. Rising coal smoke from hearths, smells of fat from pans. Every night beside their bed down there someone knelt and said, 'Bless me, for I have sinned: I murdered a girl named Zoe Coleraine'.

Among old men who had turned to the world their

118

impenetrable black shells like insects making ready for death, Adam suddenly began to lose Zoe. He would sit and try to force her back but with each further forcing she faded more until eventually his mind could not even summon up a picture of what Zoe might have looked like, not even dead, in the distance, beyond the reach of his courage, cold, waiting for him one last time, could he recall her. He tried to summon her – her skin, peach-like, her sweetness of taste and touch – but she refused to hear his call. Perhaps in Sidcup, he thought desperately, in her room, smells of her might still linger and re-make with their fragile gases her memory. It became worse. He became deprived of her name. In agony he explained to himself, oh yes, my girl, no mark on her, a bomb, I buried her, of yes, she had a name, she had.

Adam had to hurl out at all hours up the Black Mountain in night as dead as his heart, as lifeless as his memory. There he would stand out in wind blow and listen for the sound to be brought over the sea, he would listen for hours until at last it came, Zoe, Zoe, Zoe. February had loomed.

'Trouble in Africa.' Father Superior brimmed himself tea. 'Over a hundred killed in the townships.' A man of mid-sixties, his hair stood up in tufts from his bare head like the last trees in a felling operation.

'The world is in trouble,' said Father Patrick.

'Were they not better off before, I sometimes wonder?' asked Father Superior, floating on cream, just a thimble. 'Democracy is dizzy stuff, you know, if you're not used to it.'

'Trouble?' enquired Brother Walter, a gardening man.

'The South African townships,' Adam explained. 'Rioting.'

'Rioting?'

'Over a hundred dead.'

'Really. Missed that,' said Brother Walter, gently perplexed.

'Brother Adam is a man of the world,' smiled Father Patrick good naturedly. 'Isn't that right, Adam?'

Adam smiled at the old man's digging.

'He's a spy, in actual fact,' said Father Patrick, 'sent over here by the British government to infiltrate our ranks. He works for MI5, isn't that right, Adam?'

'That's correct,' Adam replied.

119

'You'd better watch out, Blaise, he's after republicans the likes of you,' Father Patrick chuckled and winked at Adam.

Father Blaise, a short, thick slab of a man with black curly hair and burning eyes did not share the joke.

'Blaise was with our mission in Somalia,' said Father Patrick to Adam gently and smiled at Father Blaise.

'You give them the vote and they throw it away or, more likely, never bother to use it,' said Father Superior, still on the townships.

'But then, isn't it their choice?' asked Father Patrick. After twenty years, his rheumatism seemed proof that he had never really left Belfast. 'Isn't that what oppression is, lack of choice?'

'A parent can hardly be held up as the oppressor of a child denied its every choice,' said Father Superior, sipping.

'But,' said Father Patrick testily, 'these are no longer children.'

'Mmmmm, it may not be in their best interests to give cornucopias of riches to people who are still essentially childlike,' said Father Superior, swallowing. 'Nowadays, I'm afraid, you find criminal elements behind everything.'

Father Blaise slammed down his cutlery.

'I wouldn't live anywhere else but Belfast,' smiled Brother Walter to Adam, 'although I grew up in Limerick.'

'In my day,' said Father Patrick for Adam, 'the Church lit up the darkest corners of sin. Now we're losing the working class, the people at the heart of the struggle here, for example. The Church's decision to excommunicate their leaders, to lock out so-called subversives into the darkness, to make their re-entry a thing of preconditions has been a disaster. We have become political.'

'Our Lord vested authority in His bishops and His Church,' reminded Father Superior and gathered together like jackdaw's nests his eyebrows. 'It is not for us to usurp it.'

Father Blaise stood up abruptly. He swept around the table, stacking the plates in a series of clatters, then dumped them on a central trolley with a crash.

'What right have we to make a judgement?' Father Patrick asked. 'In Latin America we are on one side, in Belfast on another. I look back in the confession book in the sacristy for twenty years ago. I heard confessions here two hours every morning and evening. Now I need a box two hours a week.'

120

Like a weary traveller who has reached his long-sought destination but is so exhausted he only slowly recognises the fact, only slowly did Adam grasp what was being said.

'Obedience by example,' indulged Father Superior. 'It is not for us to agree or disagree, but to obey.'

'Two hundred yards from our gates are people whose days and nights are a misery of poverty and oppression,' snapped Father Patrick. 'Are we to ignore them?'

Adam watched Father Blaise, standing to one side, skinning an apple with a sharp knife.

'One rises above,' insisted Father Superior, 'so that one can help those below. One leads by example.'

'Christ chose thieves as his last companions,' said Father Patrick grimly.

'We must not overreach our position,' said Father Superior sternly for Adam's attention. 'We must not provoke the bishops to see us as unwilling to conform.'

Father Blaise laid the apple on a plate before Father Patrick. 'Thank you, Blaise. St Paschal would have told their lordships to take a jump in the Lagan,' Father Patrick said.

'Our Lord gave no mandate to take life,' said Father Superior darkly. 'Those whom the Church has seen fit to chastise must not be given a backdoor accommodation.'

Blaise's slam of the oak door behind him shook the whole room.

'Rather than excommunicate Judas, Our Lord allowed Himself to be betrayed in the Garden of Gethsemane,' said Father Patrick.

'I love my garden,' Brother Walter beamed to Adam. 'Small, but you won't find a weed in it.'

The church was the size of a small cinema. Looking from the door, pews either side of an aisle filled the nave as far as a communion rail and then an altar. On the side walls were confession boxes of polished wood, a pair to each side; when in use the confessor hung up his name outside the central booth wherein he sat. He would have been surprised, the flax merchant of the century before, coming out on a mid-February night to listen for his horses' chomping and hearing instead men at their prayers.

'No man who practices deceit
Shall live within my house.'

121

Candles in warm cups at an altar of candles to Our Lady made the chapel ceiling weave and flicker. Mother and Virgin. Mysterious as the unfathomable mysteries of a woman's mood. As Alison's periods. The profound despair after Zoe: leave Sidcup in the morning, child and mother smiling; return that evening to Zoe wet and crying and Alison locked in the bathroom, locked because she knew Adam couldn't cope with or understand the thick globs of blood nosing from her, woman's curse, valley of tears, although he knew Alison blamed it all on Zoe; but Zoe's the lucky one, she's alright, okay?

Adam was suddenly overwhelmed by need for Angie: strong and, at the same time, soft, her skin, her mouth. Angie, beautiful and strong. He began to falter. Where was the evidence of what he had found in my report? He had exchanged Angie for this, for nothing.

'No man who utters lies shall stand
Before my eyes.'

Adam looked across the aisle and found Father Blaise looking back, giving the chanted words of the office meaning for Adam alone.

'Adam!'

At the sacristy door Father Patrick beckoned. Adam rose, genuflected, crossed the evening church of soft light.

'Come on,' Father Patrick said, a satchel in his hand. 'A shooting down in the Falls, we've been called.' He looked out at the night. 'I'm too old for this.'

Rain wet both men in the short space between front door and car. The screw of panic, begun in the church, still turned deep in Adam.

'A Mrs Gormley,' Father Patrick was saying. 'Been in bed for ten years, poor woman. Husband was a ne'er-to-do-well, I remember him. Seems this evening her youngest lad was challenged near his house. Didn't stop. They live on the Peace Line. What kind of a name is that, I ask you?'

The Fall lay under yellow light in silent menace.

'I'll tell you a good one,' Father Patrick said. 'Between us, alright?'

'Alright.'

122

'Knock on my door a couple of nights ago. Who was there but poor Blaise.' Father Patrick, laughing, wiped mist from the windscreen. 'Now, there's no one I'm fonder of than poor Blaise. But he had this face on him.' Father Patrick drew down his face like putty. ' "Father Patrick," says he. D'you know the way he speaks?'

'He and I have never spoken.'

'Well he's got this deep voice. "Father Patrick," says he, "do we really have a spy in our midst?" ' Father Patrick clapped Adam on the arm. 'He thinks you're a spy.'

'What did you tell him.'

The old priest drew back. 'I told him I thought you were.'

'Was that wise? He's been giving me funny looks.'

'Ah, poor Blaise. Biggest heart here. I love to rise him. But there's knees that kneel to Blaise in our little church that the Brits would love to see swinging,' said Father Patrick and shook his head grimly.

'Top players still?'

Father Patrick turned slowly. 'How do you mean, "still"?'

'Nothing particularly.'

' "Still" means you are confirming something you already know. What do you know?'

'Something someone said in Rome.'

'Who?'

'I can't remember.'

'What did they say?'

'I can't remember exactly.'

' "Hail Glorious, Saint Patrick," ' sang Father Patrick softly as they left the Falls Road. 'Maybe you really are a spy, Adam,' he said. 'Are you?'

'No, Father.'

'Pity. It'd liven up things around here.' Father Patrick gave a throaty chuckle. 'Talking about top players, did you hear about the two lads in South Armagh? They knew this British Army officer took a certain route every Monday morning. They knew he crossed a lonely country bridge at ten to eight. So the lads stuffed two milk churns full of Semtex and put them under the bridge and went up a wee hill opposite with the radio-controlled detonator, don't you know. Well, a quarter to eight they were ready. Eleven

123

minutes to eight you could cut the air with a knife. Ten to eight. Any second now! But no car comes. Five to eight, no sign of him. At five past eight he still hasn't appeared. One lad turns to the other and says, "I hope nothin's happened to him." '

Adam slowed at lights and turned into narrow streets.

' "I hope nothin's happened to him," ' repeated Father Patrick and clapped his hands. 'Turn left here. As long as I'm on the road, I'll tell you, Adam, the twin brother of grief is mirth. Don't ask me why. Maybe it's God's way of telling us that nothing down here really matters, I don't know. I've sat with many a poor widow for the long night of her husband's death, and we've laughed nearly as much as we've cried.'

They were passing gables of giants with hoods and lilies, slashing them with the headlight beams. Knots of men and women appeared until suddenly every corner had one, then every lamppost, then every doorway, men and women watching silently through a yellow veil of rain. Adam followed Father Patrick's directions, clipped a pavement corner over the white middle bar of a tricolour, squealed left and right with wet splashes, the lights making dancing eyebrows on the walls, around a sharp corner and skidded steaming almost into a wall of armoured cars. Over sauntered a shape in battledress, dropped helmet visor, finger hooked to a cradled trigger. Through the slanting rain three gun positions were trained on them and, as Adam opened his window, the disembodied voices from radios stabbed the night.

'Lost your way, 'ave you?'

Father Patrick leant over. 'Roman Catholic priests.'

The shape looked cautiously in at them, went around and punched up the boot, slammed it, backed off in careful, jaunty steps, signalling. A gap grunted open in the steel wall and the car was waved through. Daytime seemed trapped in the little street by the army's arc lights. Green, white and gold cardboard squares were pasted sodden and uneven on upstairs cills and windows. Soldiers holding semiautomatics crouched by doorways or lay sprawled in firing position on the roofs of jeeps. As Adam drove through police tape to Father Patrick's instructions, a very tall, caped RUC officer stepped out, straight as a lighthouse, rain bucketing off the peak of his cap, the ends of his moustache, the hem of his coat.

'Roman Catholic priests.'

'Very well. Leave the keys.'

The last house in the row but one was full: people in the hall, along the walls, on the stairs' linoleum steps. Talk ceased. From the low ceiling came sobs, falling down on the newly-silent heads like snow. A wild young man of flowing hair and beard stepped forward.

'She's keeping him aleyve for yez,' he said drily and led the way up.

The stairs shifted to one side. Adam felt the eyes on him as he climbed last. He made himself look at them, each one. Some returned his gaze but most dropped their eyes or turned their heads away. Step after step: there weren't many, it was a tiny house. Look at me! Adam wanted to shout. You owe me that much! Look at me! Zoe looked at him, a cigarette in her mouth. Adam stood. Immovable. He said, 'Ah . . .' Big, upward-sloping, almond-like eyes, persuasively curving lips, glossy, shoulder-length black hair, Zoe looked at him arrogantly. She couldn't recognise him because one of them was a ghost. Everyone was staring at Adam but he didn't care. 'Ah . . .'

'Brother Adam?' called Father Patrick from the landing.

The girl frisked her head away. Adam stumbled upward, devastated by feelings newly raw. A well-caloried, suited man with a doctor's bag was closing gently a door. He looked at Father Patrick and shook his head. Mrs Gormley's bearded son ground his teeth.

The room was dim; all bed. A woman, it had to be Mrs Gormley, lay up on pillows, black hair around her shoulders, night shift fallen loose to show her chest. A youth lay between her legs as if he always so lay, head on her belly, bare from his trousers up. Her hands were stroking circularly his face like a potter at work. The youth's eyes, huge in a straining, bloodless face, darted at Father Patrick, at Adam. From the floor beside the chimney breast came the low drone of women saying the rosary.

'Ah, Father.'

'Poor Mrs Gormley.'

'Father is here nigh, wee lad. Jerome?' his mother called. 'He was born in this vere beyd,' she hecked.

Adam held the satchel as Father Patrick unloaded a cloth and unfolded it on a table.

'Glory be to the Father, and to the Son, and to the Holy Spirit,' the women prayed.

Father Patrick took out crucifix, vial and candle, and with the cheap lighter Adam remembered from Naples, brought the candle to life.

'As it was in the beginning, is now and ever shall be, world without eynd.'

Out came a round metal dish, a plate, swabs of cotton wool and bread cubes. With huge gulping Jerome's chest suddenly began to leap.

'Ah Gawd, you took away the use of my leygs, don't take from me nigh the light of my life,' cried Mrs Gormley, seizing tighter Jerome's head as Father Patrick dropped urgently. 'Ah, Gawd, what use is another young life to you, what use?'

Over the weeping and the drone Adam could see Jerome listen beyond the dull roar of his pain as Father Patrick whispered in his ear. Jerome's eyes moved in terror, then found Adam and seized on him as if someone younger than the old priest might stop the desperate slipping he knew to be taking place. His chest heaved; he kept his eyes on Adam as if to lose him would be final. Up, higher and higher, Jerome's chest rose. Father Patrick was reaching out his thumb to the boy's eyes. Adam wanted to shout 'Stop!' Jerome's astonished eyes held Adam and both of them knew that Adam's face would be the last thing he ever saw. Father Patrick closed down the lid of each eye efficiently, then dipped one thumb in an oil vial and on each closed eye greased a cross. Down slowly sank the boy's chest gurgling. Father Patrick wiped clean his thumb with cotton wool, returned to the ear lobes, the tips of each barely whistling nostril, the lips, the palms of the hands, the crowns of the feet with their little twitchings.

'He's gone,' Father Patrick murmured.

'Ah, no. Ah, no. Ah, no.'

'He is at peace, Mrs Gormley.'

Dismay surged everywhere in Adam, threatening to overwhelm the muscles for keeping on his feet. 'I'm sorry,' he gulped to Father Patrick. 'I can't stay in here.'

Adam could isolate each noise: the low sawing of voices from the stairs and hall, solid and comforting; from the downstairs, back, cups and plates, delicate percussion; wind whispering through wood, the lonely strains of Mrs Gormley's sobs from her bedroom next door; all to where they had brought him. He dropped his hands, easing back his eyes to light. 'I didn't realise . . .'

She was sitting, looking at him. She took a cup and saucer and handed it to him. 'It's good to cry.'

'I'm sorry . . .'

'Ar eyes are the refleyct'on of ar souls.'

'Yes,' Adam replied and saw that her soul had to be yellow where it borders green. He had no idea how long he had been in the room, nor how long she had been watching him. Zoe melted away in little differences: this girl's nose was smaller, her mouth was sterner, her face broader, she was not as tall as Zoe but firmer, stronger, and simply by the way she sat you could see that life for her was much more serious than Zoe would ever have admitted. 'I . . . never saw someone die before,' Adam said.

'At least he's happy now, or so ye tell us,' she remarked drily.

'It's us who are left behind who really suffer.'

She tilted her chin at him. 'Why should anyone suffer?' she asked.

Adam said without knowing why,

' "When night advances through the sky with slow
    And solemn tread,
The queenly moon looks down on life below,
    As if she read
Man's soul, and in her scornful silence said:
All beautiful and happiest things are dead." '

The girl said,

' "The beauty of the world hath made me sad,
This beauty that will pass . . .
Will pass and change, will die and be no more,
Things bright and green, things young and happy." '

The door opened. 'Ah, poor Brother Adam, here you are,' said Father Patrick, satchel in hand. 'And who is this beauty? I think I chased you from our orchard years ago, didn't I?'

'I don't believe so,' she said.

'If there's one thing I always remember it's a pretty face,' chuckled the old priest, pleased with his game, 'and I wouldn't forget yours in a hurry, young lady. Come on now, put me out of my misery.'

She got up and stiffly took his unavoidable hand. 'Nona Lane.'

'Nona Lane, ah yes, Nona Lane,' said Father Patrick. 'You've met Brother Adam, I take it. Well, come on now, Brother Adam, we can't do any more.' Father Patrick bustled him out. 'Ah, what a waste of a young life, the poor woman, God give her the strength. At least she has all her family and friends around her. The senselessness of it all would knock you over. Goodnight, Nona Lane.'

*

At the end of the first week in March, ten days after my return from Connemara, Janet rang me. The call was overdue; I had not expected that the arrangements Janet was making for me in the north would take so long and I was impatient to see an end to things. All she said on the phone was: 'Problems.' Driving into town that day, I wondered if Janet was having second thoughts.

'It's Maguire.' Walking briskly ahead down the steps in the Garden of Remembrance, Janet took from her bag an envelope and, from that, a photograph. I saw a happy group with the high skin complexions which everyone had in colour Polaroids in the seventies: a beaming priest, a tall woman and, black hair curling over his ears, his arm around the woman's waist, Cyril Maguire. 'Dick Jennings found the photograph two days ago in an old file on Ashe we never knew existed,' Janet said. 'The priest is the current archbishop designate of New York. Maguire had just been made a senator and the occasion was a St Patrick's Day junket with the official purpose of attracting industry from New York. The woman is Mrs O'Connor or, as the New York Police Department briefing of the time points out, maiden name, Ashe. The NYPD evidently took our ritual condemnations of violence in Northern Ireland literally and sent on a full description of Mrs O'Connor's fund-raising function in Noraid.'

'He wouldn't be the first,' I remarked.

'It was a long time ago,' Janet said and stopped beneath the shoulder of a granite wall. 'But suddenly his attitude to me has changed.'

'You're imagining it, Janet.'

Janet gave me one of her higher civil servant looks. 'I'm not imagining the meeting we had yesterday. He somehow knows I know about Ashe, I'd swear it.'

'How could he?'

'Because of Connemara,' Janet said. 'Look, I'm not worried on the count of what happened there. We're both adults.'

'I don't regret it either,' I said.

Janet said, 'I just can't believe that the minister for justice is what this photograph suggests.'

'But if all along he has known what I thought was my exclusive secret,' I said, 'then the basis for our arrangement no longer exists, does it?'

I could see Janet weighing the whole thing up. I think she had exaggerated her description of Maguire's attitude to her in order to see my reaction but, at the same time, she would not have shown me the photograph if she felt she could not trust me. For a moment I felt the burden of her ambition.

'I feel lost,' Janet said, playing a more feminine card.

'What I wonder is why there is a file in the first place,' I said.

'Dick Jennings came across it in the course of some digging I asked him to do,' Janet replied. 'Republicans like the Ashes sometimes attract attention during the term of governments elected on the opposite ticket, so to speak. Ashes aren't the only ones on file.'

'Is there any reference to me?' I asked.

Janet shook her head. 'It's full of information on the Ashe building empire – which, incidentally, isn't much to talk of nowadays.'

'I thought they were flush.'

Janet shook her head. 'Not according to the Department of Finance. The two elder brothers have retired. There's an office in Dublin and some sort of factory in Belfast.'

'Where Vincent spends a lot of his time.'

'Unexplained items appear on the revenue side which Dick says could be a laundering operation for the IRA.'

'Can you trust Dick Jennings?'

'Completely.'

I scratched my head. 'Then what happens from here is really up to you,' I said.

'There's another problem,' Janet said. 'Our information is that MI5 believe and have always believed that Coleraine, wherever he is, is armed.'

'Why didn't they tell us?'

'You know the Brits. By extension, we must now assume that Coleraine will, if found by them, almost certainly meet with an accident before he's brought home.'

'Is this a polite way of suggesting I forget Coleraine and the north, Janet?'

Janet looked at me thoughtfully. 'What is it in that damned report of yours that he has seized upon? There must be *something*.'

'I have tried to think, believe me.'

Janet sighed as if the last opportunity for an easy way out had passed. 'I've already made the arrangements,' she said. 'The reason for the delay was that Edwin, my brother, has been away. Of course, that doesn't mean you have to go.'

'I want to.'

Janet seemed to make her mind up. 'Then here are the details,' she said and handed me a card. 'My brother's name is Edwin Staunch. All he knows is that you're a friend who needs help. Maguire is my problem.' She looked at me sideways and came out with her unexpected laugh. 'I can't wait to hear what you think of my Proddy brother.'

'If he's anything like his sister, then I'll like him,' I said.

We stood with the city roaring around us.

'What's going to happen when this is all over?' asked Janet quietly and I was back in the small hours in Connemara with a lonely woman. It would have hurt her then to tell her the truth. It would have been harsh to the warmth begging in her to say that the events we were caught up in had created for us a transient world, like a part of the heavens being scorched by a shooting star, that when the star had gone she would be left again in the darkness. I said nothing.

'Good luck, Brian,' Janet said and walked away, out of the stone amphitheatre.

Looking at soaring swans in stone, I gave her five minutes. Adam Coleraine armed was a different matter. I found myself wondering if Angie might not, in fact, be able to help.

Nona Lane moved down to the Kashmir on word of expected raids in Andersonstown, her home. Leaving half her supper behind, Nona went early to bed. She turned out the light. The room was really too small for a bedroom, but through two paines of glass in the roof Nona could see a flying moon in blue clouds like a brave little boat, like the boats on long days in Donegal. Jesus, how easy it was to slip back into all that old nostalgia. Nona turned into the wall and closed tight her eyes. How easy it was to remember the nice things and to lose sight of a perfectly ordinary Saturday afternoon, of a few fellas in the march with too much drink on them throwin' a few stones at the police? And the tear gas when it came, she remembered the excitement, her just out of school, the first time she felt really important. Flushed with success, they all were comin' home, her brother and herself and a friend of her brother's, for Chreyst's sakes don't teyll m' Ma where we wir. At one the next mornin' the Brits came. Oh, Jesus, forget? Forget the screamin' and shoutin' in the house that had only ever known laughter? Oh God, how many times did she go over that, see Ma's face watchin' her brother bite the soldier on the neck and then seein' him go down from the gun butt like he was dead, oh God, and Ma's screamin' and wishin' out loud to God that ar Da was still aleyve and what he wouldn't do. Forget? Acid bombs, the RUC said, had her photograph from the march. You're for Castlereagh, move it! Forget? Remember the women with plastic gloves who slid up in their blunt fingers where she'd never even put her own, pokin' like they were in somethin' without feelings, oh God, the shame a' that. Then the questions, hours at a time, lights in her eyes, and in the middle of it all in front of them her period came from nowhere, down her legs on to the floor, sittin' there in mucky underclothes, cryin' her heart out and they just laughin' at her pleadin's for water and a cloth, laughin' in her face. 'Later, Nona, maybe later, when you start behavin'.'

Nona was so tired. He kept comin' back into her head. A priest, cryin'. His big shoulders jerkin' as they led him from Mrs Gormley's room the week before. She had seen him comin' up the stairs and the way he had looked at her, into her core, like. He didn't fit. He had wept and that didn't fit. For everyone's safety things always had to fit, Nona had learned. When she went into him with the cup of tea he was sittin', his eyes covered by one hand and his head down, reminded her of the big, stone statue she used to stare at with ar Da near Donegall Place, much bigger than a real person, a man in a cloak sittin' with his head down, that was years ago. When Da died Nona used to sneak down on her own and imagine the statue was poor Da. She was sure he wasn't a priest, just wearin' priest's clothes. Priests had a kind of smell and he didn't. Somethin' about his tree-like bigness that made her want to climb into his branches and hide there. Nona crept down her left hand to meet moist softness riding bone, and she rocked there gently. Hide forever. For the long, long days. Of nothin' to get up for. Of day after day when you couldn't show your face out a doors. Of just boys in the unit, knew everythin' about solenoids and timers, nothin' else. Sniggered at her afterwards when she wanted to hold their bodies to her on account of her bein' lonely, Nona likes it nigh and ageyn surely, set her face against them to no avail, they knew. But with him as with Da she could hide her face in the warm hollows of his big, understandin' chest. Ahh. With a little gasp Nona felt a pinprick of ecstasy shoot from the vast, sweet ocean lapping within her.

Shameful. A priest. Made Nona feel guilty. Jesus, that feeling of hating yourself, Nona was terrified of that, of reading the papers the day after a mission, seeing the photographs with their names, young people just like yourself, terrifying that what you had done meant they were dead. Nona knew she wouldn't sleep that night, despite her tiredness. She slipped off but kept waking, shivering, each time from a dream in which she had been falling.

Adam lay a-bed, in St Paschal's, as the evening noises of the Falls and Shankill, of the Turf Lodge, Ballymurphy and Malone rose up the Valley Road humming. His eyes on the mountain, Adam's mind kept returning to Nona Lane. Her likeness to Zoe, her youth. She swirled around Adam's edges in pleasurable confusion. There was a fatality to her that to Adam was irresistible. Although he would never meet her again he could imagine her there in his bed, a sweetly impossible landfall. A fantasy. He knew Zoe; he knew Nona. He had seen the first look of interest that in a woman's eyes never lies. Looking out to the bare height where he had walked weeping, the stirring in Adam's pith for Nona

132

suddenly outweighed his tears. At his shoulder on the lonan, his finger would trace the line of her cheek from where fell her hair to the tip of her chin. Luminously young. She had put on layers to protect her from the world. Why? What hurt? Child lost, he would peel them all away, one by tender one, loving, like dabbing crusts of tar from the warm body of a seabird. Taking long days. Each straw of hair. Her live, young skin, his taut, the bones of her feet like soft ribbing to his thumbs, her cupped calves, the smooth of each raised knee, the overmuscles of her thighs, satin whisperings beneath his luxurious stealth, the final smooth plains running into her soft darkness, soaring tenderly, arching, making her hotly fluid. Possess.

Adam's pith crept out in a tiny flurry like unexpected snow on the side of the mountain with its pale bands of dying light.

A knock came. Adam's eyes checked the floorboards by his wardrobe before unlocking the door.

'I'm sorry if I'm disturbing you,' said a deep voice.

'Father Blaise. Come in.'

Father Blaise stood by Adam's window. He had no neck to speak of as if his head was a knot on the top of a full sack. 'I see a city in a valley down there, a river and a lough,' he growled. 'Is that what you see, Brother Adam?'

'Yes.'

'I see the spires of Clonard and St Peter's, and the Shankill,' Blaise said. 'Did you know that Shann Choill means ancient church?'

'No.'

'And Ben Madigan means the mountain of Matudan, who was the son of Muiredach, the ninth-century Celtic king of a group of tribes called the Ulaidh. They gave their name to a place called Ulster.'

'You are close to your history,' Adam observed.

'We aren't rooted in this point of time,' Blaise said deeply. 'We come from five thousand years of history. I live in the past just as the people from the past live in the present.'

'I had not grasped that aspect of Christian belief,' said Adam cautiously.

Father Blaise looked at Adam darkly, then he slowly smiled. 'I am a Christian, but I am also a Celt. Maybe that is the difference between us.'

'But what does it mean?'

'Take death,' said Father Blaise thoughtfully. 'I believe that when I die I will be judged by God and punished according to the state of my soul. Don't you?'

'I'm meant to,' Adam allowed.

Father Blaise weighed his head back and forth. 'I also believe that when I die, I'll be no different to a dog lying in a gutter. What are we except mere animals, after all?'

'Harsh,' Adam said, 'but true.'

'But, as a Celt, I thirdly believe that I will survive my death,' Father Blaise smiled. 'I do. I will return to earth and mine will often be the voice you hear laughing in the dead of night.'

Adam sat back. 'You don't find the holding of these three views at the same time . . . confusing, Father?'

'Not at all,' said Father Blaise sternly. He tapped his head. 'You see that? That's what we Irish are cursed with. Talent. Genius. We can see three things – or thirty – all mutually exclusive, and believe in all of them. We can't mind our own business, in other words. Fought among ourselves, handed it all to you, George and Harry, on a platter. Invited you in, would you believe? Feuds of blood, tribe against tribe, brother against brother, blood, that's it, too hot, not cool and useful like yours, John Bull, no fear.'

'But now . . . you're paying the price.'

'Of being taken advantage of, yes.'

'So, what is the difference between then and now?'

'The answer is, they are identically different, diametrically the same, one is the mirror image of the other's obverse, and each are always opposite sides of the same contradiction.'

'I'm no match for you, Father,' Adam said.

'You're not a spy, are you?' Father Blaise asked.

'No.'

'I didn't really think you were,' the priest said, 'but as an Englishman you have a lot of learning to do.'

'I know.'

'Life in general is highly unsatisfactory and admits no solution other than endurance,' the priest said. 'Let me leave you with a few more of our beliefs that help us come to terms with that: to forgive is divine. Do you agree?'

'Yes.'

'Murder is a sin.'

'I believe that too.'

'To be free is to be immortal.'

'Yes.'

'Man is made in the image of God; God is immortal.'

'So we are told.'

'Man's duty, therefore, to the image of God, is to be free.'

Adam shrugged.

'Therefore, a man may kill in his bid to be free,' said Father Blaise from the door. 'Knowing that, God, in His divinity, will forgive him. I'm glad we've had this chat, Brother Adam. Perhaps now we can be friends.'

February passed. There were days when Adam's frustration nearly boiled over to ruin everything. He comforted himself with time in his room, oiling and checking, replacing afterwards the board beneath the wardrobe. His resolve grew with every day into something even harder.

Belfast was to me what it is to most Irishmen from the South: a place in the attic of our minds, seldom visited and, on those rare occasions when it is, quit hastily and with gratitude. I believe it was always so. I remember reading that the linking of Dublin with Belfast by rail happened only by virtue of the intermediate points joining rather than by any grand plan.

They had not remembered among all the impedimenta of office, scrupulously recalled on my fall from grace, my old Walther of thirty years, so it sits in my palm, and the edge of the trigger guard on my finger reassuring that second Sunday morning in March as we crossed sparkling water on the viaduct for Donabate. I looked down at ships in Dundalk and thought of Angie. I had suggested she drive by the ferry from Stranraer to Larne and, from there, to a small hotel in Belfast where I would call her; she had enthusiastically agreed. Across the border the stations became more modern and the day became darker. By the time I took a taxi as agreed to Donegall Square rain was beating in a westerly slant.

Edwin Staunch's insistence that he fetch me showed him sensitive to general preconceptions about the Shankill. I had been in the Catholic Falls on perhaps six occasions in twenty years, but the Shankill was a different matter.

'Mr Kilkenny.' The back door of a black, London-type cab had opened. 'Pleased to meet ye.' Edwin Staunch took the jump seat and shook my hand testingly. My size if not yet my age, he had blonde hair and wore a ribbed, wool shirt open at the neck where hung a lucky, gold tooth from a gold chain. 'It's not often we get a chance to do somethin' for Jan,' he said as we drove away. Jan was immediately a different person to Janet: Jan had once been a girl like her brother still was, someone whose shop front brassiness brought to mind a whole race we Irish knew of but had never met, a people whose culture didn't make them ashamed of money. 'Ye'r a p'licemon dighn in the Free State, Jan teylls us, sir,' Edwin said.

'For my sins, Mr Staunch,' I replied.

'Aye,' Edwin said as if sin was always understood, 'aye. How is the wee lass?'

'Very well,' I replied.

'She's happy down ther?' he asked, a frown ready to anticipate Janet's unhappiness.

'I believe so,' I replied but thought of Connemara.

Edwin looked away from me as if to preserve the integrity of his thoughts. I could see Janet in him when he did that, or the way he crossed his legs. 'Hard t'unnerstan' other people, even a sester. Older than me but we never fought, min', an' when she came home to say how she'd decided to marry dighn ther, I told her, Jan, ye've got yer leyfe, ye know? Min' ye, it nearly killed ar pur father.'

So, even twenty years ago, Jan Staunch from the Shankill had known her own mind and acted accordingly. We had entered an estate of pebble-dashed houses built around wasteland where the lampposts were red, white and blue. Blood-red Ulster hands held out hugely through the rain from gables. At the perimeter of vision, higher buildings looked in as if into a compound.

'Ye'r welcome here, sir, an' ye always will be,' said Edwin as the cab pulled up at the gate of a house faced in multicoloured brick whose garden was crammed with storks and other wildlife in wrought iron. From the upper windows, as in the case of the other houses in the row, flapped the Union Jack.

136

I said, 'My name is Brian.'

'Well, ye'r welcome here, Brian,' Edwin said. 'An' I'm Edwin.'

Carrying my bag Edwin hurried down the path, his hips rolling in his blue jeans. The front hall was tiny, but the carpet was thick, new shag. The new smell of money floated down the stairs; the smell of polished teak floated from the kitchen, briefly glimpsed beyond the hall.

'Brian, this is ar mother,' said Edwin, wiping his feet.

'Ye'r welcome indeed. Ye can call me Mother Staunch.' Janet and Edwin's mother was tiny with the face of a small, pecking bird set off by huge glasses and blue, curly hair. 'Sit ye dighn an' I'll get tee,' she said, 'an then ye can teyll's all about Jan.'

Horse-drawn coaches driven by men in tall hats dashed across the wallpaper; porcelain spaniels, lifesize, lay either side of a stove; and a three-foot, china dalmation gazed in the direction of the window. There was a television and video, and a music centre with stacks of dials. It was hard to imagine Janet, whose expansive house in Connemara seemed to me so much part of her, fitting in here.

'This is very comfortable,' I remarked.

'Ach, there's a lot of unemployment and hardship nigh 'days,' Edwin replied, choosing to take the statement generally. 'God heylp the young tryin' to make a start. 'Twas easier in ar day. The Brits have a lot t'answer for. A crowda dipsticks. This was a gran' little province when we had it to arseylves. Always was. It was the Brits that turned us int'extremists.'

Mother Staunch brought us in a tray of tea and biscuits. 'Dublin's a feyne cetty, really,' she said politely. 'Jan's weddin' sarvice was in a Roman Catholic church, a nice one. Where was it, Edwin?'

'Donnybroo,' Edwin nodded, as if Janet's marriage was reconsidered on a regular basis.

'Aye, Donnybrook,' said Mother Staunch. 'Father wouldn't go in, we all stood outseyde with him for the hour. It wasn't that he wouldn't go in – he couldn't, ye know? He wouldn't stay in the Free State that night either. We come home on the treyn. He was sad that day, the pur mon, leavin' his only daughter ther. But, it was her choice s'far as he was concern'. That's the Protestant way.'

'Mother, Brian and I has business nigh,' said Edwin gently.

'Ach, business, business,' said Mother Staunch, finishing her tea. 'More like children's games. I'll be on my way.' She paused, turning to me. 'Ye're a neyce, big, honest-looking' mon,' she said; then, a little sadly, 'Jan always brought nice freyns her' wheyn she lived at home.'

As she said it I remembered that in some matters women have no secrets.

'So, teyll's, Brian, what can the people of the Shankill do for ye?' Edwin asked as his mother left.

I explained everything, that is everything about Adam Coleraine. I took out the photograph of Adam given to me a liftetime ago by Sir Trevor Tice and handed it over.

'As long runs a fox, he's always caught,' Edwin said softly.

'Approaches have been made about him to . . . the other side,' I explained delicately. 'The nationalist side.'

'An'mals,' Edwin said, 'beggin' yer pardon.'

'They couldn't find him – at the time.'

'I'll try for ye,' said Edwin, slowly. 'I know Jan wouldn't a seynt ye t'us unleyss we could trust ye, an' I have to teyll ye that heyplin' the Free State in any way sticks in my craw. But, that seyd, I heylp ye because ye'r a freyn a Jan's.'

'Thank you,' I said. 'Where do we start?'

Edwin laughed. 'No matter how hard ye want him, mon dear, ye'll find not a soul in Belfawst of a Sunda'.'

That Monday was jungle wetness. Adam knelt in church observing Father Blaise's penitents: two men, a woman; she stayed on afterwards to work her way, businesslike, around the fourteen stations of the cross. Jesus is Sentenced to Death by Pontius Pilate inside the door. Jesus is Scourged one side of the confessional within which Father Blaise sat. Jesus Falls. Along the way Mary Magdalene washes His feet. A whore. Compassion in her heart. Like Becky Cocozza. Stupendous legs. Without her Adam would have died that May night, his heart would have stiffened like a dead fish. Mr Adam Coleraine? Sir, I'm very sorry. Sorry, sorry. What a journey Adam and Christ had made.

Brother Walter came in from the sacristy and fussed over flowers, genuflecting each time he crossed the altar, smoothing its linen, crossing to Our Lady's altar to prise from their brass holders the butts of candles that had been offered there. Good men. A way of life not that greatly different from any other. All men were the same in their rearing penises and their realisation, growing with age, that life is nothing much to lose. Visions of churches and confession boxes leapt from Adam's youth: he had fretted about admitting impure thoughts and plots to murder Pom and robbing an old jar of sixpences; priests long dead asking in voices of stale milk for more details; the relief that came with their forgiveness. As Father Blaise emerged, Adam lowered his head in prayer until the priest had shuffled up the sacristy steps.

'He seemed a decent enough man,' said Father Patrick and put one arm stiff to the dashboard. 'Although I think he got a wee bit of a shock when I said yes to his invitation.'

They had left the Springfield Road for Lanark Way through gates in the Peace Line. Black clouds spiked the evening sky like a Chinese dinner plate. The road was a half-mile strip stuck up the middle of wasteland described by billboards either side as an industrial estate. Houses with the smoothness of new brick were set back from the bonelike emptiness and wrapped around by edged, steel fencing. With the same lack of ceremony that separates life from death they reached red traffic lights on the Shankill.

'Somebody has to make the effort,' Father Patrick said, using his elbow to push home the lock button on his door. 'The Reverend Wylie,' he said, as if he might forget. 'Right here and straight down until I tell you turn.'

They eased off on the green and the evening Shankill stretched before them. 'No Surrender' and '1690' loomed over the Protestant heartland. Leather chairs with crazy, red, crisscross cushions spilled onto a pavement. Takeaways run by Chinese and betting shops with the days' results stuck in the window sold the same food and told of the same horses and dogs as those over on the Falls.

'You and Blaise seem to be getting on well,' observed Father Patrick, looking at Adam sideways.

'I think he has decided to believe me and not you about MI5,' Adam replied.

'It's easy pull the wool over poor Blaise's eyes,' said

Father Patrick mischievously. 'Drive on Adam, you're doing a good job.'

Either side of them butchers wiped clean their day trays. A gospel hall 'Saved thru Faith'. Father Patrick indicated the turn for Adam and they branched off the Shankill Road at a wire-covered, derelict building with dozens of withered flower bunches stuck in its netting, then crossed commonage before coming to a stone church.

'I suppose you heard about poor Blaise . . .' Father Patrick began, but they had arrived at a church in stone. 'Ah, this must be it,' Father Patrick said.

Noises local to the place: children's shouts; cars back up on the Shankill Road, a sudden, whap! whap! whap!, but instantly recognisable as firecrackers. Father Patrick rang the side-door bell again.

'I hope he's remembered,' he said. 'Oh, it's open.'

The corridor to the church struggled for its light the further down it they went. Another door opened into a rectangular hall with a wooden floor, polished and marked out in white for games. A large table was laid out with dozens of cups upturned on saucers.

'Mr Wylie?' Father Patrick called, with increasing doubt. 'Mr Wylie!'

'Just a minute!'

The voice had come from behind a door with a frosted panel and Father Patrick turned to Adam with the little smile of someone who has done the business.

Beyond the white games lines were double doors: Adam touched them and they swung open. The slender windows of Reverend Wylie's church breathed down dying light on polished pews and a stone altar. Banners with vaguely military insignia hung from the rafters, robbing the place of its proportion. Without candles, flowers or lights, its smells were those of recent ghosts. Had they brought Counsell to a place like this? To lie cold but always arrogant beneath the flag of his old regiment? Counsell's justice had been the right kind after all, but would Adam ever get a chance to follow him? Water crashed and overhead tanks and pipes squirted as ballcocks dropped into action. Adam turned back as the small door opened and a young man in an overcoat with an upturned collar slouched out.

'Oh,' Father Patrick said.

'How're ye doin'?' the minister asked. He stood hunched as if always cold, hands in coat pockets. Between flying sprays of rusty hair, a sharp face looked out like an Irish setter from a kennel. Just visible at his throat was a white round of collar celluloid and below it the tiniest patch of purple.

Father Patrick said, 'I thought. I'm sorry. I. Mr Wylie.'

'Mr Wylie's away for a few days,' the minister said. 'He'll be back on Friday. I'm Roy Mackie. What can I do for you?'

'He and I met last week,' said the old priest in confusion. 'He invited me here this afternoon, at least I think it was this afternoon. I'm sorry, we're from Paschal's. I'm Father Patrick, this is Brother Adam. It is . . . Reverend Mackie?'

'Yes, it is. How're ye doin?' Reverend Mackie gave them a brief handshake and returned the hand to its pocket, managing as he did so to look at the watch on his other wrist.

'I'm sure it's me who's mistaken,' Father Patrick said and tapped his head. 'It's not as reliable as it used to be, you know.'

Reverend Mackie nodded very slightly. 'Would you like tea?' he asked.

They stood silently as the kettle began to hum. Adam noticed Reverend Mackie's furry, blonde, thin wrist, the way the purple vest intruded higher than the plastic dog collar, the washed-out blue of the eyes and the way the hair bounced so you could see his ears only when he moved. The minister reminded him of Giorgio.

'Milk and sugar?' asked Reverend Mackie.

Everyone took milk; Mackie took two spoons of sugar, his left hand remaining in the sanctuary of his overcoat; Father Patrick smacked his lips as if this was the best cup of tea ever. 'Are you from Belfast, Mr Mackie?' he asked, as if that might be the key to something.

'Shankill born and reared,' Reverend Mackie replied.

'I hope you can come to St Paschal's with Mr Wylie,' said Father Patrick. 'It's a homely place,' he said, but it came out as a condemnation of where they stood. 'You'd love it.'

'I daresay,' Reverend Mackie said and drank down his tea in a slurp. 'I'll tell Keith. Mr Wylie,' he added with a touch of impatience.

'We've put you on the spot,' Father Patarick said, putting down his cup as if to hurry on. 'But I don't apologise,' he added with a good-natured laugh. 'When I was you young fellows' age I had plenty of friends up the Shankill, plenty. There was no Peace Line then, no line at all. We came and went, we played together like any normal group of young bloods. That's the times we want to see again, Reverend. No lines, no divides. Hands joined together. Boys and girls. We're all the same in Christ, after all, don't you agree?'

Reverend Mackie looked at Father Patrick with eyes consisting of many rings within rings. 'Are you talking about ecumenism?' he asked.

'Oh,' said Father Patrick, keeping up the jollity, 'yes. If you like.'

'I don't.'

'Don't like. . . ?'

'Ecumenism,' said Reverend Mackie into a sudden, little pool of silence.

'Oh,' smiled Father Patrick, as if it might still be a joke he had not yet the hang of. 'Why is that, now?'

'It's very boring.'

'Boring. . . ?' asked Father Patrick in a shrinking voice.

'Very,' Reverend Mackie affirmed.

'Are we talking about the same thing?' asked Father Patrick valiantly. 'Ecumenism, surely, is Christ walking along the Peace Line.'

'I've never seen Him, but if I did I'd tell Him he'd be much better off looking after the people,' Reverend Mackie said.

'You mean, teaching them love,' said Father Patrick.

'I mean, helping the poor buggers get from Monday to Tuesday,' replied Reverend Mackie. 'No harm to you, but I wonder where ecumenism gets the lady I found this morning. Choked sometime in the last three days on her own vomit. I counted a hundred empty sherry bottles in what she called her kitchen.' Reverend Mackie shrugged and his hair bounced lightly. 'I have a job here. I'm trying to help people rediscover their own dignity. I get letters every day about marches and goin' to Lourdes and singin' Christmas carols together, and puttin' on dances for Papists and Prods, and linkin' arms, and concerts and talks and everythin' else under the sun. I just throw them away, they're

142

boring beyond belief. I've got my Sunday congregation up to nearly two hundred – and that's taken three years to do. I'm not goin' to throw all that away with a march or mixed marriages or the Virgin birth or puttin' your fingers into Christ's side. If someone has something to say, then say it is my motto, but don't drag other people into it, especially those who may be too polite to refuse.'

Father Patrick was gripped as if by a seizure of confusion, compounded by old-fashioned principles about accepting hospitality. 'So, ecumenism is dead,' he managed to say.

'Just boring,' Reverend Mackie replied.

'May I make a point?'

The two men turned.

'As an outsider,' Adam said, 'it seems to me that both sides here, Catholic and Protestant, concentrate too much, if I may say so, on religious differences. A person from another culture – from China, say – would not even be aware of such differences, so minute are they.'

'It's these differences we're trying to resolve, Adam,' Father Patrick said.

'What's minute to a Chinaman may be far from minute to a man from Tiger Bay,' said the Reverend Mackie. 'I'm sorry, I didn't catch your name.'

'Brother Adam.'

'Brother Adam's from England,' said Father Patrick by way of explanation. He added with a nervous laugh, 'He works for MI5.'

'There are many points of indisputable fact that both communities are equal heirs to,' Adam said.

'For example?' blinked the Reverend Mackie.

Adam smiled. 'You both live in one city.'

The Protestant minister shook his head slowly. 'That's where ye're wrong, Brother Adam. Belfast is not one city but a number of cities.'

'Well,' Adam persisted, 'you all live on one island.'

'What is an island?' asked the Reverend Mackie. 'An Ulstermon is British. He can stand at Donaghadee on a fine day and look over the Channel at the tops of the Rhins. If he waits till evenin' he can see the lights come on in Galloway. He doesn't regard Ulster as an island separate from Britain.'

'But it is,' said Adam like the desperate manager of some failing enterprise.

'You're mistaken,' said the Reverend Mackie unperturbably. 'A stretch a water's nothin'. The only island for an Ulsterman is the one that starts with the wee hills he sees when he stands lookin' south from Fermanagh.'

They drove home in silence, back up the Shankill, past the gospel halls and takeaways, across the Lanark Way and through the Peace Line where a checkpoint of soldiers and RUC were funnelling people into the Falls. 'You never know with young people nowadays,' said Father Patrick, regaining some strength as they drew near Paschal's. 'Mr Wylie seemed a decent sort, though. I'm not giving up.

"Hail glorious St Patrick, dear saint of our isle,

On us thy poor children bestow a sweet smile . . ." '

Father Blaise's face floated from left to right across an upstairs window as they parked.

'Poor Blaise,' said Father Patrick, wincing in anticipation of the aches that getting out of the car would bring. 'You've heard, I suppose, that he's being transferred this weekend to Rome?'

I spent the Monday indoors on the Shankill, chatting to Mother Staunch and waiting for Edwin to return. Mother Staunch kept coming to me with fresh snacks of tea and biscuits and hot sausage rolls as if to a favourite son home from boarding school.

'How's Jan?' she asked quietly.

'She seemed well when we last met.'

'I mean, how is she really?' Mother Staunch nodded. 'She rang me, Brian. I know.'

The fact that Janet had told her mother our secret, even though it would ensure I was looked after here in Belfast, confirmed to me yet again that Janet always played to win. 'I admire Janet greatly,' I said.

Mother Staunch sighed wistfully. 'An' she you. 'Twas a rebel thing she did. I told her "Go and have yer fling with him, childe, but don't marry him." It only drove her further from me. He's not a bad mon, I suppose, but I will never know what she saw in him. They have three beautiful children, let me show ye.'

Together we went through an album. Janet's husband once had

144

a chubby, boy-like face that with the years had turned fat and made his eyes small. Janet's look beside him was always one of defiance. The children grew up through the pages as if the great compromise that had been made did not affect them.

'And ye've yer own family,' said Mother Staunch quietly.

'Yes.'

'I sometimes ask the good Lord, why did Ye make life so troublesome?' said Mother Staunch.

Edwin came back that night after ten. 'Nothin' so far,' he said. 'But it's early days.'

On the Tuesday morning, when Edwin had left again, I went into Belfast. It had always seemed a place apart to me, although I'm sure its apartness was only in my mind. The Catholics may have owned the land but the Protestants built the city on it. Everything was Protestant to my eyes that drizzly morning: the Union Jacks, the uniforms of the police and army, the names over the UK shop chains that we never saw at home, even the sky, I imagined, was cold and decisive in a very Protestant way. On impulse, at the back of a shopping centre, I took a taxi going up the Falls.

The Divis flats were ugly, the graffiti on the houses sinister, but this was the Belfast I remembered from my brief visits. The taxi was a shared affair, stopping to take people on and let them off like a bus. We went up the Whiterock Road where children played on their school break in sudden sunshine; we curved around by the Springfield Road and made our way down again, stopping and starting, people biding each other the time of day with familiarity, asking after children, nodding pleasantly to my strange face. In heavy traffic, on the way down to Milltown cemetery, I disembarked. The morning mist had gone and, in front of me, at the extremity of vision, the white block of Stormont distorted ideas of distance with its exact perfection. Ahead, spread out opposite the gates of Milltown, were four armoured carriers, a dozen soldiers, and RUC in green flak jackets, hands on their hips. A hearse was up-crawling to them, bright wreaths on its roof making gay chin frills for the grim faces behind it. I felt a sudden anger that any death should be so attended; as if my consorting on the Protestant Shankill was an act that needed remedy, I fell in with women, children and old men with younger men supporting them, getting out of cars and taxis and pressing through the gates.

Hearse and one car led us, shoulder to shoulder in the unexpected warmth. From up in the Turf Lodge Angelus bells dealt down chimes in brittle, marble fragments. Everything sparkled: the hearse and car behind it, the white, white headstones, the cars flashing back and forth under Milltown on the M1.

We outpoured downhill to form a circle around a mound of fresh earth. Young men set down on planks the coffin and the wreaths were brought in armfuls. A priest circled, sprinkling.

'Lord who gave your servant, the gift of life . . .'

How easily I fitted in here at the burial of a total stranger, how comfortable I felt in the common heartbeat of familiar prayer. There was a homing-in that I had never thought I would be part of, that could never happen to me on the Shankill, nor at home in Dublin, for that matter. It was as if, in this final act, someone's burial in the bleak landscape of Milltown, the crux of Northern Ireland was laid bare as bones and blood.

As if to delay my return across the divide, when the burial was over I fell in with the crowd walking back down the Falls. I had a sense of inviolability. I saw troops body-searching some boys against a wall: the combat gear and accessories of the soldiers looked ugly beside the youths' shirts and jeans. Some men in the dispersing funeral crowd spat on the ground and my instinct was to do the same. Where was the resolve I had shown in Connemara, I wondered? How Vincent would have laughed if he could have read my mind.

We turned off the the Falls Road and down a street several hundred yards in length. The crowd thinned as people went into houses or up other streets or narrow entries. Under a mural depicting the Mother of God, Bobby Sands and a Kalashnikov rifle I decided to press on. I had in my mind a picture of West Belfast; if I kept going I would come out on the Shankill. Rounding a corner I came face to face with a red brick wall painted in giant, white letters: 'BRITISH SOLDIER YOU ARE DEAD.'

Miles overhead a chopper choppered. I passed shops of grocers and bookies and drink emporiums, their windows caged like bulging lenses. I felt I knew this inner, Catholic heartland. Although I had never been there before I had written about these streets and the people who lived in them; I had delivered their names and addresses, if only they knew it. Ardea Street, Adrigole

Street. Satellite dishes sprouted from houses like tree toadstools. Front doors emptied directly to the pavement and, in each window, hung lace curtains. The streets were honeycomb-like, each one, it seemed, ending in a vista of adorned gables: Ahakista, Ardgroom and Aughlis Street. I stopped in Aughlis Street. It was one I remembered because in Aughlis street had once lived James Pierce Doyle. Two women on a corner looked away but they saw me, they saw everything, the anti-terrorist manuals the world over were bursting with them, these women and children of Belfast and of the Gaza Strip. They dehumanised strangers with their eyes.

'Excuse me,' I said, 'Doyles'.'

One of the women said a number and pointed to a door. I rang a bell. It was a remote chance that Adam Coleraine had come here, yet it seemed too obvious to pass. An old, dishevelled man stood in the doorway, white stubble like bristle on a worn brush patching his face. The hall behind him was clean with small, smooth tiles and, on the stairs, there was red lino.

I asked, 'Does James Pierce Doyle live here, sir?'

The old man hunched like an animal unsure in light. 'Pierce. . . ?' he began, confused, looking behind him as if the man I sought might be there, looking back again at me. An equally old and small but springy woman came into the hallway. 'Pierce . . .' the man said, uncertainly.

'What de'ye want?' the woman asked. 'I'm Mrs Doyle.'

'Does James Pierce Doyle still live here?'

'Not any more.'

'Where does he live?'

'Ye's beyst ask th'IRA that,' replied Mrs Doyle tightly. 'But don' ye ask th'RUC or the Bretish Army, because they won' heylp y'anymore than they heylped us.'

I said, 'Why?'

'Why?' she cried. 'I'll teyll ye why, whoever y'are, because th'IRA took a decent wee lad and turned him int'a'monster, that's why. An' seynt him t' Englind, that's why. An' when he thought he'd won his case below there in Dublin, preteyned to heylp him, an' took him off . . .' Mrs Doyle's tears had overtaken her words. 'They took him off . . . an' because they thought . . . he was a danger to them . . . put a bullet in his lovely heyd . . . that's why!'

'I'm sorry.'

'Sorry's a lot a good,' she sobbed. 'Wh're'ee anyway? Ye'r not the first t'ask after Pierce.'

'I'm sorry to have intruded.'

'The Brets were here askin',' Mrs Doyle said. 'I'm askin', wh'r'ee?'

'I'm just a friend,' I said, knowing it was unwise, retreating.

'Ye're no freyn',' said Mrs Doyle; then, for her own reasons she cried: 'Ye're another Bret!'

I turned from the door and walked for the corner; the two women were in the same place.

'He's a Bret!' cried Mrs Doyle, out on the street. 'He's an informer!'

I tried not to hurry. A gable with the Mother of God beckoned me, her sorrowful, young eyes downcast on a map of Ireland, bright green, valley of tears. Green, white and orange on the kerbing bricks swung me beneath the mural: 'Hail Holy Virgin.'

'Bret!' cried Mrs Doyle.

'Bret!' cried one of the women in support.

There was a little shop in someone's front window selling daffodils. Easter soon.

'Bretish informer!'

With the comfort of the corner between me and the women, I began to run; but my direction was lost and halfway down the street, to my dismay, all three women and a teenage boy burst out ahead of me from the mouth of an entry between buildings.

'Ther he is!'

I passed them at full tilt and took the first turn left and left again. Row upon row of marzipan iced with giraffe brick went past, entries burrowing deep to footlink neighbourhoods. The smell of soot mingled with that of cooking. Infants crawled on scrubbed door steps. At my back came a sudden smack: two boys whacking between them a leather ball on ash hurleys. Without hill or horizon I turned corners, running over broken glass, skirting waste ground where all that remained of houses were hearthstones. The area was extensive. Street led into street. I wondered if I was running in a circle. The children looked all the same and I saw the hand of the same artist in the dark eyes peering from the hoods of different murals. The only constant was the chopper. I changed direction down an entry between houses back to back and

148

arrived abruptly in a square where half a dozen youths were dismembering a motor car.

Everything stopped. Tricolours hung out of windows and, daubed in the same colours down one side of an end house, were the words 'OUR DAY WILL COME.' The square, an abutment of small gables, spilled with youths. Eyes slid behind windows like crabs under rocks. Then, as if the Falls were a huge maze and I the only one in it without the plan, Mrs Doyle and the women, now grown into a group of six or seven, arrived twenty yards opposite where I stood.

'Ther he is! Ther's the Bret informer!'

A teenager of shaven head, his ear lobe weighted with a gold crucifix, tore with slow deliberation all the trim from along the car's side and threw it, chrome curling, to the road. The air had auto-charged. The ones in the middle had formed a line and I could see those behind scooping into their skinny arms rivets and other assorted car parts. I could have pulled the Walther on them, but I realised the statement it would make.

'Fuckin' Bret.'

I bolted as the first pitch caught me solid over the eye. I ran as metal sang at my legs and either side of my feet. I could hear them pause to throw and then their chasing feet. Hit simultaneously in the back and on my ankle bone, I threw myself down the length of a shoulder-wide entry. Out its other end there was an empty street with another entry opposite. My shoes echoed like wing beats in the tunnel as I made its length, turned right down another street of small children on toy cars and girls with bows and dolls who stopped to gape at me. Looking back at my empty wake, I made another corner, rounded it and slowed to a walk, hands on my hips, dredging for air, slowly conscious of hot blood seeping down my face.

I walked, turned to check, dissected noises of blood pounding from those of the surrounding city, local and distant, turned again, freeing my red vision with a wipe of my sleeve and wondered what had become of my inviolability. Gradually air cooled my lungs and I began to see. At first it was blood, I was sure, stalactites of it before my eyes; I knuckled them. The bars remained, constant in my twilight. Blinking, I saw the locked gates and whirled, sick with certainty. Swollen in numbers to twenty or more the youths used the full breadth of the street like a creeping wedge. I sprinted over the gap and shook at the gate's bars, sheer and twenty feet. There were cars, distantly, moving behind the gates, across wasteland, up and down the Falls. I tried to jump, to climb, but spikes, designed to stop just such enterprise, revolved at my grip. I turned as the approaching flanks quickened at me. The time was coming when the gun would have to be produced, but there was an intent about the crowd that told me it would have very limited effect. Cursing my stupidity, amazed that kids so young could be so murderous I lunged through the bars of the gate for a bottle and, smashing it, swept it in an arc. They fell back momentarily, but only to take their aim, then in they came with rocks and rivets, excitement radiating from their hungry young eyes. Then two of them fell like skittles and the rest waved back in a huge, reflexible ebb. Keys rattled and the gates were hauled back.

'You can call that a close one, mate.'

Blood on my face and head must have been a mirror in red of the black smears camouflaging the soldiers' faces.

'Hop in 'ere and we'll run you to a hospital.'

I edged past them. 'No. Thank you. I'm alright.'

'You're cut, mate. Don't be bleedin' stupid.'

'No,' I said, backing away, breaking into a run.

'Bloody 'ell,' I heard a soldier say.

Wednesday morning on the path up the mountain Adam could hear the deep, rising gongs of iron settling down in the crane's ambit, could see dying black and red light flashing up from the shells of a thousand cars piled at the lough's side. The cowled figure that he had seen up ahead fifteen minutes before had disappeared. Adam climbed. The path rounded under a bluff to a waterfall. By the ruin of a stone hut through whose gaping hole of a window Adam could see old stone tables and wheels, evidence of past industry, sat Father Blaise on a rock.

'I knew him well,' Father Blaise remarked. 'Roland. A Protestant. He cut limestone for me one day up here, not just to let me see the mollusks and the shells, but to smell! Four million years and the smell of seaweed was as rich as on the beach in Carrickfergus. Isn't that wonderful?'

'Wonderful, Father.'

'I prefer to confront my maker in a place like this, somewhere that's stood the test of time, so to speak.' Father Blaise smiled weakly at his joke. 'I suppose you've heard the news?'

'Yes.'

'Rome won't be so bad, I suppose,' said Father Blaise. 'Decent food, vino, but . . . I don't know. This is the cauldron, know what I mean? Life is never so present as when it's side by side with death.' He looked sadly at Adam. 'I'm sorry. I like this city. Being a sinner, I'm most at home with sinners.'

Rain ran down the gable of the hut and into the churning stream; rain fell in droplets from Father Blaise's hood.

'Men who blew up hospitals. Men whose victims were children. Men who would have given you their last pound if you needed it, whatever your religion, but shot Protestants, not because they disliked them personally, but because of what they represented. Men who shot members of the British army and fed the bodies to their dogs. I absolved them all.'

'You did what you thought right.'

'Yes, because we all need inner healing. I performed one of my Celtic tricks. I detached myself from the reality of their sin. I asked myself, what is reality? I answered, it *doesn't exist!* Only images exist. They are the reality! Whose are the words spoken by an actor? The actor's? The playwright's? Are they rightly those of the character whom the actor represents? Or of the character whom the character represents? *Who is speaking?* It is an *image!* That which separates blood from the soul and allows us breathing space and sanity. The image is in everything from religion to canned food, God bless it. The image was my ally. It followed me to forgive.'

'What happened?'

'I went to Somalia for ten years. Three years ago, when I got back here, I was told that the men who had once come for confession no longer did so. It was such a relief to me.'

Adam felt his heart and that of the priest beat in step. 'But . . .'

Father Blaise closed his eyes 'But it wasn't so.'

'Not . . . for you, you mean?'

'No, it wasn't so for me.'

Adam asked, 'Who?'

'One man.'

'One?'

Father Blaise nodded. 'He talks, I listen. He doesn't ask God for forgiveness, he *persuades* God that he *should* be forgiven. It's been going on for many years. He . . . I shouldn't be telling you this – '

'Please, go on, Father.'

'He brings me photographs of the people who have died because of him.'

'Photographs?' asked Adam.

'Cut from the papers,' the priest affirmed. 'Sometimes a couple, sometimes a dozen. He carries them around.'

'Then he's crazy,' Adam said.

'He's the sanest man I know,' Father Blaise replied. 'He has it all worked out. The photographs are the proof of the evil he has done. They are his confession. He makes himself confront the faces of the people he has killed as if to hurt himself. He cries sometimes, particularly when there are women or children involved. At that point he is probably genuinely sorry. He needs my forgiveness in order to sustain him for the next batch of photographs.'

'These photographers . . .' Adam began.

'Men and women, soldiers and children,' Father Blaise said. 'Some shot at point blank range in the Shankill, others killed by car bomb somewhere in England or in Europe. I take on his sin in its entirety. It's a burden, I can tell you.'

'So much sin – so many photographs – must mean a position of authority,' Adam said.

'Quite,' said Blaise tersely.

'Are you . . . afraid of him, Father?'

'No,' replied the priest. 'Why do you ask that?'

'It seems this man is a weight on your mind,' Adam said. 'I could understand how you might fear having to tell him you were going away. He might react violently to the thought of your going beyond his reach, so to speak, with all his secrets in your head. But if you are not afraid of him, then you should be happy that you will no longer facilitate his twisted world.'

'That is the problem,' the priest said. 'I can't. That is what I dread. Having to look at him and say, this is your last confession to me.'

'Why do you so dread it?' Adam asked.

'It will be like cutting off his air,' Father Blaise replied. 'It will kill him.'

'But it has to be done.'

'Easily said.'

'You have the courage, Father.'

'To kill him?'

'Yes.'

Father Blaise looked at Adam, his faced ravaged. 'How can you do that to your own brother?'

*

On that Wednesday in a shed in Dunmurry, Nona Lane stood watching a hearse come to life. Skinned to bare metal it regrew like a miracle under the solder and seal of the lifer out on a ninety-six hour pass from Long Kesh. The shed's outer bay opened responsibly to a lane; the access to its inner workshop was hidden by a ten-foot wall of scrap metal. Under a light and to one side from the hearse waited an open coffin. Hearse and coffin had made the long trip north like Darby and Joan, and Nona had watched them both stripped – the coffin down to its tar – and rebuilt, the hearse to its old magnificence, the coffin with steel panels inlaid, every edge and screw bevelled and countersunk. The work absorbed Nona: the need to create in order to destroy was a proposition with meaning for her, containing within it its pure opposite, the necessity to destroy before one could create. The lifer rolled out on his back and dusted off his hands. 'That'll do her nicely, nigh,' he said. 'I can't be late back'r they'll cut me good beheyvur.' His young face at odds with his white hair.

'Teyll's 'geyn, what've ye leyft?' Nona asked him. She knew the joke.

'Three hundred'n seyvny-two years,' replied the lifer, straight-faced, as she showed him out.

She liked that, Nona, being an equal with a man who had admitted in court to the price of a British soldier's life being ten thousand pounds. Made her feel secure. Like the work in the shed with its defined objectives, the hearse and the open coffin that would in hours be laid down tenderly with home-made explosive –

ground fertiliser and nitrobenzene – and the danger that it entailed. Like field trips as part of an active service unit, camaraderie in the enemy's heartland and the sharp-edged thrill at the time of knowing that what you were doing was right. Nona never felt fear at such times. Fear for her was something closer to home: failing in the tasks she had been set; guilt when she read the papers; wondering what was in Uinsionn's mind when he looked at her.

Nona turned from the coffin and hearse. At times she longed for the sameness that seemed to link the girls in Donegall Place. Lunchtimes together, a desk job, a miniskirt, a handbag with the wage you earned and little tubes of luminous lipstick. A young lad waitin' till you both had enough saved and were ready to make a break, maybe, with this whole, sad place and start up fresh and rear kids without having to worry forever that someone was goin' to put a bullet in them. Such thoughts always brought Nona back to the reason for her being different, and the longing for sameness was replaced by a heady sense of her place. But was it impossible to believe, as she did, to lead the life she did, and to have a baby or two? Gifts from God, better they come into the world with her to protect them. Give them strong beliefs, they might be the ones who turned history back. People scorned, saying, 'Can't be done, the clock won't go back,' but they were wrong. When the colonists went home the clock would go back to the day they had arrived and they too, in a funny way, would get their freedom. You could not be free if you enslaved, there could be no freedom built on blood and an old sin.

That was owed to the lost generations. Did their hearts too beat to the same drum of excitement? Did they break under the same agony of doubt when the prospect was snatched from them again and again? Would anyone remember their pain? Without children to follow her, would anyone remember Nona Lane except a few young fellas in Long Kesh or curious strangers paused a stride by the republican plot in Milltown? So young, they would say. Why? What drove her to be different? Nona ran her hand along the hearse's gleaming, black wing and felt all the silky skin that sat tight up to her womanhood contract. Important. That was. Now.

A hundred pounds of home-made explosive in a coffin. Up in the

Shankill on Wednesday night we'd heard the noise like distant thunder.

'Atrayshus,' said Edwin Staunch. 'Make ye wanta cry. Every winda from Cromac Square to th'eynda May Street gone. The new shoppin' precing at the corner a Gloucester Street has all the fron' ripped from it and every shop destroyed.'

That morning, Thursday, Edwin and I went into town. Amid the tapping and tinkle of glaziers at work, some RUC men in heavy flak jackets greeted Edwin familiarly. His type, I thought, big-boned men with a sense of proprietorial regret. Whispered words went with the understanding nods of business unresolved. What meetings would take place later under the guise of common blood when uniforms had been discarded, I wondered? Their city, theirs and Edwin's, with his tight-waisted, leather bum-freezer and his lucky gold tooth. I rang Angie from a call box; she had sounded very down when I told her that it looked like Adam was not in Belfast.

'Sinn Fein are cryin' out for jobs an' invesmen' while's th'IRA are blowin' the country to pieces. It's crazy,' Edwin said. 'Will ye teyll them that dighn in the Free State, Brian?'

'Brian is not some sort of official repisentitiv from the Free State, Edwin,' Mother Staunch scolded.

'What would be my qualification if I were?' I said. 'A degree in history – or a degree in forgetting history?'

Edwin said, 'Ach, let me teyll ye about history. In 1969 the governmint a this province should a stamped out trouble the very seckind' it began rather than panderin' to the Free State an' every other namby pamby that raised his voice an' lettin' a bunch a crim'nels – 'cos let me teyll ye, that's what they were and are – lettin' them brazen faced into the city that'd supported them from the creadil to the gree'iv.'

Mother Staunch smiled at me as if we were two adults and Edwin a child. Father Staunch, God rest him, must have been a big, strapping man like Edwin, but Janet's brain had come from her mother.

'That seyd, I hate no mon,' Edwin frowned. 'That doesn't mean, mind, that I don' abjure popery and everythin' that goes with it. I do. But I forgive all men, even th'IRA, for the evil they're caught up in.'

155

'There's evil on both seydes,' said Mother Staunch.

'Ach sush, will ye, Mother?' Edwin said.

'I'll not be sushed, I'll have me say,' the old woman snapped and Edwin blinked as if he had been slapped. 'Pride is ar dighnfall in this place,' she said for me. 'Pride forfeits the right to know love.'

'You're all Christians,' I said, like the broker in some faltering deal.

'Mother . . .'

'It's pride keeps us in this place!' Mother Staunch cried. 'If exchanging love for pride meant going, then, in the name a God, we should go!'

'Why should you?' I asked with the Irishman's curse of being unable to mind his own business. 'Any more than the Catholics should go South?'

'There's many of them want to,' confided Edwin, 'but the South can't afford to take them.'

My time had come. From that small, cozy room on the Shankill with the evening outside buoyed up and stretching with the promise of Spring, Ballyvoy seemed irresistibly wild and pure. 'South is where I have to think of,' I said. 'I appreciate your kindness.' I wondered if Adam Coleraine, wherever he was, was happy.

'Ah,' said Mother Staunch sadly.

'We tried our beyst,' Edwin said. 'I'm sorry.'

'He's not here,' I said. 'It's that simple.'

'When will ye go, Brian?' asked Mother Staunch.

'On this evening's train,' I said.

'I'll bring ye dighn to it,' said Edwin as footsteps down the front path were followed by the doorbell's chiming and Mother Staunch went out.

I could not find a man who wasn't to be found, I thought, as Mother Staunch's head came around the door. 'Edwin.'

I was looking forward to home, to Dublin accents after those of Belfast, to the sight of all your faces which, as I hadn't needed Arty to tell me, were all that mattered in the end of the day. The concerns raised by Tice and his crew back in those meetings in November now seemed far away and insignificant; I had begun to feel a sort of relief that my life was free of such people, although I'm sure the feeling was compensatory.

156

The door to the kitchen opened and Edwin looked in. 'Could I see ye, Brian, please?'

I wondered why the kitchen was in semidarkness as Edwin closed the door behind me.

'Sit dighn, please,' Edwin said. 'Brian, this is Brigadier White.'

Another man was sitting between me and the curtained window. All I could see was that he was small and broad and that his head was smoothly round.

'Detective Superintendent Kilkenny, Brigadier,' Edwin said. 'Free State p'lice.'

'Mr Kilkenny.' The brigadier had one of these whispering voices. 'I'm sure y'unnerstan', sir, that yer country and ars is at war?'

It crossed my mind that this was some sort of joke. I looked for Edwin but he was, as far as I could see in the gloom, standing to attention. 'I'm sorry but I do not consider that to be the position,' I said.

'Weyll, ye'r wrong, sir,' the brigadier retorted. 'Wheyn one countra sends agents an subversives t'undermine the foundations of another, that's an act a war. That's the position, sir, between your Free State an' Ulster. We're both on a war footin'. I'm an off'cer in Ulster's people's army. Ye'r an agent of ar en'my, set on underminin' Ulster. Ye can be executed for yer crime.'

It was impossible to believe this lunatic serious, yet a glance at Edwin, rigid as a flagpole, was enough to confirm that belief in the impossible was suddenly very important for me.

'I would beg to enquire the nature of my crime, Brigadier,' I said, slipping into his quasi-military speech.

'Infiltratin' ar ranks,' whispered Brigadier White. 'Mr Staunch is a very good freyn a ars, a loyal off'cer, but he allowed himseylf to be used by ye as an agent a the Free State. He nigh understans that, isn't that a fact, Mr Staunch?'

'Yes, sir!' Edwin snapped off.

'Any act that undermines the Union undermines Ulster,' the brigadier confided. 'Any attack on the United Kingdom or its inst'utions is an attack on Ulster. The army of Ulster's people exists to defeyn' Ulster from attack. Ye, sir, stan' convicted in a time a war of attackin' Ulster, by virtue of yer bein' here to illegally kidnap a fug'tive a Crown justice and bring him to yer country for yer own illegal eynds. That's a ver' serious matter.'

'Are you referring to Adam Coleraine?' I asked.

'This mon her',' the brigadier said and took out the well worn photograph.

'With respect, Brigadier, Adam Coleraine was very recently the subject of a request of us by the British Home Office,' I said. 'We helped them as any neighbour would. That's still the case.'

'No, it's not the case, sir,' Brigadier White spoke. 'Actin' on ar freyn Mr Staunch's request, we've been makin' enquiries about this fug'tive, and we've suddenly found arseylves in a very embarr'sin position. We suddenly find ar contacts in high places want this mon very badly. They want to know why *we* are askin' after this mon ye'r here to kidnap. We can't teyll them because that would put ar freyn Mr Staunch in a very embarr'sin position, him havin' been infiltrated by ye. Isn't that right, Mr Staunch?'

'Sir,' Edwin affirmed.

'We know where this fug'tive is,' the brigadier said softly. 'We can now solve the problem by handin' him over to the proper forces a law 'n' order.'

'You know where Adam Coleraine is?' I asked, incredulous despite the nature of my position.

'The Ulster people knows everythin' that's happenin' in ther own back yard,' the brigadier said. 'Furthermore, sir, this mon rep'sents a speychel case. In his former position in London he was workin' under a mon who was, the Lord reyst him, a very good freynd a the loyal people of Ulster.'

He was talking about Counsell. 'The quality of your intelligence is most impressive, Brigadier,' I said.

'That's what the en'my don't unnerstan'. That's why ye'll never win this war,' said Brigadier White. 'Nigh. The only problem remainin' is yerseylf. Ye must be dealt with, sir.'

I wondered had Janet run to Dublin twenty years ago to get away from the Ulster run by the Brigadier Whites.

'In normal cir'stances, ye'd never leave this house,' the brigadier said. 'Ther's a company a men within fifty yards, watchin', that'd blow ye to bits at a second's notice. But Mr Staunch has pleaded yer case. I remember his sister, Miss Staunch, a bonny lass before she supped with the devil. Ar freyns mean a lot t'us, sir, ye can be thankful.' The brigadier stood up. My first impression about his size had been correct. His head came no higher than the cill of the kitchen window. 'Ye're not wanted here, sir. In three hours if ye're still in Belfawst, ye'll be a dead mon. Rules a war.'

Clicking his heels loudly together the brigadier saluted Edwin. There was a bit of parade-ground stamping. Edwin snatched open the kitchen door to the hall and the brigadier marched out.

In the same black cab that had brought me to the Shankill the Sunday before, in silence we crossed the Westlink at three that afternoon by Peter's Hill. Edwin sat on the jump seat with a look on his face of a man who will not shirk his duty.

'This is business, Brian, y'unnerstan',' he said, more than once.

Beforehand I would have thought the centre of Belfast safe as a fortress, surrounded by hostile camps of warring tribes. That morning I understood the opposite: only with the tribes in this city were you really safe.

'An' don't try anythin' silly, will ye, Brian?' he said. 'Ye've upset the nerve cell of Loyalist Ulster.'

Nothing tired you like failure and I was exhausted. I would have gone home, as intended, happily ignorant of Adam's existence, if the ridiculous Brigadier White had not rubbed my nose in it. I was tired beyond belief. I wanted a drink. I wanted to stand in a southern-speeding Irish train and raise a glass of whiskey to Belfast and shout 'Good riddance!' I said to Edwin, 'I'm just sorry that I got you into an awkward position.'

'Ach, I should'a known better,' Edwin said.

'What will happen to Adam Coleraine?'

'Brigadier White will see what th'establishment wants to happen to him.'

'The establishment would like to see him dead.'

'Then . . .' Edwin did not finish the sentence. He looked out the windows of the cab at the barricaded facade of the Law Courts. Belfast was enjoying the spell of good weather that had begun earlier in the week and I got the impression, looking at a group of pretty girls passing an army checkpoint, that despite the army and the barbed wire and the general appurtenances of war, the human spirit would always triumph and that all was needed was a little sunshine to bring it out. We swung left and over a bridge before u-turning to a halt at Central Station.

'It's nothin' pers'nal, I hope y'unnerstan', Brian?' said Edwin as we shook hands.

'I do,' I said. I meant it. I hoped he wouldn't wait to see the train away: I wanted to ring Angie before I left. I had made up my mind that I would lie to her.

'Teyll ar wee lass we think about her often,' Edwin said when we had shook hands. 'Teyll her that she can always come home – if it went wrong dighn there or anythin'.'

I stood and watched the black roof of Edwin's cab join others heading back over East Bridge Street for the Shankill. Janet might well take him up, I thought, if her roots in foreign soil of half a lifetime were suddenly torn up. I was turning to enter the station, about to ring Angie, thinking about Janet and Edwin, wondering about a man called Adam I had never met, someplace in this city I would never find, when I heard my name called.

'Brian!' The voice came from a black cab pulled into the kerb twenty yards back from the station's door. 'Over here.'

I walked cautiously down the footpath. I transferred my bag to my left hand, leaving my right free for the gun. From the dark square of the cab's back window came a woman's hand. 'Come here, Brian lad,' said Mother Staunch.

Dinner finished at two. Adam returned to his room. Removing his habit he dressed in black trouser, a shirt and a pullover before putting the habit back on again. It felt tight and made him sweat. From beneath the floorboard at the foot of the wardrobe he removed the padded envelope he had sent to the poste restante in Belfast over six months before, took from it a Smith and Wesson wrapped in an oil rag, stuck the gun in his pocket and, taking a brown paper bag from within the wardrobe, stepped into the corridor. Because his heart became suddenly the dominant noise in his life, his other movements took place in apparent silence. This great cardiac accompaniment also played tricks with his vision so that his hands – holding the bag; locking his door – were distant and tiny and robotic. The corridor itself telescoped abruptly, like an endless tunnel, although from where he stood to the top of the stairs was fifteen yards at the most. Adam took half a dozen of his new, phantom-like paces to Father Blaise's door.

'Come in.' The priest looked up from reading. 'Ah, Adam, come in.'

'I hope I'm not disturbing you, Father.'

'Not at all.'

'I've brought you a small present,' Adam said, and held out the bag.

'Ah, you shouldn't have, goodness me,' Blaise said, taking the bag and lifting out the bottle. 'Ah, my goodness, malt, ah God, this cost a fortune. I can't. No, come on, I won't.'

'It's nothing,' Adam said.

'It's too much,' said the priest. He looked at his watch. 'At least you'll join me in a glass. It'll just be one, though.' The priest spun off the cap and filled tumblers. 'Slainte.'

'Slainte.'

Father Blaise let slip down half the contents of his glass. 'Ahh,' he said, leaning back and closing his eyes. 'You never quite hunt out the ghost, you know. You learn to live with it, that is the most, I believe. Some are lucky, go through life unaware that they are never alone. Intelligence comes into it, of course, or the lack of it. Sometimes I wish I were a fool.' The priest looked happily at his glass, drained it; Adam recharged it with silky amber, shielding his own with his hand. Blaise said, 'A fool indeed. Imagine the bliss! The sun rises, your bowel moves, the sun sets. Cursed, cursed, all of us. We only hunt out that ghost the day he and e become one and the same.' Father Blaise's pupils rolled up slowly and whitely into their sockets, then like someone who has practised soft landings, forward on his table he feather-like slumped. Adam caught him and lifted him onto the bed. Heavy. The opposite to Alison. Or had that been a dream? Tipping the glasses into the wash-hand basin, Adam's hand bucked as he emptied the bottle after them, then held it to the tap for flushing, the mouth of the bottle jumping this way and that as all trace of his doctoring was sluiced into Belfast's sewerage. Time now meant everything: how long Blaise would stay out cold; whether the penitent for whose confession Blaise had put his name down in the sacristy book would come on time; the length of time Adam would have in the aftermath to get away. He descended the stairs of red linoleum for the last time, feeling a strange loneliness for the place. Paschal's, empty of men, seemed suddenly and unaccountably warm, the

161

long corridor leading to the church with on one side its high windows was spliced with bars of sunlight and within them danced motes of dust. The irreversible nature of what he had upstairs set in motion, the fact that now, even if he wanted to change his mind, he could not weighed Adam down. The empty church spread out before him, ten times the size of a cathedral. He shuffled down three steps of marble and along the side aisle. What if the wrong penitent came? What if he had picked up wrong what Blaise had said? Candles at the altar of the Blessed Virgin became living bulbs where time, now so precious, could be examined, each second halted and broken into fibres at leisure. Adam saw people dancing in the flames, civilisations thought long extinct fallen into limbo like crumbs through cracks on a table; the instant between when the bomb went off and when Zoe was struck suddenly fertile ground where none had previously been apparent. Time stopped and became something you lived in, an enlarged and infinite now. A hundred years ago the splitting of atoms would have been unthinkable. Perhaps, he thought, he did not really exist. Perhaps this was what this revelation meant. If he didn't exist, he couldn't suffer any more. Who was there to confirm his existence? Reaching the confessional he put out to hang the sign with Father Blaise's name, then sat in to smells of teak and old, sorry breaths. Adam felt a rush of illogical uplifting. All this, as Father Blaise had once said, was just an image separating blood from the soul, a nothing land of painless illusion. The door of the lefthand cubicle opened. Adam, gun on his lap, slid the panel back.

They came straight up the Falls in a red Escort at half past three, Nona in the back seat and a young lad from Derriaghy driving. There was no word of patrols or checkpoints, the lad was clean and the car was shining, one year old, his father's.

'D'ye expeyct any trouble, Nona?' The lad looked at her in his mirror, seeing not Nona but a woman in a headscarf and glasses.

'Ach, no, not at all,' Nona replied. 'Are ye nervous or what?'

'I'd never be nervous s'long as ye'd be with me,' said the young lad from Derriaghy shyly to his mirror.

They went through Andersonstown and Ladybrook and down through Twinbrook until they came to smart factories with long cars parked outside them. Although the young lad had not been told anything except that he was to drive, all Nona's mind was on Uinsionn. The thoughts of meeting him, even for a wee drive, gave Nona little pains of apprehension in her chest. At a nameless junction of roads linking windowless factories, the car pulled up on Nona's instruction. The road was as empty as the scrubland either side.

Uinsionn made Nona afraid in the same way God had when she first went to school: a person always in control of you, cold and calm, who always knew more than you and about you, courteous in a way that made him untouchable, up in clouds you could never reach with a view of a dreadful abyss beneath your feet where beasts and serpents howled in waiting. A relationship founded on fear made liking or disliking irrelevant: you didn't like or dislike God; Nona feared Uinsionn. She wondered if Uinsionn feared God: he had to, this was the second time she was going with him for his confession.

Nona suddenly saw him in the wing mirror, a tall man in a blue overcoat, walking up from a factory unhurriedly. The mirror gave no clue as to distance: one moment he was miles away, the next the door beside Nona was opened.

'Nona, Nona.' He slid in and sat with one leg under the other, facing her. Nona always felt cold at his smile. 'How beautiful you are, Nona. A beam of sunshine into our dark lives.'

'St Paschal's on the Valley Road,' Nona rapped out to the young lad from Derriaghy whose mouth hung open.

'Was your journey alright?' asked Uinsionn solicitously as they moved off.

'We had no problems, Uinsionn,' Nona replied. Feeling self-conscious, she took off the thick spectacles.

'Ah, that's good, Nona.' He was so relaxed but Nona was balanced on a knife. 'I want first to tell you, without any delay, how pleased I am.'

Nona felt herself glow. 'Thank you.'

'No, no, Nona, you deserve it,' Uinsionn said. 'Have you seen the papers? The whole world listens now when we speak, Nona.'

Nona didn't want to say that she never read the papers afterwards, that she carried out orders, that she could never feel the way he did.

'It's like a roar, Nona, isn't it?' Uinsionn said and smiled.

'A great, sea roar, a fury whipped up that is beyond containing.'

His hand came down on hers for a moment and Nona started. It felt dead. They passed Ladybrook on the way back up. The sensation of his cold flesh made acid rise from Nona's stomach. She felt so small in his presence, as if he knew everything about Nona there ever was to know. Like God did. Passing in by the gates of St Paschal's, Nona tried to think of a prayer.

I thought, as I rang Angie from the station, that every pair of eyes behind a newspaper were for me. I had always known there was a good chance things would be squeezed in the end, but not so tightly as they were turning out.

'Is yer mon a Roman Catholic, Brian lad?' Mother Staunch had asked.

Even then I didn't understand. 'What man?'

'Ach, the mon ye'r her to feyn,' Mum Staunch said, 'the mon that Colonel White came about.'

'Adam Coleraine,' I said, 'yes, now that you mention it, I think he is.'

'The colonel met a Church a Irelan' min'ster this mornin', a Rev'ren' Mackie, I heard him say to Edwin,' said Mother Staunch. 'Rev'ren' Mackie's one a these young lads with hair his wife should cut if he had a wife. Rev'ren' Mackie told the colonel yer Mr Coleraine's a priest or a brother be the name a Brother Adam in St Paschal's up on the Valley Road.'

My damned and damning report. One line at the most and Adam had seized it like a salmon from the bed of a river rises to flick from the surface a single, juicy fly: a fruitless raid by the RUC five years before on St Paschal's, allegedly to apprehend IRA fugitives known to confess there. The action had been widely condemned; I had mentioned it in my report as an example of the lack of sensitivity which the security forces showed for the Catholic community's beliefs. I had watched the back of Mother Staunch's taxi ten minutes before, and my main feeling, Gilly, was that of all the sins I stood guilty of, that of needless stupidity was the least excusable.

'Adam's here in a religious order,' I said a quarter of an hour later, in the passenger seat of Angie's Alfa-Romeo. We passed the back of City Hall. 'Turn right and then left.'

'What start have we got?' Angie asked when I explained that my information was not exclusive.

'None,' I replied.

We went out by the Divis Flats and up the Falls, Angie driving as if all the energy she had bottled up in waiting needed to be dispersed in revs.

'I'm sorry it all took so long,' I said. 'What did you do all that time?'

'Sat staring out my window at Scots Guardsmen hurtling up and down below me,' she said grimly and stood the Alfa on its nose at the lights on the Springfield. 'Looked at the rain squalls tumbling down the mountain. Avoided the glass when the window of the room I was staying in was blown in by a bomb.'

I knew that if I stopped to think about what I was doing, I wouldn't do it, but somehow, against all my expectations, the presence of this headstrong woman was a sudden comfort.

'I worked out what I will say to Adam,' Angie was saying. 'I'll tell him that uncertainty is worse than bereavement. I'll tell him that uncertainty breeds hope and that can be very cruel.' She drove grimly, arms straight out to the wheel. 'I'll tell him that to be alive is to ache but it's the best way to be. I'll tell him how the best of our lives is still before us, there for us to make the best of.'

We passed the gates of Milltown and forked right. I took the gun out and checked its chamber; Angie saw it but didn't comment.

'I'll tell him I thought that if he was dead too then it wouldn't matter, I would be with him,' said Angie, gunning us uphill, 'except I hadn't thought that I believed in any of that, but that in the end I was a coward. I wanted to die if he was dead, because that was the only way I thought I would meet him. I'll tell him.'

Listening to her, my eye on the road behind us, my mind on the task ahead and my hand on the butt of the Walther, I was struck by how coldly possessive some women are in matters of the heart. We drove up the Valley Road until we came to pillars of old brick and handsome entrance gates. There was a drive flanked by laurels and grass verges, forking to a Y after fifty yards where signs pointed, 'Church' left, 'Residence' right. We followed the tarmac, right, to the porch of a large, Victorian house. The bell on ringing echoed inside as if along miles of hard floors and lofted ceilings. Belfast had become invisible and inaudible. I rang the bell again.

'Good morning.'

Around the side of the house an elderly man in working clothes and boots had ambled. His 'good morning' was from the South.

'Good morning,' I said. 'We're looking for a friend. Brother Adam.'

'Ah, Brother Adam,' he said. 'I saw him going towards the church ten minutes ago.' He beamed. 'He'll enjoy a visit.'

'He's well, then?'

'Oh, yes,' he replied. 'Very well. Doesn't say much, you know. But it's all up here.' He threw his eyes up the way happy caricatures do. 'A bit like myself. I'm deaf, you see, so I don't say much, but that doesn't mean I'm not, as they say, with it.'

'Of course not.'

'I'm Brother Walter,' he said and came to shake our hands.

'Pleased to meet you,' I mumbled and Angie did the same.

'I'm sorry, I didn't get it?' Brother Walter beamed.

'From Dublin,' I countered.

'I'm Limerick,' said Brother Walter warmly, 'near Mungret. You know it maybe?'

'Heard of it,' I acknowledged.

'Everyone's heard of Mungret,' Brother Walter chuckled. 'Limerick. The Shannon. Kilkee. The Clare Glens that aren't in Clare at all but out at Newport near the Benedictine Fathers. It all seems very far from here, doesn't it?' he said with expatriate familiarity.

'Certainly,' I agreed. A sudden hatching of panic told me that this accessible, innocent place could not possibly hide a man for all these months; that if there was a Brother Adam, then it had to be another man; that if this Brother Adam were the right man then St Paschal's would be crawling with Colonel White's loonies. We should get back into the car, I thought, and not disturb the peace of a blameless man at his prayers.

'Can I help you?'

Behind us the porch door had opened and a priest whose face was round and wrinkled like a pale chestnut stood there.

'Father Patrick, these good people are friends of Brother Adam.' Brother Walter smiled down apologetically at his boots. 'I think he's in church. They're up from Dublin.'

'Ah, that's very good indeed,' Father Patrick smiled. 'Won't you come in?'

'Thank you.'

'Hopefully you can stay,' called Brother Walter.

'Next time, I hope,' I said back over my shoulder.

'Did you come up today?' politely enquired Father Patrick as we proceeded three in a line through a dark hall and past a statue.

'Yes,' answered Angie and I both.

'Ah, good,' responded Father Patrick.

'Is Adam well?' asked Angie. 'Brother Adam?'

'I suppose we all have to find ourselves at first,' replied Father Patrick. We turned into a corridor tiled in swirling mosaics with, along one side, tall windows overlooking a yard and, at its end, oak doors with panels of coloured glass. 'But I am glad to see he has friends. He's a deep one, Adam, you know.' The priest paused, his pale blue eyes on us. 'We had some good chats together in Naples, he and I.'

I met Angie's eye. We both remembered the telephone call in November.

'Tell us,' Father Patrick was saying, 'does Adam really work for MI5?' I must have stared because the priest burst out laughing. 'Oh, dear God, if we stayed serious here, we'd all go mad.' He chortled and both Angie and I joined perfunctorily in. 'We have great laughs, Adam and I. I introduce him as our resident British spy. He's a great character. You're from Dublin, you say?'

The question was for Angie and made her blush her innocence of Brother Walter's introduction. 'Not exactly . . .'

'Thought I got the accent,' Father Patrick smiled and rested his hand paternally on Angie's arm. He leaned back and gave me a wink. 'Perhaps you're Adam's case officer in MI5,' he said to Angie.

'She's the head of the whole thing,' I said.

'And where does that leave you,' asked Father Patrick, turning on a sixpence.

'I'm the Papal Nuncio,' I said.

'The Papal Nuncio.' The old man's laughter made his eyes stream. 'You never know, do you?' he said, opening the door to our left. 'Our little church,' Father Patrick said, papally spreading his hands.

Through crisscrossed hatch wires Adam saw a man's bowed head.

'Bless me, Father, for I have sinned. It is two months since my last confession.'

Adam heard a voice deeply melodious. Leaning his elbow on the ledge as the darkness became diluted between them, Adam covered his side face with his hand and nodded his head.

'There have been more deaths, Father. All on my head.'

'Who?' whispered Adam.

'British soldiers. A civilian. All unavoidable.'

Through his fingers Adam saw a sheaf of photographs held up.

'I have wept for them all, Father. Tears have run down my face and I have cursed anew the first day that an Englishman ever set foot in Ireland. For that was the day, all those years ago before any one of us was born, Father, that fate put the cross of a violent death on these people. I will never forget their faces.'

Adam felt the strength run out of him.

'But they are not the only deaths in the time since I last confessed. Four of our own have also died – young lads who didn't choose to but did so rather than live in shame. When I feel the wood of their coffins bite my shoulder, I know that only God's forgiveness, through your kindness, Father, stands between me and despair.'

Adam wanted to burst away; he tried to think of Zoe.

'I have learned from you, Father, that there can be only one true God, the God of love and truth. God is truth, He is love. Freedom is also truth and love. God is immortal. Man, a mere mortal but shaped in the image of God, strives for immortality through truth and love – through freedom. In such striving man becomes, however briefly, God-like. In other words, man free takes on the image of God. Those who deny us freedom also deny us the most cherished of God's gifts. It pains God to see such injustice since it flies in the face of His image. Therefore to take up arms against injustice, although in itself painful, is less so than the cause of such arms taking and is, in the eyes of God, forgivable.'

Adam gripped the gun.

'I hate what I am forced to do, Father. It is so hard, my life. God is my only comfort. God is on the side of the slave, the downtrodden, the disenfranchised, the abused, the exploited and the weak. He said, "Blessed are the meek for theirs is the Kingdom of Heaven." It is for them I fight, Father. I ask you to forgive me.'

Adam brought up the trembling muzzle of the gun to the hatch. 'I cannot speak for God, nor for those whose deaths at your hands He has facilitated. But for Zoe Coleraine, killed at the age of twenty last 17 May in Paddington by a bomb dispatched by you, here is your penance, and may Almighty God have mercy on your soul.'

'Uinsionn!'

For the tenth of a second, no more, Adam's attention was caught by the voice outside.

The kneeling man gasped: 'You!'

Adam fired.

I saw from the top of steps in the three-quarters light from eaves windows: a small church with pews blocked either side of a nave; a main altar to our right; beyond that an altar to Our Lady with candles flickering; two sets of confessionals along the walls. A woman in headscarf and glasses, we could see each other plainly, was near the back, looking at me strangely, why?

'Now, if he is here we should see him,' said Father Patrick going on down three marble steps. 'I think Father Blaise is hearing confession.'

The woman had all my attention: she reached her right hand across and inside her coat in a movement I instantly understood.

'Watch out!' I called, bustling Angie down the steps. We sprawled behind a pew.

A handgun went off. Vincent Ashe burst from the confessional. He was dressed in a long, dark-blue overcoat tied with a belt. He saw me and his mouth gathered in a worm. A dark form erupted out beside him, there was a blurred hand chop, the shape fell and Vincent, a gun in his hand, looked left and right.

'Adam!'

Angie scrambled headlong down the aisle, past gaping Father Patrick. I shouted, 'Angie, no!'

She was making for the inert form, between Vincent and me, thwarting any shot I might have had. Vincent reached and grabbed Angie by the hair and yanked her back to him, burying the nose of his gun so hard into her throat that she began immediately to choke.

'Nice try, Brian,' he said calmly. He took two steps backwards, looking to his both sides. 'What have they put you up to today, aye?' The woman was sweeping the gun in double-handed combat mode, a controlling arc. Vincent took another backward step for the door, Angie's round mouth in the crook of his arm. 'And you knew nothing when you led them to the border? You disappoint me, Brian.'

'I'm not after you, Vincent!' I called.

'Am I to believe that, Brian?' Vincent asked and he sounded genuinely injured. Perhaps he heard something in my voice which told him I had traded his cover for my job. They were as far as the door when a car's engine could be heard from the front of the church. Behind Vincent appeared a young man wearing an anorak and I heard him gasp, 'I don't know – Branch maybe,' fear in his voice. I chanced a wide shot and caught him in the shoulder, knocking him.

'Throw down the guns!' I shouted. I added, 'Irish police!' for the woman's benefit. But Vincent had Angie off the ground in his grip and, with the woman making a closed knot of the three of them, was coming back up the church.

'I will kill her, Brian,' Vincent spoke. 'I swear to almighty God I will have to unless you drop your gun. Now!'

Betrayal was everywhere and reason no longer a factor. Father Patrick was standing near the steps with a look of someone whose worst suspicions had at last been realised. I skidded the gun over the tiled floor towards Our Lady's altar. Vincent was at the bottom of the marble steps where Father Patrick was blocking his way. 'Move!'

Father Patrick was shaking his head. 'I always knew it.'

'Our of our way, Father,' Vincent called.

'For God's sake, is this a joke?' the old priest cried. 'You can't do this to a woman.'

'Vincent, take me!' I shouted.

'But who would care about you, Brian?' Vincent asked. 'Move aside, Father!'

'Take me, I'm too old to worry about dying,' said Father Patrick and, bracing the gap with his arms, he actually smiled.

I saw Vincent's eye. 'Do as he says, Father!' I yelled as I saw two men in coats slip in by the main door, moving like pros. All I could think of was Arty and Tice and that I had been used again. Then in the space above Father Patrick's shoulder appeared another face. It was that of a squat-shaped priest with a head of black hair. He looked down at Vincent and cried out, 'Uinsionn! No!'

Vincent shot Father Patrick at two feet. I dived for Our Lady, both to deny Vincent a target and to regain the gun. When I came up, the steps were empty and Father Patrick was lying in a ball at the foot of the steps with the black-headed priest bent over him. A bullet from a semisilenced gun thudded the wall plaster behind him. 'Irish police!' I shouted at a man crouching, aiming at me again. He answered with another shot and I saw he was covering for his colleague who was dragging the inert body that had to be Adam Coleraine to the door. Whether I forgot I was no longer in my own jurisdiction or, more likely, reacted with outrage that here, in my island, in a Catholic Church, were two British agents making off with the man I had risked so much to find, I cannot tell; I just knew I would not allow it to happen. 'Let him go!' I shouted. Adam had begun to struggle. I squeezed off four or five shots over their heads, shattering in the process a stained-glass window which burst most dramatically and fell both inside and out like a brief but deafening rain shower.

It was enough for them. They dropped Adam and bolted. A moment later tyres bit noisily outside. I caught Adam and made him stand.

'Oh, my God!' he said to Father Patrick's dead form.

'Adam,' said the kneeling priest, tears running down his face. 'Oh, Adam, my God, what have I done?'

We ran together, Adam and I, up the steps of the sacristy and back out the way I had come in, through the residence to Angie's car. The morning was as when I had arrived fifteen minutes before: sunny, peaceful, a thousand miles from troubled Belfast. As we drove out, Brother Walter, rising happily from a flower bed, waved.

Reports from Coastal Stations

In her office on St Stephen's Green, Janet stood looking out on her city of adoption. A helicopter racketed up from the roof of Government Buildings. There was now more in Janet's file than she wanted to digest: a tapestry of illusions and unprovable deceits. From 1983 came a forgotten story, an accident in which a woman pedestrian had been killed by a car whose driver was one James Ashe. James, Jimmy. The state's action for dangerous driving was struck out because the prosecuting guard failed to appear in court. In 1983 Janet had been a mere higher executive officer in the Department of Justice and Arty Gunn had been the chief superintendent in the metropolitan district from which the prosecuting guard had been transferred. Threads came together to give Janet a different picture of a place she had dared to think she knew. She saw the blurred edge of republicanism, itself like a border, a place of shadowy men who all looked like Cyril Maguire, feudal lords from little crossroads villages where you couldn't buy a loaf of bread or post a letter or have yourself prepared and buried without your money passing through their fingers. Everywhere Janet looked she saw fresh evidence until evidence was all she saw, blotting out all innocence, all trust.

Although her understanding of politics was consummate, Janet recognised how her natural background was a handicap to the high goals she had set herself. Wide spaces intruded. Reactions in basic circumstances: to religion, to freedom of expression, to history. Scots Presbyterian versus Irish Catholic, they did amount to more than labels, after all. Janet cooled her eyes with drops from a little bottle; then she walked the thirty yards from her office to that of the minister for justice.

'Ah, Janet, thank you for coming at such short notice,' said Maguire as Janet was ushered in.

'Minister.' With his hair like a set of tar and his mohair suit and white cuffs, Maguire reminded Janet more of a model for a man than a real man. 'My pleasure.'

'How are you, Janet?' asked Maguire, locking eyes.

'Well, thank you, Minister,' Janet replied.

'Ah, that's good. I'm relieved.'

'Minister?'

'Don't get me wrong, don't get me wrong, Janet,' Maguire chuckled. 'It's just that over the last couple of weeks I was wondering whether you were entirely happy.'

'I'm extremely happy, Minister,' Janet smiled.

Maguire made a big, exaggerated shrug. 'Good,' he said and laughed, then turned his attention to his desk as if the purpose of their meeting lay there. 'I'm only the caretaker landlord here, really, Janet. I suppose you could say the same about any minister. I'm the people's choice to oversee for a short time their affairs being managed by you – the professionals.'

It could have been his patter to sell a car in his garage in the midlands, Janet thought, which is what he had been doing before he became the people's choice.

'I suppose in one way, the power vested in such a transitory office is disproportionate to the item for which it is occupied,' said Maguire magnanimously. 'Compared to yourself, for example, I'm only passing through. But that's democracy, warts and all, Janet. A minister in his brief stay can try and put his personal stamp on policy. He can also influence the shape of the department after he has gone by the appointments he makes within that department. You with me, Janet?'

Janet realised in one unpleasant jolt that the job she had strived for all her life suddenly lay before her like a trinket on a dealer's rug. 'I think so, Minister.'

'We're a young country,' said Maguire expansively. 'Up to very recently most of the cabinet could claim descent from someone who was out in 1916.' The minister sat back contentedly. 'To hear the old people speak you'd think that 1916 or 1922 was only last week – and it's not, in fact, all that long ago, Janet. I love hearing that old chat. Men whose fathers were born in the last century handing it down to ourselves here, about to go into the next millennium. I don't know, it gives you confidence to think you're a part of a chain. Anyway,' the minister gave himself a little, chuckling reprimand, 'I mustn't go on. What I want to say, Janet, is that I imagine in my mind the events of those times as an old battle from which we have since been retreating. The years are miles, you with me? Now, in a situation like that, you never get all your troops home at once. Some of them are captured by the enemy, some are wounded and some still want to stay and fight, even though the treaty has been signed and the war is over. What do you do with such men? You can't abandon them with the stroke of a pen. Not when you know the sacrifices they have made. Not when you know that these will be the very people you will depend on in the event of war breaking out again – which is always a possibility.' Maguire upraised his hands to include Janet in the utter reasonableness of his thinking. 'We must show compassion,' he said.

'There is compassion,' Janet said carefully, 'and there is the law.'

'Often a young country cannot afford to indulge itself in the very fine distinctions,' Maguire remarked with a frown that said he was doing his best in difficult circumstances. 'Law is words in a book. Compassion comes from the heart. The law always has to be interpreted, otherwise we would not have courts or judges. It's not absolute, therefore. Compassion is what your gut tells you. The greatest men in the world have followed their gut. Take a hero from, if I may so describe it, the tradition you were once part of, Janet. Admiral Nelson. The orders telling him not to fight were fluttering bright and clear from the signal ship, but Nelson chose to put his telescope to his blind eye. That's what I'm talking about, Janet. In the context of ourselves, today, in the circumstances we find ourselves in, one foot in the future, one in the past. The law flutters, telling us one thing, our gut rumbles and tells us another.' The minister for justice slowly placed the palm of his hand over his left eye, and making a tube with the fingers of his other hand he brought it up and set it against his hairy knuckles. 'You with me, Janet?'

As always when she was off-balance Janet laughed. 'I think so.'

Maguire smiled as well. 'It's a queer old world,' he said and shook his head as if they had both come to the sudden and satisfactory end of a difficult assignment. 'Janet, we got side-tracked. I'm sorry. I wanted you in here because, as you know, in twelve months time the position of secretary to the department will change due to retirement. It is normal in such circumstances to establish the availability of candidates before drawing up a short list. Janet?'

'I . . . I am honoured,' Janet said.

'I too am honoured, Janet,' smiled Cyril Maguire.

In her own office, thirty minutes after a division bell had taken the minister at speed down to the Dail, Janet sat and considered not the choice with which she had been just confronted, but another choice she had made, twenty-one years before. In terms of starkness it had been the same. The Shankill or the South. Her virginity or the exotic. The known for the unknown. Janet's decision had taken her down a path on which turning back was impossible. Now, no less. Janet had decided she needed a night with her feet up and a video to occupy her mind when her secretary came in from the outer office. 'The Branch are getting in news about a shoot out in a church in Belfast,' the man said.

I would like to set the record to rest on my intentions that evening as I fled west with Adam Coleraine across Ulster, Gilly. My paramount goal was to get out of the North. I knew I had broken the law being up there with a gun, but equally I knew the consequences both for Adam and myself were we to be apprehended by the Brits. Adam, whom I felt a responsibility towards, would never be heard of again and I would be used as a scapegoat in whatever were the political manoeuvrings of the moment. I gambled that we would be less expected to go west than the more direct route south – but either way, we had to cross the border.

There were other thoughts which I allowed myself indulge for brief space: the obvious danger to Angie's life was one, but I also dared to let a small ember of impending success warm up my heart: I had achieved what I had set out to and, furthermore, despite the tragedy in St Paschal's church, Vincent Ashe was now a hunted man. Back over the border there would, I felt, be a resumption of my old role. People could no longer ignore me.

We were south of Dungannon before five. Every time music on the car radio stopped I expected news of us, but there was none. I also expected road blocks and so left the main road and began a loop under Omagh. Adam, out of his religious habit, sat in the clothes he had worn underneath, staring unseeing at the road ahead. I could feel some of the remorse that he was feeling and the great wave of grief that it had swelled up again in him. Grief, I knew then, is the greatest leveller of all, greater than death even, because whereas death holds the possibilities that are intrinsic to the unknown, everything in grief is known, everything in all its impoverishment.

These were the smuggler's routes we were driving on, the nighttime conduits for pigs and cattle, the wooded lowlands where we skipped back and forth over the years, a leg in both countries. At a little after six that evening we entered Castlefinn. We passed no sign, no mark, no checkpoint or watchtower to say we were over. I pressed on, eager to put extra distance between ourselves and any possible pursuers. The outskirts of Ballybofey were adorned by little aluminium and glass factories. Buds on trees were broken out at their tips whitely and flesh-like and cut grass smells made their way inward to us through the car's ventilation system. I drove directly to the Garda Station with a clear picture in my mind of the justice that had to be done.

The door was locked; there were no lights showing. I rang the bell, looked at my watch, then went to a telephone kiosk on the far side of the road with the intention of ringing Garda regional headquarters in Letterkenny. Something made me dial the number to Janet's office instead.

'I have him, Janet,' I said, conscious of the triumph in my voice.

'It's no good.'

At a hundred and fifty miles, her voice was cold as a gun.

'Janet, we have a case at last against Vincent Ashe. He's shot a man dead. There are six witnesses.'

'At least two of whom say you tried to kill them.'

I couldn't understand this. The Janet I thought I knew would have trusted me against the world. 'I suppose their story is that they were in to say the stations,' I said drily.

'The RUC are in the process of issuing warrants. For your arrest.'

'As you said yourself, you know the Brits,' I said in disgust.

'You can't behave like you did on people's own backdoor.'

'I suppose these warrants will be pursued in Dublin,' I said.

'With relish.'

176

I wondered who had got at her – was it Edwin, her brother? Or Maguire? Or was what I was hearing for real? 'Am I the only one wanted?' I enquired. 'After all, a priest was shot dead by Vincent Ashe.'

'We know,' Janet replied with the finality of a bolt going home on a door. 'The RUC apprehended a wounded subversive in the church. He told them. All ports and airports here and in the north have been sealed – for both of you.'

She made it sound as if Vincent and I were on the same side. 'As long as there's fair play,' I remarked bitterly. 'What does Cyril Maguire think of all this?'

'We haven't discussed it.'

'I can see how my arrest would be a grand diversion,' I said. 'Is Maguire really serious about going after Vincent?'

Some hesitations make you wonder after them if they took place at all. 'We haven't discussed it.'

'But, your impression? I mean, there was that photograph.'

'I have every faith in the law.'

'Don't we all?'

'Brian?'

'Yes, Janet?'

'My advice to you is that you and Adam Coleraine should come in.'

'And trust Vincent to Maguire? Thank you for your advice,' I said and hung up.

I tried to imagine people like Janet who had clawed their way to the top and the different faces along the way they had had to show as the occasion demanded; I tried to imagine how, at night, they managed to close their eyes and sleep with a clear conscience.

An old Guard was ambling up the far pavement. He had a professional look at Angie's car and at Adam in it, then he climbed the steps of his station, one at a time. I crossed the road and we drove away, wordlessly, south. Down the slim neck of South Donegal where there is only five miles of Ireland between the border and the sea, the feeling of being a fugitive in my own country became hard to accept. I had only a vague idea where we were going, but I knew I should not let them capture me. As we crossed the Erne at Ballyshannon and left the radio frequencies of the North for those of the Republic, the first, patchy news reports began to come through and, with them, the reality. In Ballina I lurched off the main street to avoid a guard on a corner and was amazed how complete my sudden transformation from hunter to hunted had become. I hated it. I hated the fear that I suddenly could not control. I hated hearing what Janet said. I hated whatever had driven us all to where we had ended. Through Mayo, along roads without borders where the only lights were our own reflected in the eyes of sheep, I hated fate for the hand I had been dealt. It was a night for the falling stars that I had wanted to tell Janet about but now never would. I hated Ireland as we made our lonely arc. I hated Vincent Ashe with a hate that knew no bounds.

The journey would never end. Air in cold spears flew in when they stopped and Uinsionn got out. Tyres bit grit when they pulled away again. Nona's head spun under the twin weights of tragedy and exhaustion. She liked it better when they were moving. Gears: five; tyres: four. Nona's head was an engine, oil-like blood pumping thickly, her eyes spinning like ball bearings, what beautiful machines our bodies really are. On the floor at her feet the Brit woman started struggling again, such a nuisance, bound and gagged and wedged face down, but the stupid bitch couldn't accept it.

'Shut yer fuckin' mouth!' Nona said and stamped on her and closed her eyes again. A bond grew between Nona and the road. She had this crazy idea that if the car stopped they all would die. Like a moth to a light her mind kept returning to the church, to the sight of *him* eruptin' from the confess'nal, to the sight of *him* goin' down under Uinsionn's gun, to the cry from the Brit woman runnin' up the church, to the look in the old priest's eyes the second before Uinsionn shot him; like a moth Nona's mind flitted away. They had killed a priest.

'Nona?'

No matter what you thought or believed in, you could never forget that, that went against all blood, that was a higher price than anyone wanted to pay.

'Nona?'

Uinsionn's voice came from the front in the disembodied, snatchy way of one radio ham calling another across oceans of ether.

'Yes, Uinsionn?'

'Are you alright?'

'Yes.'

'We had no choice.'

'No.'

'It was a trap and the priests connived. Can you believe that? Abusing one of Christ's sacraments for something so base? And using a man not even a priest at that.'

Nona yearned for a warm bed and for sleep. For a respite. But Uinsionn's words made her frown and she recalled the same thoughts she'd had in Gormley's. 'Do you . . . know him, Uinsionn?' she asked cautiously. 'The mon in the confess'nal?'

'Yes, I know him, Nona,' Uinsionn replied, 'I know him.'

Nona felt so inadequate in Uinsionn's presence.

'What choice had we?' Uinsionn was asking again. 'The old priest tried to prevent our escape. What were we meant to do? This is a war. Having put his church at the disposal of the enemy, did he expect us to lie down like lambs and be slaughtered? Because that was what would have happened, Nona, have no doubt. Have no doubt. They were all armed, including the one in the confessional. His role was not to give me penance but to execute me – in Christ's confession box! Everything we did was justifiable. We came back to ask God's forgiveness on our knees. We were attacked. The bible doesn't ask you to lie down and be killed, it says you must save yourself. That's all we did, save ourselves, Nona.'

A humming axle joined Nona's ears. With the ripple of the car's passage Uinsionn's words ruffled the thin veneer of her sleep the way raindrops do the surface of a lake.

'But it won't be seen like that, Nona. We will be hunted now forever.'

Nona did not want this new union she heard in which she and Uinsionn were one in everything. 'No one there . . . would rec'nise me, Uinsionn,' Nona dared to say.

'The boy from Derriaghy, Nona,' said Uinsionn gently as if to a forgetful child. 'He'll tell them everything they want to know, the boy will.'

The car's headlights cut through a winding landscape of hedges and trees that made no sense to Nona. She wondered in silence

179

how she could have forgotten the young lad from Derriaghy, his terrified face lookin' up at her from the church floor. Tell them everythin', of course he would. Why had a small part of her persisted in the belief that she was any better off than Uinsionn?

'We must get out, if only for a short while, Nona. We will,' Uinsionn said. 'It won't be too bad. Anything will be better than this. We have friends, Nona, friends you never knew of. They'll help us. It is the right thing to do. We were born to survive. The merest animal fights to the last breath, heroically. Life is all we have in the end and we fight. God gave us our life not to squander but to keep at all costs and we will do that, Nona, you and I.'

Without warning the Brit woman reared from the floor and nearly knocked the gun from Nona's hands.

'I – want – to – stop!'

'Jeesus!' Nona cried. 'Uinsionn!'

Uinsionn drew into the side of the road. 'Let her out for a moment,' he said.

'Lie still!' Nona orderd and undid the cloth binding the woman's hands and mouth. 'Get out, nigh,' she said, stepping out herself onto a wet margin of grass.

'Shoot her if she tries to run,' Uinsionn said from the car, loud enough for the woman to hear.

Under trees fog turned to rain in steady drips. The woman lurched, retching, into briars.

'Jesus,' Nona said.

Done with pukin' the woman hiked her skirt up and balanced on the wet grass.

'Thank you,' she gasped.

There was a moon somewhere above the fog because the fog had a kind of shine to it that made it weird. Beyond the ditch a ewe called and a lamb answered.

'Thank you,' the woman said again. 'My name is Angie. What's yours?'

'Ye shut yer fuckin' mouth!' Nona replied.

The journey would never end. Time became something eaten by the road that ran straight up the middle of the church where Nona was a bride. Her honeymoon was a sleep of lulling words. Children. The sea. The sun. The dead. The dead. A priest blessing her marriage. Nona looked but there was no one at her side.

People laughed. The priest's face was sad, he was the old man from Gormley's, he was the priest they had killed. He was sad for Nona. She looked up again. *He* was at her side, a priest, cryin', at her side. He didn't fit. Nona came awake as the car stopped and she scented a different quality to the air.

'Do you smell the sea, Nona?'

Nona could actually taste it as well as smell it when she got out. The fight seemed to have gone out of the woman and she allowed Nona to walk her towards the outline of a house. Funny how Nona could taste somethin' like that soon's she got down here but never notice it in Belfast. Some people claimed they could smell the sea in the middle of great continents, Nona had read. Down here made her shiver, an emptiness with all of Ireland sittin' on top of it. Nona saw the woman into a windowless room, used now like the whole house for hay storage, and dragged over the door. The prim way she'd said 'Thank you', 's if pissin' was such a big deal!

'Sit with me, Nona,' Uinsionn said.

Like the heads of monster children bushes outside began to slowly appear. One bird opened its account, then two. Wind busied itself around the roof eaves and windows as if wind and the house depended on each other in this place. Nona drew a bale out and sat on it with her knees up to her chin. She could see quite clearly the texture of the hay, saved greenish the summer before, and Uinsionn, sitting with a gun in his lap. They would never be able to go back. Like the hay, all they would have of the past was its smell. The things that a single bullet could put in motion.

'We are safe here, Nona,' Uinsionn said. 'We are safe here among our own.'

Nona could never feel safe down here. Uinsionn's people could never be hers.

'You were superb today, Nona.'

'Thank ye, Uinsionn.'

'A long day tomorrow, Nona,' Uinsionn said. He took some turf shags and built the fire with them.

Nona nodded.

'I mean long in the way the day we are born is long, or the day we die. We spend the days between like a drunkard spends his shillings, but those days are made all of gems, every second,' Uinsionn said. Nona could see he wanted the time to his leavin' to

181

be a slow thing. 'Do you think the Englishwoman overheard anything that might give our intentions away?'

'She was too fuckin' busy worryin' about herseylf,' Nona said.

'I wonder,' Uinsionn murmured, his face drawn to the orange flames.

'I have only two rounds short of a full chamber, if there's trouble,' Nona said.

'I haven't even that,' Uinsionn said.

'There's half a pound of Semtex,' Nona said.

'Aye,' Uinsionn said, looking curiously at her. 'Look out there, Nona, and tell me what you see.'

Through the window were stars chased upwards by the dawn. 'Stars on their way,' said Nona, and suddenly knew she could not be a further part of this man's plan.

'More stars than every child ever born to a mother, Nona, can you believe that? How insignificant to a star whether a man moves from one place to another for a space of time, or dies a thousand deaths.'

Uinsionn had turned his face to Nona and he was a stranger, different to the man she thought she knew. Why, Nona could not tell. She felt in the grip of a terrifying unpredictability. All she knew was that she would not go.

'Nona, we will be safe.'

'I'm sorry . . .' Nona said, rigid.

'Don't be afraid. I'm not like other men.'

Nona didn't want to hear. She stood up. 'I'm sorry, I'm tired. I'll sleep with her inside.'

'I understand, Nona,' Uinsionn said.

It was not sleep that Nona needed but empty time to wash slowly through her head. The heavy revolver in her hands, Nona curled into a soft corner inside the door of the first room, six feet from the woman. Side by side with the bales stood a dressing table, big and chunky, all its drawers in place and the oval mirror in its headboard streaked a dirty white by the shit of swallows. The piece of furniture made Nona pensive; innocent vanity clung to it and in the mirror Nona could see her own face fracture, perhaps just as another woman had seen her lips on the morning of a fair day, had powdered up her cheeks to mask weathered veins, had knotted a scarf beneath her chin before walking for miles beside a man she loved. She was lucky, that ancient woman.

182

Nona saw the Brit woman come awake although there was something too easy about the way it happened, as if she had been choosing the moment to open her eyes.

'Nona?'

'Shut yer mouth, d'ye hear?'

'What's going to happen to Adam?'

'I seyd, shut yer fuckin' mouth,' Nona said, but she knew her voice lacked resolve.

'I blame myself,' the woman said. 'I couldn't feel the way he did when Zoe died. You can just observe and pity and thank God or whatever you believe in that it's someone else, not you, however much you love them. That's natural I think.'

Wind, risin', fallin', a dog howlin' at the moon.

'There's no anger in grief,' the woman said. 'That's how I saw him in those days, soft. That outraged me at the time because I didn't understand.'

'Didn't unnerstan' what?'

'That softness and hardness coexist in all of us, whether you're the one who plants the bomb or the father of the girl it kills.'

'What bomb?' Nona asked, shaking her head.

'The bomb last May in Paddington,' the woman said. 'It killed Adam's daughter, Zoe. It's why Adam's here.'

'Ye'r a lyin' bitch,' Nona laughed, getting up.

'It's the truth,' the woman said.

'Bitch,' Nona said curtly and hit her down once with the pistol butt on the lower nose, doubling her.

'Nona?'

Nona swung round. 'Bitch,' she said to Uinsionn. 'Was tryin' to get away.'

Nona saw the mockery in Uinsionn's eyes again, as if he had overheard everything that had been said, as if the idea of this crumpled woman being a match for Nona was laughable, as if the most private parts of Nona's soul were such a public affair.

'I understand, Nona,' Uinsionn said.

From the big window of Janet's house outside Clifden the ocean defied you to take seriously man and his entanglements. Seagulls hovered, calling, at eye level. Occasionally boats come in way below us to haul pots, two men in yellow oilskins to each, glinting specks on a sea of alive, deep green. I wondered what Janet would think if she knew the refuge I had chosen. The keys had been in the flowerpot when we arrived in darkness the night before; we hid Angie's car in the garage, beside an old Fiat that Janet's family must have used to go on summer picnics; I poured myself a whisky and drank it with a peculiar, grim satisfaction.

In a way the events of January had prepared me for the news headlines I now heard. Listening with a certain detachment as if my life were a thriller being told in instalments, I was determined not to be diverted from my objective.

The media gave much more prominence to me than to Vincent; I tried to work out from the bulletins that Friday morning what Vincent's movements were, but Arty or whoever was in charge was keeping a tight cap on it. As I sat in the unheated house, watching the light change with the morning on the sea, listening to the radio softly on, the extent of my predicament asserted itself. But at the same time I had this totally illogical belief that a break was coming my way.

A Dublin voice was giving out the forecast: reports from coastal stations: Malin Head to Howth to Rossclare. Adam sat on the floor, his arms around his knees. He looked very vulnerable. We would have to go our separate ways: I was the fugitive here, not Adam. He would have to find himself a good solicitor and ensure that he got the full protection of the Irish State. I did not overestimate the chances of his easily agreeing to this course of action.

'I'm very sorry about Zoe,' I said.

He barely flickered. If he wondered how I might have such knowledge he did not show it. Roches Point Lighthouse to Valentia, the soft voice on the radio said. To Belmullet.

'You know one of those films where everyone is trapped together in a plane and the only thing they have in common is their appointment with destiny?' I asked gently. 'That's what we're like – you and me, Counsell and Ireland and Sir Trevor Tice, my report and seven hundred years of history. Like it or not, we're all locked up together, the living and the dead.'

I knew he was in his early forties, but Adam looked ten years older than me that day. His crazy plan was none of my concern, nor even his attempt to shoot Vincent, but I was intrigued to know how he had nearly pulled it off.

'I know you took my report,' I said, 'and I know that it gave you the idea of St Paschal's – it was stupid of me not to have remembered. But did you know in advance that the man you would try and execute was Vincent Ashe?'

He may have shaken his head, he may not. I reckoned he needed, amongst all the other things, medical attention. There was news again on the radio, with a reporter describing what he knew of the two manhunts. I grabbed a map. Activity was reported from Buncrana in Donegal; from Tallaght in Dublin; from South Armagh. Ports and airports were being guarded around the clock. Gardai had swooped on Birr when a hill farmer, out the night before at his lambing, recounted how he had heard women talking on a quiet boreen before a car drove off. I drew a rough line on the map from Belfast to Birr, and projected it south: the line ran into County Clare.

'I thought I was okay.'

The voice was barely above that on the radio. He wasn't looking at me but out over the sea, an endless cap of shining, wrinkled plastic.

'Everything was smooth, responded properly. I was in control, I thought. I had plenty in reserve. Now I know there were signs I saw but chose to ignore. The man who sold me the paper every morning in Sidcup station, for example. For countless years. Handed me out the *Guardian* folded. Then one morning there was a boy in his place. I never asked why. I never realised how transitory everything is, never saw the signs.'

The voice on the radio was now that of a seanachi, a storyteller, comforting: '. . . in my father's father's time.'

'A man off the Strand used to cut my hair and trim my beard when I had one. Mr West. He had angina, poor chap. I liked him, made him laugh. I went in one day and a woman offered to cut my hair. I never went back.'

'Fadó, fadó,' said the seanichi. Long, long ago.

'Time is really people, isn't it? There they are in a long queue going back to the beginning. So many of them. Niches in the rock face. Toeholds. I try to think of all of them to see if anything makes sense. My parents, their friends. All the people who made up their greater world. For example, as I was growing up in Carlisle, Atlee was in Downing Street. There was a war in Korea. Do either of those things explain anything to me now? What about Kennedy's assassination, the seminal event? Or the Beatles? Who now knows what Carnaby Street was? I smoked pot with Alison whilst people died in Vietnam and felt not the remotest guilt. Zoe was born under Labour, grew up and was killed under the Tories. She would never have heard of Jimmy Carter. She might have registered Watergate because there was a movie. Chairman Mao was sort of like Che Guevara, except he wrote a book. Zoe's landscape was so different from mine. Instant, global communications, the present as a miniseries, film stars run the world . . .' He wept. 'Every knows John Denver. War is something on television. You pay by card. You just . . . go!'

Adam shook, binding himself tighter, crying.

'It took Zoe's death to make me see I had nothing. A wife I no longer knew nor loved. A job I could no longer believe in. A house I disliked. No beliefs, no values. No real friends – not even Angie. I'm just her project and look where I've got her. I never imagined it would really end like this. Failure in everything, including hate. Failure to be what I pretended in other men's eyes. A man whom I liked and who liked me died yesterday because of what I am – or perhaps because of what I'm not. Even my dreams are doomed. I dreamt about a girl and she turns out to be a killer. There should be some consolation at the bottom but, believe me, there's none.'

The radio news shifted over the day to higher ground: the country, were it a commercial enterprise, would be wound up, someone had said; Ireland must never join a military alliance; and the latest reports from coastal stations. A picture of Vincent's intentions was becoming ever clearer in my mind. Vincent would not stay and fight a case he could never win; Vincent would never allow himself to be bound with the chains I had heard so much about. Vincent would run. That meant out of Ireland, but it also meant, since everything had happened so quickly and unplanned, that he needed a breathing space to put arrangements in place. That breathing space was what Maguire would give him to pay off whatever old debts were owed. Vincent would take that space in County Clare, I was sure, but where? When the only light was out to sea, a purple band an inch high and a hundred miles in length, I said, 'I'm going after Vincent Ashe, Adam. For your own sake, I

186

suggest you give me six hours, then go straight to Dublin and employ a solicitor to get you the protection of the Irish courts. It's your best bet.'

At first he didn't react at all, then he slowly shook his head.

I said, 'You're not safe here, Adam. I'm leaving tonight. It may only be a matter of hours until Tice's men find you. You know what that will mean.'

'I'm not going into court or to any solicitor.'

I was tiring of Adam Coleraine. 'Why not?'

'Not with Angie still out there on my account,' he said quietly.

'I can't take you with me.'

'I may be of some help.'

I considered the other options: they amounted to nil. I felt my sense of responsibility to him coming to its limit.

'The girl's name is Nona Lane,' he said. 'The girl in the church with Ashe.'

The name meant nothing to me. 'How do you know that?'

'I met her once.'

I couldn't see his face in the darkness, but I could hear his voice with something beyond mere interest in it.

Then he said, 'I can find out where Ashe is.'

I thought I had misheard him. 'You can what?'

'Find out where Ashe is.'

There was a sense of happy foolishness, like people discussing how they will spend the Lotto. 'Is that a fact?'

'Yes.'

'How?'

'If I can find out, can I come with you?'

The prospects of him knowing seemed so remote that I said, 'Alright.'

Adam said, 'Father Blaise in St Paschal's is Father Blaise Ashe, Vincent Ashe's brother. He is also Ashe's confessor, but if he knows where Ashe has gone, I think now he will tell me.'

I felt the the only boy in the class who doesn't know the facts of life. 'Then ring him,' I said. 'But for God's sake don't tell him where we are.'

'I don't know where we are,' Adam replied, standing up.

The voice on the radio was busy and sharp, one of these bright young city lads talking about that day's financial markets in Dublin and London, New York and Tokyo. The Irish pound and sterling; the dollar and the yen.

'Father Blaise, please.'

The next time I heard this radio report, I swore I would spare a thought for some poor wretch on the run someplace, holed up on his own, wondering how at such a time anyone could worry about the value of money.

'Father Blaise, it's Adam.'

The weather report would not be denied. A rain belt moving in from the Atlantic, would affect all areas before dawn. I looked out at the moon in a clear sky and a sea so flat you could skate on it. They had it all wrong, I laughed, wrong completely.

'Superintendent.'

Adam had come back from the phone without my hearing or seeing him.

'Father Blaise says Vincent will go to a place called Cullen,' Adam said.

I took out the map and lit a match. I found Cullen in the middle of County Clare, the eye of a web of little roads. 'Did he say why?'

'It's the family's ancestral farm,' Adam replied. 'Vincent has always gone there before he leaves Ireland, and when he returns.'

I quenched the match between my fingers. 'How is Father Blaise taking it?' I asked.

'Slightly better now, I think,' Adam replied. 'He said to tell you that he's praying for us.'

We left in Janet's old Fiat within fifteen minutes, creeping away from the cliffs and the sea, through Clifden in its yellow street lights that leave no shadow. That a man was praying for us in Belfast was suddenly a source of tremendous comfort and courage. We would need his prayers, I felt, all of them. On the car radio they were playing the national anthem.

I spent endless hours trying to repair the walls of an old garden. Janet was helping too, but her part was a tidy house in Monkstown. She kept hoovering, saying, 'But this is the world of real importance, Brian.' Janet's hoovering overlaid my efforts, like the sound of the sea, and it caused me great frustration, because every stone I put into the wall fell out again, until I cried.

I was awake for a minute before I opened my eyes. It was very pleasant sitting back in that old Fiat with the strengthening sun on my eyes, feeling whole and refreshed after a few hours sleep. All the great days from the past returned in crystal clarity: the day I married; the day I got my commission; the celebrations at subsequent promotions; the quiet pride that I was part of something worthwhile. I'm a morning person, I know, but that morning I had no doubt that the course I had taken was the right one.

Down over austere miles of limestone escarpments, swans were caught like ice chips on a distant lake. the fields, where they existed apart from the rock, were marked off with stone walls as delicate as threads: two cattle grazed in one field, in another there was a magpie. Adam sat outside the car on an outcrop, staring back towards the sea. The weight of his loss, borne in solitude, was merciless, even to me, a stranger. My self-interest was niggardly beside his tragedy. His child had been ripped from him, whereas I, awaking late in life to the venality of men's intentions, had lost only my pride. I had lost nothing, *nothing*. I topped the Walther up to its seven rounds and got out. There was birdsong in the air all around Adam's head. 'Let's go,' I said.

It has been said of me with reference to subsequent events that I acted impulsively and was irresponsible in regard to other people's safety. The facts do not support such charges. I had made it quite clear to Adam that his coming with me was based solely on his agreeing that he would not be present for any confrontation with Vincent – but even that suggests that I intended to confront Vincent by myself. I did not. I planned first to establish that Vincent was, in fact, in the house that his brother had described to Adam. I wanted to know who he had with him and, particularly, Angie's position. With these facts in hand my intention was to rally the local gardai – giving myself up in the process, if it came to that – and to see Vincent apprehended and Angie safely released.

We came through Clare towards Cullen by way of roads barely two cars' width that twisted up and over hills of holly and rhododendron and down between little fields of snipe grass. Unless someone had tumbled to the different car in Janet's garage, the Fiat was perfect for the job: without a description of the car in which your quarry is travelling, planning a manhunt of the type underway for us would be a nightmare. You rely on random checks and, most of all, calls from the public. To minimise the latter, any time we went through a village Adam dipped down out of sight.

Wind got up and we drove into a slanting rain. Houses seen half a mile back when reached proved derelict, their windows solid with concrete blocks, their surroundings overgrown. The chimneys of occasional holiday bungalows were smokeless, their facades sterile. We rose and dipped and rose again and suddenly the belltower of a church stood out on the near horizon like a scaffold.

From behind the wheel of the car I scanned the landscape. If there was in Ireland a crucible of Ireland the Nation, this was it. This was De Valera's Ireland: the idyll of self-containment, maidens dancing at crossroads and the Atlantic nearby as the rich garden. There was no compromising down here. Men slipped in and out, questions were never asked or, if they were, never answered.

'There,' Adam said and pointed.

On a slight rise of ground half a mile west of where we were parked a pocket stand of pines rose and, just visible among them, the gable of a house. From the pine trees to the village, a distance of another half mile, the fields ran bare and poor. I followed the road for the village. It curved down and around the slight rise making a hill of it and ensuring that sight of the house was lost from the road. There was an entrance with an aluminium gate chained across it. A muddy boreen twisted up into trees.

I kept going into Cullen. I wanted to dump Adam before beginning my reconnoitre and I also wanted to establish the existence or otherwise of a Garda station in the village. Speed-limit signs a hundred yards away stood out like red and white eyes of robots landed in an alien vista. With the vigour of the Atlantic behind it, rain quickened. The grey of the sky and the stone of the church seemed hewn from the same rock. Both were suddenly splashed with ultraviolet blue as a strobe directly ahead of us came to life.

I reversed. The blue light was growing. I hit the aluminium entrance gate at twenty, bursting it back. Adam jumped out. As I pitched up the boreen, he dragged the gate to and ducked as the Garda patrol car shot past.

We came out onto level ground. A rough yard of sorts for collecting cattle had been made on the hill. A tractor stood in the yard with a load of wet, abandoned dung. I got out. Sea smell, deep and distinct, hung in the air, but the noises were all in the fiefdom of the rain. Rain cancelled out every other sound; rain gave a voice to the soft grasses and a song language to a thousand hidden pools; rain made music on the roof of the car and on the canvas cab of the tractor we had passed. To unseen pieces of metal and machinery in fields and ditches, rain gave notes of irregular percussion. Ahead of us the boreen dipped sharply, disappearing under the hill we had stopped on, before resurfacing some hundred yards on its final approach to the house. It was obviously unlived in, but a couple of generations ago it had been a proud place when the pines had been planted as a windbreak or in a poor man's defiance of his own mortality. The roof was intact. From where I stood I could see the scalloped asbestos roof tiles dripping like an ever-forming string of glass beads the full length of the eaves. By the front door where haggert had not yet encroached, a concrete water tank stood, its inside walls scoured deep green from years of stagnant water. Only the ghosts of Ashes lived here, I thought. This place below me and all about was just a lost dream to grown men and women who had gone as children to distant lands and who had made of it in their memory something reality never could.

The tractor behind me came to life with a roar. With its loaded trailer it steamed across the boreen, blocking it. A man jumped from the cab and ran.

'Hey!' I cried. 'Police!'

Jumping back into the Fiat, I swung in reverse.

Adam cried, 'Look!'

Swelling up at us from the dip was a JCB, its shovel fixed like a battering ram. It breasted the hill yellowly and at full throttle came for us.

'Get out!' I shouted.

The speed at which it was happening seemed impossible in this lost place. I hauled out my gun and at the same time swung the car forward, trying to find space beside the metal shovel. I met it square. The Fiat went backwards like a pram and hit the trailer. The digger kept coming so that the steering wheel drove into my chest. Then the seat mountings went and my next perspective was from near the back window, three feet from the groaning metal face that wanted to embrace me. We rose. I say 'We' but I could not see Adam anywhere; the Fiat and me went up as if on hydraulics. All at once all that was left to my world was a shrinking, metal space. The digger's revving engine had a madness to it. I thought I heard another engine. I heard scraping metal. Oh yes, and the rain. Despite the fact that I knew this was it, over the sound of my own fear I could still hear the rain.

Janet awoke to the ringing blows of hammers securing scaffolding to the house next door. Two men in yellow hard hats, almost up to eaves level in the first light; Janet repulled the window curtains, showered and dressed. Her neighbours were away on holiday. There was no refurbishment plan that Janet knew of that would require scaffolding. Drinking a cup of coffee, standing, her family in morning clatter around her, Janet struggled to reassert her sense of inner authority. When she had come home the evening before, her eldest daughter had remarked that earlier the telephone had been dead for fifteen minutes. Janet left half the cup behind her and hurried out.

Friday morning traffic was slow after Blackrock; the grey sea always looked higher than you sitting in a car. Without premeditation at Merrion Gates Janet swung the Granada in behind the cars turning right and saw a dark blue Cortina four cars back do the same. News on the radio carried no mention of the Garda manhunt that was taking place. Howth looked green and inviting out between the two steaming rock sticks of the Pigeon House as Janet crawled in along Sandymount Strand, past the Martello Tower built for the defence of the nation. Now it was all James Joyce this and that, Dublin intelligentsia. Janet's reading when she had the time was history, the great Queens of England, poor Queen Mary's courage after the deaths of all those children. Cruel times, but were these any better?

Janet took a left turn quickly, down a sleepy street that she did not really know, and hung on the next intersection long enough to see the Cortina make the same turn from Strand Road. Instead of right Janet went left. She drove faster than she liked down residential roads with trees, narrow from cars parked either side.

White reversing lights inched inexorably out twenty yards ahead and kept coming despite Janet's hand on her horn. Full weight on the brake, the Granada sat down with a high pitched shriek. Behind Janet the hurrying Cortina did the same, five yards from her boot. Two sun visors clicked down. Janet nevertheless recognised one of the men as being Harcourt Square. Turning full around in her seat she stared back at them: then traffic in both directions made her resume, slamming through the gears of the big car in her anger.

Janet could rationalise away the dead telephone, the sudden appearance of scaffolding next door, but not the Cortina with the two Special Branch men. Having accepted that forces were moving against her, Janet then had to explain why and could not. Janet did not like Cyril Maguire's political philosophy as crudely explained to her by the minister for justice, but she rationalised that too on the basis that Maguire's tenure of office was limited, that one man's view would have no bearing on the long-term future of the department under her stewardship, and that anyway there was now a nationwide search taking place for Vincent Ashe which Maguire could do little to stop even if he wanted to. That logic led Janet to regard my position as, although regrettable, ultimately futile. Having helped me in the north as much as anyone could be expected to, Janet wasn't now going to compromise her life's ambition by gambling further on a cause clearly lost. As she slowed to enter the car park at the rear of the Department of Justice, and a red Mercedes with Arty Gunn's pink head behind the wheel left the same through the exit gates on the other side of the building, Janet decided she needed to test the new alliance between herself and Maguire.

'Good morning, Assistant Secretary.'

'Good morning,' Janet said to her secretary. 'Has the minister arrived yet?'

'I understand he has gone directly to cabinet,' the man replied.

Janet entered her office with its two windows through which you looked directly over St Stephen's Green as from the drawing room of a country house. All at once a great sadness overtook her. She refused to believe that her following was more than a temporary aberration, a mistake in the chain of command; but then why did her sadness persist?

'Was Assistant Commissioner Gunn here this morning?' Janet asked as her secretary laid out before her documents requiring her attention and the morning's items of correspondence.

'Not to my knowledge, Assistant Secretary,' the secretary replied. 'Do you wish me to contact him?'

'No,' replied Janet quietly. 'But let me know when the minister returns.' As the man closed the door behind him Janet dialled a number in Harcourt Square. 'I'd like an update on the operations current,' she said when she was put through.

'I'm afraid I've been instructed not to give out any information on the telephone,' the briefing officer said.

'Do you know who you are speaking to?' Janet asked.

'Yes,' came the reply.

'Thank you, I'll remember this,' Janet said, immediately regretting her asperity. She dialled again. 'What's going on?' she asked Dick Jennings.

'Little,' Dick Jennings replied.

'Has anyone been caught?'

'No.'

Janet frowned at the curtness of the usually affable Jennings's replies. 'What is it?'

'Nothing.'

'Dick!'

'It's just, I don't know,' Dick Jennings said. 'It's just as if Brian is the main culprit, d'you know what I mean? He's the focus, he's the effort, as far as Arty is concerned. This Ashe man, I don't know, it's as if he's a secondary target.'

Janet put on her electric kettle and made herself a pot of tea and sat down determinedly, hiving off her feelings of conflict and unease, and dealt with her correspondence and applied the full weight of her mind to the draft of a constitutional amendment which sought to make subtle alterations to Ireland's status of neutrality. She loved Ireland. She loved the identity that came with being Irish, something new to her because in the North identity was a provocative thing, but down here it was no more an issue than air or daylight, just a quality that people took for granted. She was surprised how quickly the morning had gone when, without a knock, Arty Gunn walked in.

'Assistant Secretary.'

'Assistant Commissioner?' Janet frowned. She tried to read from Arty's face the reason for his uninvited entry, but Arty, as ever, was smiling sadly as if this was just another day set aside for the end of the world.

'I hear you were on inquiring about our hunt for dese subversives,' Arty said and sat down and crossed his legs. He was wearing the blue suit he normally reserved for meeting people he saw as important.

Janet said nothing.

'Ah, that's not an aisy one.' Arty shook his head dismally. 'It's a pity your friend Brian doesn't accept that the game is up.'

Janet could not retain her position and accept such impertinence. 'I beg your pardon, Assistant Commissioner?'

'I think it's time we all recognised the bad egg in your bashket, Janet,' Arty said.

The use of her first name, the disrespectful familiarity in the heavy, Mayo vowels, caused Janet to catch her breath. 'I—'

'There's no one blamin' you, Janet,' Arty said, the soul of reason. 'I'm not suggestin' you told him anythin' you shouldn't have, that would be out of the question, or that you're concealin' anythin' he told you, but Brian's a bloody rogue, he pulled the wool over all of us.'

'I most emphatically resent this intrusion,' Janet said. 'Now, if you wouldn't—'

'Look,' Arty smiled, and his little eyes flickered knowingly, 'I know about you two, alright, Janet?'

'Are you suggesting, Assistant Commissioner,' said Janet, with emphasis on 'Assistant', 'that you have been scrutinising my movements?'

'Brian's dealings with subversives has been under scrutiny for over twelve months,' said Arty mournfully. 'It was for your own good, Janet. You never know where the contact with dese elements will lead.'

'This is outrageous,' Janet said and stood up.

'Is it outrageous, Janet?' Arty asked, like the betrayed father of a once-loved child. 'If it was outrageous would Brian be out there now on the run with another criminal, a man whose betrayal of his own country is well known to us all, I think?'

195

'What crime is Brian Kilkenny meant to have committed?' Janet snapped.

'The RUC say attempted murder, Janet, but maybe you know otherwise.'

Janet, at the window, her window, her office, fought for equilibrium. 'Brian Kilkenny has devoted his entire life selflessly to the service of his country,' she heard herself say. 'He does not deserve this treatment.'

'If it wasn't for the Home Office business he'd a been gone on early retirement last Chrishmis,' Arty said.

'That is the first I've heard of it,' Janet retorted. She could not believe that the man installed opposite her was an integral part of the hierarchy she aspired to.

'He's gone outa conthrol,' said Arty miserably. 'The fact that this man Coleraine might have his report has driven Brian mad. He went so far's to bring over a woman from London to Belfasht, this man's doxy, and now he's put her life at risk as well. Brian's days of innocence are long over, Janet, as I'm sure you well know.'

'I resent your tone and I resent your uninvited presence in my office,' said Janet fiercely. 'I am also sickened beyond description by your eagerness to continue the character assassination you began in January of a man who was your loyal colleague for twenty-five years.'

Janet had come to stand over Arty who had remained seated. Without warning he reached out and caught her wrist. 'He had an illegal gun,' he hissed, 'in a place he should not a been, ya bitch! Dere's a priest dead. Your friend Kilkenny's now no bether than the dirt he's been lyin' down with all his life . . .'

'Let go of me!'

'. . . an' you, Assistant Secrethery, have aided and abetted him every inch of the way to satisfy your desires. Now, you know the way this works, Madam Janet. You can have it hard or you can have it aisy.'

Janet managed to free her arm and leaned back against her desk, gasping. 'Get out!' she cried. 'Get out of this room!'

'Where is he, Janet?' asked Arty, on his feet.

Janet fumbled back for her telephones, but Arty slapped her hand away.

'Are you telling me you don't know, Janet?'

'I do not have to entertain your illegal presence here,' Janet panted.

'I'm afraid you do.'

'Show me your authority.'

'My authority is veshted in me by *my* State,' Arty said with venomous unassailability. 'I'm conductin' a murder investigation which you are hinderin'.'

'That is ridiculous . . .'

'Then tell me you haven't been in touch with Brian Kilkenny in the last three days!'

'I have not,' Janet said and wondered if she was going to faint.

'Nor he with you?'

'No.'

'And even after due consideration of the position,' Arty said, 'having been informed by me that warrants have been issued for Brian Kilkenny's arrest on a capital charge, do you still insist you're innocent of any knowledge of his plans or his whereabouts?'

'Yes,' Janet panted as bells began ringing from church towers for the noonday Angelus.

'Then what was he doin' in your house in Belfasht, Madam Janet?' said Arty and thrust his face within four inches of hers. 'An' when he eshcaped with a wanted fugitive, what was he doin' in your house outside a Clifden? Or shall I call it, your love nesht, wha? Should I, Madam Janet?'

With a cry, Janet pushed Arty back on his heels and rushed from her room, past her silent secretary, down the corridor and into the suite of rooms wherein presided Cyril Maguire.

'Assistant Secretary . . .' began the minister's personal private secretary, but Janet was through the doors and into an office twice the size of her own.

'Janet. . . ?'

'Minister.'

Cyril Maguire jumped to his feet. His eyes went from Janet to the door which Arty Gunn was closing.

'Minister, I'm arrestin' Janet Moriarty under the Offences Against the State Act,' Arty said.

'I'm sure that won't be necessary, Assistant Commissioner,' Maguire said.

'Minister,' Janet heaved, 'there are certain aspects of the current case involving Detective Superintendent Kilkenny which have come to my attention.'

'Very good, Janet,' Maguire said, statesmanlike.

'Brian Kilkenny has for fifteen years carried a burden on his shoulders for his country,' Janet heaved. 'He has, as you know, been invaluable to the effort against subversives. His source of information all that time was Vincent Ashe. Now Brian is in trouble directly as a result of Ashe, but it appears that the main effort is directed against Brian Kilkenny, not against Vincent Ashe. You cannot preside over such a misuse of the law. Brian Kilkenny should be given the protection and help of this State, not hounded like a beast. Ashe is the man you must bring in.'

'I see, Janet,' said Minister Maguire slowly, and Janet saw that he was looking straight past her at Arty.

Dead fern ran up in stubble to where miles of mountain began. On their west-facing tips, blonde swathes of larch caught evening sun and brought it down rippling from the peaks to the tree line that leaned over rushy land like a black cliff. Beside a two-storey house a small field of broken cars and tractors was the site of a white trailer whose aluminium stack oozed smoke. Out at them dashed a dog, frantic, and running behind it a man in his shirtsleeves, one moment peering in at them, the next scampering up ahead of the car, dragging back a gate, waving them through into the shelter of the trees as he checked the empty hillside below to emphasise the priority he attached to vigilance.

'The trailer for the prisoner,' Adam heard Ashe say as they got out.

'No problem, no problem.'

Deep smell of pines after rain filled Adam's lungs painfully. His chest hurt where the wing of the Fiat had struck it; another two seconds and he would have been beneath the wheels of the JCB. He had watched the machine ram the Fiat savagely – no one could live in that – and then saw a big Vauxhall come slowly up out of the dip from the direction of the house. The next minute meant little to Adam: one moment Angie was standing by the side of the car, screaming his name – something had happened to her face, it was swollen almost beyond recognition – then he was being forced at gunpoint to lie on the car floor. He assumed Angie was going with them. He passed out. He had awoken once in a tiny village where Ashe had stopped to make a telephone call and, again, just minutes before.

A path led by way of planks across a stream. Adam followed the shirtsleeved man who kept muttering to himself. At the trailer, a younger, thick-set man came down the steps, staring at them. Adam turned to Nona but she looked quickly away.

'Up!' Ashe said, looking strangely from Adam to Nona.

Stale body smells clung to shabby fabrics on chairs and windows and to the blankets of a bunk folded out. Under Ashe's instructions, as Adam sat on the bunk, the man in shirtsleeves ran a steel clasp around his ankle and fastened it by way of a chain to the bolt which secured the bunk to the trailer's wall.

'Thank you,' Ashe said. 'You may leave us for a while.'

Adam put his feet up on the bunk to take the weight off the chain and lay back, hands behind his head.

'I know who you are, Adam,' said Ashe.

Adam looked at him.

Ashe said, 'I want to tell you that I am sorry about your daughter.'

What hate there was in Adam had been sunk under the weight of his failure.

'I know the pain in your heart, lying there like a cold hand, God, I do,' Ashe said. 'I apologise. Ireland apologises for your loss.'

Adam turned his head towards the wall.

'Can you see, Adam?' Ashe said. 'How God marked me? If I could say to Him, mark me twenty-fold and bring that poor girl back, then I would do so! Gladly! I despise the system that makes us enemies, that results in deaths like your daughter's. Despise it, Adam!'

To himself Adam recited, 'When night advances through the sky with slow and solemn tread . . .'

'What was her name, Adam?'

'. . . The queenly moon looks down on life below, as if she read man's soul . . .'

'Your daughter's name, Adam – what was it?'

'. . . and in her scornful silence said: all beautiful and happiest things are dead.'

'Dear God, history is strange,' Ashe said. 'What happens today is as insignificant to the story of the world as whether or not it rained before or after lunchtime – and yet it is such details that constitute the history of the world. Isn't that strange, Adam?'

Adam lay, hearing nothing but his own heart and in his head the surprising words, 'The beauty of the world hath made me sad . . .'

'It was unavoidable! The van would have been discovered!' Ashe said urgently. 'There was nowhere to go with it. They couldn't waste it. These are the hard decisions you make in a war situation.'

'. . . This beauty that will pass, will pass and change, will die and be no more . . .'

Ashe sighed. 'The great men were often despised in their own time. Caesar, Charlemagne, Napoleon. They took the hard decisions, saw beyond the horizon. They fought great battles, many of which they lost. They rode across fantastic landscapes whilst their fellow mortals scurried in the burrows. Hannibal tamed the very Alps to his purpose. They often died in brutal circumstances or in exile. The present in no different, Adam, to the past, the burden no less on those who fight for nationhood. I'm talking about torture, damn it! Do you think I'm any less human than you? Why do you think I confess? I'm *torn* apart inside.'

'. . . Things bright and green things young and happy . . .' Why did she think that way, someone so young?

'Adam. Do you accept my apology? I think I deserve an answer.'

Youth was like O'Casey's lovely human orb shining through clouds of whirling human dust.

'You have lost your daughter, I have sympathised. Do you think that puts you on a pedestal? Do you think that makes you any better than the thousands of poor creatures who are still grieving for loved ones murdered by the forces you work for? Does it excuse you from basic manners? Does it make you better than me?'

Age had a duty to youth. Adam felt a thrill of sudden hope.

'I do not blame you, Adam, yet because of you we are all here tonight, hunted like animals. You are my captive, yet I do not threaten you, although a little over twenty-four hours ago you tried to kill me. Why? Because I forgive you. I understand what you have been through, how your mind might lead you to attempt something as foolish as you did, but, as a fellow human being, I forgive you. I would like you to accept that, Adam.'

What had there been in her quickly-averted look outside? Something other than the cold solidarity with this man that might be expected, Adam was sure, but what? A cry for help? The pain of guilt from murdering a priest? Something.

'You are on such high moral ground, aren't you, Adam?' Ashe said slowly and stood up.

Turning, Adam saw that although the pupil in Ashe's eye had become more intensely black, the rest of his long face had actually relaxed into a crooked smile.

'You are so wronged, you can do no wrong, Adam. It must be wonderful to be up so high, to never slither down into the pit. Perhaps the gap between us will not always be so great.'

Adam waited until Ashe had left, then he stood up. The chain allowed him a few feet, no more. Distant valley pinheads of light flickered. With the clatter of a long bolt being drawn, a woman came to the back door of the house below and threw out water. The man in shirtsleeves followed her; he held a shotgun self-consciously and made a business of performing sentry duties before they both went back inside. Adam struggled to put aside his despair and to grasp the hope, elusive as a shaft of light, that Nona had presented. Why? Across her eyes outside had come the same look as that day in the Falls when she had been sitting on the stairs and Adam had thought she was Zoe. Was there a purpose beyond mere reason that dictated they should both be in the same place this night? Adam felt a jolt. Beyond reason was the realm that had chosen Zoe, that made dogs bark in the night. In moonlight he saw the doorhandle turning. He went and lay on the bunk.

'I was told to bring ye this.'

Adam saw a plate of white, buttered bread and a mug of tea. He swung out and, as she looked on in silence, drank and ate, feeling the sweetness and the starch sharpen and revive him.

'Ye despise me, don't ye?'

Adam put down the mug. 'No.'

'Ach.' Nona tossed her head. 'Ye'r like all the Brits. Ye see us here's common crim'nals. Say it. But if we're just common crim'nals, then why's Belfast the only city in the western world

201

where there's been troops on a war footin' for near on thirty years, I ask ye? Is that common? It's not surely. It's uncommon, in fact, and so is our sitye'ation.'

Adam nodded.

'Are ye really a priest?'

'Why?'

'Priests come into the houses walkin' 's if they're Gawd himself. Priests stood back for four hundred years and leyt the people be shet on. The priests is frightened of th'IRA, because they know th'IRA's th'only chance the people has for ther freedom – but I don't understan' ye.'

How could Adam persuade her where her freedom lay? 'You must get away from this place, Nona.'

She frowned. 'What'r ye talkin' about?'

'Ashe is a psychopath. If you stay with him, you'll be killed.'

'Shut ye'r filthy mouth,' and went to the trailer's door. 'He's a great mon.'

'A great man condenses the feelings of his people into his own heart; in Ashe's heart those feelings would die of cold. A great man's visions are those of compassion and mercy; Ashe's vision is a cruel, withered thing, dead for want of pity.'

'Ye'r the psychopath,' Nona jeered from the door, but something held her there.

'You know I'm right.'

'He's sure of his place in history, more than ye'll ever be.'

'Run, Nona. Get away.'

'Why should ye worry what I do?'

'I care.'

Nona looked sharply at him as if he had no such right. She came back and stood over him. 'Who are ye?'

'A man.'

'A priest?'

'No.'

'Why did ye come over here?'

'To do what justice says should be done.'

'To Uinsionn?'

Adam looked up at her. To her face full of childish suspicions of an adult's motives he wanted to bring both his hands warmly so that she would know the depth of love that she was missing. He wanted to bring hs lips to her wary eyes full of tempted fascination so that when she closed them for sleep she could do so unafraid. 'I want to help you, Nona.'

'How can ye help anyone? You're a pris'ner.'

'Leave here, now. Take the car, or run, just get away. Everything here is bad.'

'Shut yer mouth.'

'I'm not thinking of myself. You're young, you could be my daughter, for God's sake. Get out! Now! He'll not pursue you. He has too many problems of his own.'

'Why did you say that just nigh about yer daughter?'

'She is your age, Nona.'

'She . . . *is*?'

'Yes.'

'Do ye have another daughter?'

'No. Just Zoe. She's like you in many ways.'

Nona seemed to relax. 'How?' she asked.

'The same hair. Similar around the eyes. Zoe's taller than you, but you both move the same way, walk the same way.'

'Is she . . . pretty?'

'Everyone said she was the prettiest girl they had ever seen.'

'What do you mean?' Nona snapped.

'Just that.'

Nona's eyes darted as if looking for a trap. 'What does she . . . do?'

Adam shook his head. 'She's dead. She was killed by the IRA bomb in Paddington last May.'

Nona led with the knuckles of her hand across Adam's face and bowled him backwards. 'Ye'r sick! Ye disgust me! Talkin' like that 's if to trick me, preteyndin' someone's aleyve when they're dead!'

'For me she's alive.'

'Ye'r sick! Sick! Sick! I'm tellin' ye, mister!' cried Nona, back at the door of the trailer. 'I should a known.'

'Is there no one dead who's still alive for you, Nona? Alive every minute of your day?'

'Ye'r the fuckin' pox!' Nona sneered. 'Tryin' to turn me ageynst ar own.'

'There is someone, isn't there, Nona?'

'I don't have to talk to ye.'

'Who is it, Nona?'

Ireland's night ticked by, sleeping seconds.

'Ye'r nothin' but trouble. Uinsionn says ye'r a Bret agent, seynt her' to kill him.'

'Do you remember what you said to me the first time we met, Nona?'

'I don't want to remember nothin' about ye, mister. Ye'r sick.'

'I was crying, because Jerome Gormley's death reminded me of Zoe's, and when I looked up you were there, and you said, "It's good to cry. Our eyes are the reflection of our souls." Only someone who believes in the soul would say that. You believe, Nona, because you have lost someone dear to you, as I have. Isn't that right?'

'Why should I stan' her' and talk t'ye?' Nona said.

Adam said, ' "The beauty of the world hath made me sad,

This beauty that will pass . . .
Will pass and change, will die and be no more,
Things bright and green, things young and happy." '

Fighting the tears in her eyes, Nona said, 'Ye'r lookin' for a bullet, d'y'know that?'

'People who have lost those they love can talk to each other, Nona. It helps. Like crying. Who was it?'

She sighed. 'My Da.'

'Still alive for you.'

'Yes.'

'Although he's dead. When?'

'Eleven years.'

'I'm sorry.' Adam could see the outline of her head. She could have been any girl, or one.

'Ma said 'twas the chill of a summer's evenin' from where he'd slept be a winda. He went slowly first, then rapid, hour by hour, almost till you could see his very elbows. There was nothin' of him left in th'eynd, couldn't even sup the soup I tried to make him take. Suddenly I was big and he was small. 'Twas a . . . cryin' . . . shame.'

'I'm sorry.'

'One mornin' I woke. Everyone's eyes were red. They never called me. Ma said he just gave a little sigh and that was him away.'

She sat on a chair at the end of his bunk. 'Why didn't they call me?'

'They didn't want to hurt you.'

'He used bring me dighn with him to Donegall Place to see the statues. One of them was a man in a cloak sittin' with his head down, much bigger than a real person, and when ar Da died I used sneak dighn on my own and imagine the statue was poor Da.'

Adam reached to her shoulder. 'Sometimes I think the pain is the price we have to pay for keeping them alive inside us.'

'When I first saw ye, d'ye know who ye put me in mind of? Of Da. Of that statue.'

'You must get away from here, Nona.'

'I can't.'

'You can.'

'Ye don't unnerstan'.'

'Understand what? I can see you're terrified of him, but what can he do to you, Nona, if you run?'

Nona bit her lip. 'Ye don't unnerstan'.'

'He'll use you and then discard you.'

Nona looked at Adam and, through her tears, she laughed. Reaching out she touched his face with her fingers. 'Are ye really worried about me?'

'Yes, Nona!' Adam said. 'I've lost Zoe, but if you were to break free from Ashe then the balance would be put back a little, somehow.'

'Ye'r worried about me,' she said and laughed again. 'Ye'r really worried about me!'

'Think of what your father would want for you.'

Nona looked at Adam as if he had not grasped those things most fundamental to life. 'Ye don' unnerstan'.'

'I want you to be free, Nona.'

'Ye don' unnerstan', ye don't unnerstan'. Were we to sit here for a hundred year, ye could never, never unnerstan',' she said and laid her two hands either side of his big face, and shook her head. 'Not in a hundred yeras, not in a thousand years, never, never,' and she began to kiss his face, first in little, different places and then urgently as if each new kiss would die unless another was quickly planted. 'Not in a million, million years.'

Adam cupped Nona's head to him as they fed from each other's mouths, adjusting with gentle necessity. Nona opened the buttons of her shirt and came out of it, the luminous shade of her body altering the mixture of different darknesses in the trailer. Her knees either side of him she brought his head in to each of her breasts in turn. From his waist at the back she pulled up his shirt over his head. Adam lay back and unbuckled her, and Nona wriggled down her jeans from her backside, and her pants. Adam went further on his back and drew her over him, feeling her thighs at his face. With the tip of his tongue he parted her bush and found, first dry, then sweetly wet, her vulva. All his mouth's flavours changed to her taste of woman-child. Nona clasped with both hands Adam's head. She pushed him softly back and went to his waist, unclipping his trousers. Hands on his chest she went astride and guided him. Adam lay back, every device of him embalmed lusciously. Nona first arched back stretching both of them to an extremity, then hooped forward and kissed Adam deeply as he came, all their juices mingling, hot and cold, sweet and spiced, young and old.

A cold bell in Ennis struck three. An old, crouched nurse opened the door and threw me a look. Out in the corridor I could see the regulation shoes and blue trousers' ends that marked the lower extremities of the Garda sergeant whose Friday night had been sacrificed for national security. The nurse left the room and I heard words exchanged before she loped off to her next inspection.

It had been Angie, of course, who had saved my bacon. The patriot from Clare on his JCB had no answer to the venom of this enraged Englishwoman, her face swollen like a turnip, whose screams of abuse and flying handfuls of stone and dirt had sent him steaming away down the wet boreen in the rivering rain. She climbed up and got me down. I was dizzy and my neck hurt but, like an old football, I'd just been kicked around the pitch a bit more than I was used to; it was Angie who needed attention, her nose was badly broken and paining her. 'I'm bringing you to a hospital,' I said. I tried to find my gun and couldn't. We went back down the boreen with Angie babbling on about how they would take Adam with them, out of the country, away. We climbed the gate and had walked halfway along the shining tarmacadam towards Cullen when the squad car picked us up.

There comes a time when you make, in an instant, all the accommodations that you have struggled for ages to resist. Pain was floating from me upwards dizzily in palpable bubbles of release. The drugs, I suppose. Staring at the door between the foot of my bed and the corridor I was suddenly and irrationally happy that I was about to surrender all my responsibilities. Brought to the hospital in Ennis where a young houseman, broaching no interference on his turf, ordered we both be held for observation overnight, the last I saw of Angie was her being pushed away in a wheelchair, large tears on her cheeks. I kissed her goodbye. She was grateful that her pain would soon be at an end, but she understood our failure too, and it sat uneasily on her. By the time the local lads had contacted Dublin and told them who they had, and I had been charged, and people in Harcourt Square decided what to do, it was eleven and the greater part of Ireland who might on a weekday have been interested in my fate had clocked off for the weekend. I used my call to ring my solicitor at his Dublin home. He sounded terse and I didn't blame him; I was acquiring the knack of living up to my reputation.

Even in defeat you soon seek out warm corners. I was beaten, but I wasn't dead. I was in Ireland; Vincent would soon be gone. A sort of twisted justice in that, I thought. Did he ever really believe in the things he had told me? Would he find someone in his exile to persuade?

I awoke to a familiar but not identifiable noise. My immediate sensation, like someone waking after a bender, was accelerating dismay. For Adam. For myself. I thought of Vincent and I felt revulsion. I thought of my misplaced euphoria of earlier, then heard the bell strike four and realised I had been asleep for less than an hour.

From the corridor came the sergeant's voice, then the sound of him hanging up a telephone. Its electronic trill was the sound that had woken me. A big man, the sergeant came into the room tugging down the frocks of his jacket in a bolstering of authority.

'You're to dress yourself.'

'Why?'

'Just dress yourself.' He was uncomfortable. 'Orders from Dublin, Superintendent,' he said by way of hedging his role in something that might in the future work against him.

I was pulling on my shoes and worrying about the media – did they invent shame? – when a young guard came in, tall and green as an ash, and muttered to the sergeant.

'We're coming,' the sergeant said and the guard left.

'I'm ready,' I said.

'Put your hands out together.'

'Are you serious?'

'Those are the instructions,' said the sergeant grimly and clipped down the cold braces of handcuffs on my wrists.

We went downstairs and out through a glass-walled reception in which a young fellow was sitting, bleeding from his head and smoking a cigarette, beside a very pregnant woman. There was no doctor or nurse to see me off, no discharge procedure, no cameras or reporters with mobile phones. Wait till Dublin, I thought, to hell with them, I had my life to live. Backed up to the hospital door was a gurgling, black Granada. The young guard guided me down into the deep rear seat and locked the door. I heard him say something to the local man, then come around and get in the other side. We drew away, around a circular flowerbed, and out the gates.

'Do you have a discharge form for the prisoner?'

I sat forward and stared like a moron into the front of the car where the high headrests made sight of the driver difficult.

'I wasn't told . . .' the guard began.

We stopped abruptly on the empty road and began to reverse back to the hospital's gates.

'You had better go back in and get a discharge form. Otherwise this removal could be irregular,' said Janet to the obliging, young guard.

In bleak fields either side of the road our headlights picked out skeletal castles and bushes straining away from the winds of the Atlantic.

'I've never done anything like this before – legally or illegally,' Janet said and handed me the handcuffs key.

'You're a promising beginner,' I said, climbing into the front.

'Are you alright?' she asked.

'I'll survive,' I said and told her about Cullen. 'What about you?'

'I won't survive,' Janet replied and slammed down through the gears for more speed. 'I've been put on suspension pending an internal investigation into that oaf Arty Gunn's allegations about me. My career is over. They're both in this, Arty and Maguire. You know what they say about taking on City Hall.' Janet slammed her hand down on the steering wheel. 'It's grotesque! But I was damned if I was going without a fight.'

'Where are we going?' I enquired.

'To stop Vincent Ashe leaving the country,' she replied.

I looked at Janet and remembered the snippets Angie told me she had overheard. 'Good,' I said.

'I brainstormed the thing with Dick Jennings last evening,' said Janet grimly. 'Dick's on our side – more the fool him, but he is. Maguire's not going to arrange Ashe's getting out – he's not going to give him the government jet – but at the same time he's not going to put too many obstacles in Ashe's way.'

'There's meant to be a nationwide effort going on,' I remarked.

'There is, in a halfhearted sort of way,' Janet said. 'But since Maguire can't transmit his real intentions to the rank and file on the force, Ashe cannot risk going out by conventional ports or airports. Dick and I both agreed that. Neither will he risk the border.'

'Which leaves unconventional ports and airports.'

Janet nodded and passed a truck. 'What would you do? You'd make for somewhere without an extradition treaty with here, wouldn't you? Even better, somewhere you're already known. What country or countries qualify as far as Vincent Ashe is concerned?'

'The Middle East. Libya.'

'No extradition to Ireland,' Janet agreed. 'A supplier of arms to the IRA for over two decades. Run by a man every bit as screwed up as Vincent Ashe. One problem: how does Ashe get there?'

'By boat. We ship cattle to Libya.'

'Unfortunately, no longer,' Janet replied. 'Like the rest of Europe, we've been embargoing Libya for five years. The only place in the Middle East we now ship cattle to is Yemen.'

'Then he'll go to Yemen first and then Libya,' I said.

'Exactly,' Janet said. 'But there's only one boat. It leaves weekly, every Saturday from Waterford.'

I looked at the break in the sky that the dawn was making; I looked at my watch. 'Leaves at what time?'

'They were vague,' Janet said darkly. 'Without giving the game away, we couldn't press. Dick has gone down directly to find out more. He's meeting us there.'

'You've made a brave choice,' I said quietly.

Janet let out her unexpected laugh. 'There was never a choice,' she said.

Down the length of a slowly-brightening valley, the mountains on one side, partly wooded, partly shaved, were like the heads of punk kids you see in Grafton Street. How one death, a footnote on a busy day a year ago, had changed everything.

'What are you thinking about?' asked Janet quietly.

'I was thinking about how you read about a bomb somewhere and then flick on to the page with the television programmes,' I said. 'Yet what you have read may have changed your life utterly without your realising it.'

'It's terrifying.'

'And it's also somehow wonderful. It means people don't die for nothing. It means life isn't ever cheap. Doesn't that give us some hope?'

'What hope is there for us?' Janet asked.

It was the question I was hoping she would not ask. She was so vulnerable now. I wanted to believe that what she was doing was all for concepts like justice and respect for the law and the principals she worked for; I did not want to believe that I was any more than peripheral to her equation. 'I don't know, Janet,' I answered.

'It's not your fault,' she said and shook her head in frustration. 'I've spent over twenty years trying to master another culture and learned, when the real test of my success came, that I had learned nothing. I've spent over twenty years married to a kind and gentle man, and discovered that a part of my life has been wasted.'

I did not know what to say. I reached over to reassure her and she caught my hand and brought it to her mouth.

'Damn it,' she said hoarsely. 'Where's the justice? A murderer sails away and we're left behind. What can't we go, you and I? Jesus, Brian, I would, I'd go now, this minute, forever. I mean it. Leave the lot, vanish. Oh, Jesus, I would.'

In flat, open country where river had made a wide delta of mudland and rushes, I knew that Janet was the one who would get nothing from the bolt that had catalysed our lives. It was so unfair. She must have known I could never give her what she wanted, which was all of me, but then her life had been spent reaching for the unattainable and it struck me that if she ever got everything she wanted, then Janet would no longer be the Janet I knew. I was about to say something to the effect that life is unfair when the mudland suddenly became a mighty river with banks half a mile apart and I realised we would soon reach the sea.

The man in his shirtsleeves dozed in the corner, the shotgun artlessly by his side. Nona heard the back door creak and felt a void opening under the floor of her stomach. She heard the long bolt going back home.

'Do you hear the wind, Nona?'

Not wind eating at the forgotten eaves as in the house in Cullen, just a sighing of the turbulent earth. 'I hear it.'

'All of Ireland is in that wind, Nona, all the voices of the past.'

Nona could hear her father's voice, light with laughter, and other voices too from the past, her own, uncertain, and Ma's, distraught. Ma was someone Nona instinctively wanted to see at a time like this. Ma knew about such things.

'This time tomorrow we will be away, Nona,' Uinsionn said. 'Out of Ireland.'

'Uinsionn . . .'

'Yes, Nona?'

'I don't want to go.'

The silence was to make her look at him before he would reply. 'Don't want to go?'

'No.'

Uinsionn crossed his long legs. 'I see. Why?'

'I . . . just . . .' Nona stammered.

'I can't make you come with me, Nona.'

Suddenly Nona could not bear Uinsionn's proximity, nor the way he looked at her, half smilin'. It was 'sif the stain from his eye was spreadin' everywhere, stickin' everyone to him, all of them.

'They'll put you away for a long time, Nona.'

How could Nona tell him she couldn't think that far? Or even if she did, that she didn't care anymore?

'First Castlereagh. Then remand ahead of a trial. Five of six years of a sentence. Strip searches every other day. Is that what you want, Nona?'

'I just can't go.'

Embers red as blood gleamed out from the ashes in the grate.

'Adam and I had a long chat yesterday,' Uinsionn remarked. 'Before you took him his tea.'

'Oh?' Nona said and kept her eyes on the fire.

'He is a sad man. I expect you know why he tried to kill me?'

Nona nodded and her stomach moved.

'His daughter. The bomb in Paddington that time. I *told* him, there were no options, it had to be done. His daughter was a casualty of war. I really feel for Adam. I tried to get him to see it from our point of view, to look at us, diminished, on the run, forced into exile. I could not get him to see it, Nona, as hard as I tried.'

Nona felt so small with Uinsionn, she was just a child that he could terrify at will.

'Then this morning I had an idea,' Uinsionn went on. 'I hate to leave a man like that without him having the full picture, you now? I had the idea that we would all have a chat about it, Adam, myself and you, Nona. We can talk in the car later, about Adam's tragedy, the details, why from our point of view it was unavoidable, why we consider it was excusable, and so on. What do you think, Nona?'

She felt so lonely at a time when she should have been weak from joy.

'Nona?'

'No.'

'We won't tell him?'

'No.'

'I understand, Nona. And, you will reconsider your decision about coming with me?'

'Yes.'

'Ah, that's good, Nona,' Uinsionn said, 'I knew you would. I knew.'

They left the glen with light promised from the east – only the man in shirtsleeves to see them away, hurryin' to tend the gates, in his excited eyes the years of legend that lay ahead – and drove south, Nona at the wheel, Vincent in the back with Adam whose ankle bracelet had been transferred to the seat mounting.

'Drive faster, Nona,' Uinsionn said. 'We can't be late.'

They went ever southwards with darkness lifting off the fields like mist either side of their way, and sheep with their lambs grazing, and cottage chimneys beginning to smoke, and no clouds in the sky that was swept bare in front of the coming sun from the horizon ahead to the tree-fringed mountains to their right. Suddenly Nona saw everything differently. Here was peace. Here was freedom. She knew. A richness of spirit seemed to throb from the waking landscape. Flatlands stretching widely either side, thick with cattle: dun, white and black, sleek, dark mustard. A king's beasts. Before, Nona's aspirations for all of Ireland had been tinged with a resentment against the people down here for their smugness and isolation, but now the sight of Munster's calm hinterland made her crave for them to be a part of it: Adam, Nona and the child Nona knew was in her belly.

'Shall we tell Adam what you have decided, Nona?' Uinsionn asked.

Nona gripped tightly the wheel.

'Nona has decided to come with me, Adam,' Vincent said. 'Haven't you, Nona?'

Nona's 'Yes' was a whisper, her head forward near the windscreen as if straining to discern the road.

'Why should she stay here and face a rigged trial?' Uinsionn asked. 'There's no justice anymore, there never was. Did I force you, Nona? Is not your choice to come with me entirely of your own free will?'

Nona tucked in to her throat her chin. 'Yes.'

'She's a child, Ashe. She's terrified of you.'

'Ah, he can speak. Are you, Nona? Terrified of me?'

'Don't answer, Nona,' Adam said. 'You have nothing to explain to me. Nothing to be sorry for.'

'Nona knows that, don't you know?' Uinsionn said.

'It's so easy, isn't it, to terrify a child?' Adam said.

'Nona has not been a child for a long time,' Uinsionn said. 'Nona knows things that children could never know. Don't drop your speed, Nona.'

In the driver's mirror Nona saw Adam's face. She wanted to reach back and bring him the comfort that would take his mind from his grief. A repaying and repaying. For as little time as an idea can exist to earn its name, the possibility that she and Adam might somehow overpower Uinsionn had presented itself to Nona, but then she had switched her eyes in the mirror and found Uinsionn's half-smiling face, and side by side with the terror of knowing she would never have the courage to confront him was the abject dismay that came with knowing that he owned her.

At six o'clock dogs scavenged at refuse sacks in a pretty village not yet awake. Uinsionn went to a telephone box.

'Nona.'

Uinsionn was speaking on the telephone. Nona turned.

'You have done nothing to make you go with him!' Adam said urgently. 'Run while you can! Now!'

Nona's mouth was tugging down on one side as if in a battle with itself. She said, 'I'm . . .'

'Drive, Nona! Not for me, but for you!'

He had made love to her as if to life itself. Nona opened her mouth to explain why she could not run, but she could never explain.

'Then shoot him, Nona! No one will ever blame you!'

She gasped, 'I'm pregnant!'

Adam said, 'That's wonderful!'

'Shut up,' Nona whispered as the phone box door slammed and Uinsionn walked back to them.

Nona drove. He had said 'wonderful' when she had been worryin' about havin' led him on, worryin' that the man-need that had driven him like all the others would, like them, wither in shame with the light, but he had said 'wonderful'. She was goin' to give him somethin' back that no one, not even Uinsionn, could take. At the wheel of the big car with its surging response to the touch of her foot, flying between hedges and along open roads, Nona knew she would not go with Uinsionn. She would pretend to Uinsionn but she had a gun and she would not go. She wanted to rid them of Uinsionn like you would rid your body of a dead part of it. Adam had said 'wonderful'. Like the speck of life in her, his words were the first seeds of hope that together they might somehow, someday, make somethin' of it all, no matter what

214

Uinsionn did or said. Hope came to Nona in a heady wave. It didn't matter now about Uinsionn. She carried hope within her. After Uinsionn left she could go and hide and then, later, months or years later, she could face Adam with the miracle they had made.

'Pull in up ahead.'

A cutting ran up through trees into an area of open fell, hidden from the road. Stone chips rattled the underside as Nona drove in and turned.

'Take out the ignition key and come back with me, Nona.'

Nona, as Uinsionn got out, suddenly wanted to scream. She knew these places, how it worked. The choice of remote location, the fact that their destination would soon be reached, that Adam was a witness to murder. Would Uinsionn make Adam kneel and give him a bare minute to make peace with his Maker? The camp trainin' hadn't mentioned this, how she would feel, lookin' in the mirror at him starin' back at her – did he know too? – the sudden tears in her eyes, his smell. Nona got out, dizzy. Uinsionn was at the boot, lookin' in for somethin'. His gun was pocketed. Nona felt for the outline of the Heckler and Koch in her jacket as she walked back, sound crashing through her ears giddily. She saw Uinsionn through a miasma that stood between her and freedom. The gun hurt she held it so tight. It weighed hugely as she brought it around. Stay back so that if the first shot didn't work, she'd have a second.

'Nona?' Uinsionn turned up from what he was doing.

It was as if the gun was too heavy to come up all the way. 'I . . . I heyt these places,' Nona stammered.

Uinsionn was smiling curiously, the smile Nona now hated more than anything.

'They . . . make me jumpy.'

'I understand, Nona.' His hand reached very slowly out into the gap of air that separated them. It mesmerised Nona, like a snake. 'You can give me the gun, Nona.'

Nona watched every movement as he took it from her, the sound in her ears thundering, sound of sadness, his eye like a light that had caught her in the darkness.

Uinsionn let slowly out his breath. He looked at Nona's gun, pocketed it, then smiled bravely at her as if everyone had to put their best foot forward. 'I had the woman make this up last night, Nona,' he resumed.

He was holding out a jacket that lacked sleeves. Nona had not seen it before, she couldn't really hear right, she could not even remember her own name.

'The Semtex is sewn into each pocket,' Uinsionn said. 'I joined both pockets and wired in a solenoid.' He held up a black box the size of a pack of playing cards. 'We have to make Brother Adam work for his living, don't we, Nona?'

They left the mountains for hills with near horizons. With the ageing of the morning came cloud. Nona wondered why she had not shot him there. Before then, only Adam had been threatened. Now, with Adam bound into the jacket, they all lived at Uinsionn's pleasure in the prison he had created, a world within a world where even a ray of light just breathed on by God faced death before ever it could gleam, a bomb all of them in Uinsionn's hands. She drove and drove as if away from the hope of the dawn until they came to the sea. Twice Nona looked in the mirror: once to see Adam, and he smiled at her; once to see Uinsionn and she met his eye that quivered alone, absorbing her, his head nothing but an eye, cold and pitiless.

Harsh, new factories and perfunctory rows of public housing faced each other in the deadness of Saturday morning's sleep. In the lee of high walls we crept into Waterford and came to the quay of a river. I had expected to see a boat, but spikes of high water licked at unattended moorings and the quay stretched empty of any vessels to a bridge; even across the wide expanse of river where there were timber yards with cut trees stacked in thousands like cheroots, and grain silos, and downriver from them containers strewn brightly beneath giant grab cranes, not even a dinghy existed that I could see. Janet pulled in behind a black car and Dick Jennings, dressed in an anorak with the hood up, got out of it and walked back to us. Inside a wall between us and the water, expanses of concrete were being hosed by men in oilskins.

'She's sailed,' Dick said, sitting into the back. 'But if he's on it, don't ask me how.' The Department of Justice legal adviser looked as if working such long hours did not suit him. 'I saw the boat in last night, I saw it go out. There's been a garda presence and customs people here throughout the loading and unloading, and no funny stuff went on, I'd swear to that.'

I asked, 'When did the boat sail?'

'An hour ago,' Dick replied, addressing Janet as if I was someone he really shouldn't be speaking to.

'Well, that's it, isn't it?' Janet said to me.

'It seems to be,' I agreed. We had suddenly run out of everything: opportunities, space, time. Breakfast seemed like a good idea.

'It was always a gamble Dick, but thank you,' Janet said.

Dick Jennings looked to be wrestling with some personal dilemma. 'Assistant Secretary,' he said reluctantly, 'it may be totally coincidental . . . but soon after the boat sailed . . . I may be completely wrong . . . but I could swear that it was Assistant Commissioner Gunn I saw driving past here.'

Janet and I are still looking at Dick Jennings.

We took off coastwards out of the city under a sky that was too deeply, perfectly blue for the coming day to draw any lasting comfort from it.

'Dick will be alright,' Janet said, by which I took her to mean that whatever her fate she would not draw Dick Jennings in any further or make him pay for his allegiance.

Suddenly, on a hilltop, we saw the coastline below us. The river had spread into a great estuary and tight shadows on the distant shoreline took a moment to become villages clustered in the adjusted perspective. From where we had paused to the boundary of the land a field of cattle stretched and, from a rise of yellow gorse behind us, a brown horse grew like a monument. Upriver the water was a half-mile-wide cutting between deep slopes, partially obscured by the contour of the land; down estuary an ever-widening took place that only ended with the hazy silver plate of the sea.

The road seemed to follow a course directly for the cliff. An unexpected dip gave the excuse for a curling turn and when we resurfaced we were hanging on the very edge, staring down without a word. We both got out. Below us a boat was set on a mid-channel course for open sea, cleaving the flat greyness into lazy, rolling folds. It was a white boat. I could see hay stacked high on every deck space. The boat glided without sound, a miniature,

217

changing the calmness of the whole estuary into a wake of disturbance disproportionate to its size. It seemed unassailable. From near the funnel, a little, white smoke explosion shot up abruptly like a puff from a pipe, and a flat, reverberating blast, at odds with the vessel's modesty, broke the stillness.

We turned for the car. The imperative, it seemed, was to keep the boat in view.

'You drive,' Janet said.

The road sank with the cliff and the boat stayed no longer a toy but grew as big and as long as a terrace of houses. Beneath our feet a tiny village appeared, clasping the water to the land. We came under the cliff and out by a footpath with tubs of flowers, bright and busy as confectionery. A lane ran between the gables of two houses and ended in rectangular blue like the long window at the end of a nave. We came out on a dock where bobbed the masts of small boats and where, wedge-like, a car ferry of empty deck was flush to a concrete slip. The ferry's engine fumes made the view distorted: but either the ferry was edging left, or the village was floating downriver. Then over the stern gates I saw Vincent.

'They're moving!' Janet cried.

I pointed the Granada and put my hand on the horn. I never thought about a slipway. I was doing forty and could not have avoided Arty. He appeared suddenly between us and the ferry, on the edge of the quay, pointing at us with a gun. He looked sad, then vanished. For a moment we were weightless as the ferry leapt up at us from the sea. We caught the back of the deck, just, buckling inward the flimsy gates with comforting impact.

Although I was sure only seconds had gone by, we were half way out into the channel on line for the cattle boat when next I looked. Myd concerns were Janet then Arty, in that order. Janet was moaning, head back and dazed, but all I could see of Arty on the shrinking dock was his red Mercedes. Vincent was thirty yards away on the other end of the deck, standing beside a car, holding up something. I got out.

'Brian!'

Vincent had not moved. He had his hand in the air. To his right stood Nona Lane. In the back of their car I could see Adam's head half turned towards me. A man was looking down in confusion from the bridge. The cattle boat hooted.

'Brian, stand where I can see you, hands in the air!' Vincent shouted.

'I'm not armed.'

'This is a detonator, Brian. So help me, we all go up!'

I felt the ferry's revs drop as the true situation dawned on the man up on the bridge. 'Detective Unit!' I called up to him. 'This ferry is under arrest!'

'Continue for the boat, Captain!' Vincent shouted. 'I warn you!'

I put my hands up as bid. There was no noise over that of the ferry; it replaced breath and heartbeat as it crabbed out through the grey, choppy water. Nona walked down the open deck. There was a lonely purpose to her approach, like someone crossing a bridge in the hostage transfers you read about.

'Ageynst the cawr.'

She searched me. She led me ten yards over to the bulwark on the other side of the deck.

I whispered, 'Nona, where's the bomb?'

Her eyes were deep yellow, light green. 'On Adam.'

She went to the Granada, looked at Janet who was still out of it, probed the dash and door pockets and ran her hands beneath the driver's seat. We were approaching the cattle boat remarkably quickly, slipping sideways on. The captain throttled his bow into the incoming tide to prevent us being taken past.

'Adam!' I shouted. 'Are you alright?'

'Shut up, Brian!' Vincent cried. 'Nona!'

Nona ran back the length of the deck. Railed steps had been let down from the cattle boat to a platform almost level with the water.

'Vincent, there's no way you can get away with this,' I cried.

'Brian, Brian.' He looked at me with feeling. 'What have I ever done to you, except once save your life?'

'Do the right thing,' I said. 'I swear you won't be hurt.'

'What have I ever done to my country except loved it, Brian?' he asked. 'Is this what I deserve?'

I had the odd feeling that this was something we had all been through before. We came side on to the much higher vessel and a deckhand scampered down the boat's steps and with a rope made fast the platform to the ferry's stanchion. I took a step nearer, although I was still twenty-five yards away.

'Come on, Brian, why not?' Vincent was holding towards me both hands together in an offering. 'Come on. I'm not dying in any filthy Irish jail.'

'Stay where ye are!' Nona shouted. 'He'll use it!'

'Brian knows that,' Vincent said, 'which is why he'll not stop me, isn't that right, Brian?'

With a massive crash Adam came to the inside of the car's door with his shoulder and stood up, one foot on the deck, hands bound behind his back. 'Call his bluff, Brian!' he cried. 'I'm the only one certain to be killed and I'll die gladly rather than see him escape.'

'What's another life now, Brian?' Vincent asked and held the detonator up. He turned to appraise the position of the cattle boat and I chanced another two forward steps. It was Nona who spotted me.

'Stop!'

Vincent whirled, pointing the detonator like you point the remote control at a television. I froze. So, I think, did everyone.

'That might just have done it, Brian,' Vincent said. 'Next time it will, for sure.' He threw one leg over the side, the deckhand and he grabbed arms and Vincent was pulled up on to the platform. He turned. 'Come on, Nona.'

The noise of the boat's engines and a sudden wind seemed to whip words away like specks of foam. I knew I had to get Adam out of the jacket before the boats separated.

'Nona!' Vincent was calling. 'Come on!'

'No.' She was shaking her head. 'No, Uinsionn.'

'Nona . . .'

'I'm not goin', Uinsionn.' She was standing, her hand on the car.

'You can't stay on the ferry, Nona. Do you understand what I mean?'

'Why do you want her, Ashe?' Adam shouted. 'Haven't you done enough?'

'Do you want her, Adam?' Vincent asked.

Dark faces had come to look down at us from the boat's deck. Without warning its hooter let out a massive blast.

'She'll go if you throw away the detonator, Vincent,' I shouted.

'No deal, Brian,' Vincent called, his lips drawn back. 'She comes anyway. She knows why she has to.'

Nona was standing her ground. 'I'm – not – goin' . . .'

A deep revolution of the cattle boat's engines made white of the water beneath us and the deckhand made to cast off. Vincent grabbed him back and shouted above the noise. 'Nona, you know why you have to come!'

'I'm not goin', Uinsionn!'

I was level with the car, although ten yards across the deck from it. I wondered if, using the car for cover, I could get to Vincent on the platform.

Vincent's eye danced. 'D'you know who Nona really is, Adam?' he yelled.

Nona screamed, 'Uinsionn! No!'

Vincent seemed to smile. 'Nona, Adam, is the person who primed and left the bomb in Paddington that killed your daughter.'

We were making for open sea, together. Sprawled back on the car seat, Adam stared up at Nona from a face cracked in a thousand splinters. Vincent held his place, waves washing over his feet. Up on the boat deck a man screamed down obscenities.

'Wait!' Nona cried. 'I'll come!'

She ducked into where Adam lay. Vincent was trying to get a view of them, but from where he stood the car's roof blocked him. The detonator aloft, he held me venomously in place. We were sloshing along, water running the length of the ferry's deck. I could see Nona. She had undone the ties on Adam's jacket and hands and was pulling the jacket over her head. She was bending to Adam's feet. I could hear our engine's straining in reverse, trying to free us. Vincent's eye was brightly on me as I moved. I saw his face, not the face I remembered, but a grinning skull. Beside Vincent, the deckhand threw off the rope and sprinted up the steps. Nona had the jacket clasped to her as she made a bound over the side of the ferry. I was ten yards from her.

'Nona!' Adam called.

She turned to him and Adam shouted something. I know because I saw Adam's mouth as another jarring blast of the boat's hooter drowned his words for me, but Nona heard them. I saw her face. I thought as I moved that I might get to her in time, but she was going for Vincent, whatever it took.

The sky became white stars and wet thunder. I could swim

221

forever. I was a fish, at home in cool, consoling depths. Here I would stay, safe, swimming. Air filled my lungs and made me rise, but I cried out long and loud in protest for all I wanted was the comfort I had found on the bottom of the sea.

Postscript

Memory is one of God's greatest gifts. It is a landfall on which I spend most of every day. I live in my memory, Gilly, swooping in and settling like a big, invisible bird there, waiting and waiting until the images begin their peeping out. I take incidents such as the day we married, or the day of my commissioning, or a first communion, and I dissect the minutes one by one. People come out to me whom I had long forgotten. Faces appear like kind friends come to help me along another little step of the way. I can tell you every stick of furniture in a room thirty-five years ago and recount without flaw who sat there on a certain night and what they said. It's a marvel, this solitude. I never knew so much could be carried in one head.

I'm well treated, by the way. Granted there are some nasty screws but in some matters, such as post in and out and visitors, I have been allowed some privileges denied to the subversives. I have the impression that in the rank and file there is more than a little sympathy for my predicament. Arty was never popular. He had butted his share of egos in his singular ascent and if he had thought that Maguire would have made him Commissioner, then Arty would have swum to Liverpool. You remember he fought for four days, his battle progress given out hourly on the news. That was the worst time for me, Arty's battle to live. I prayed for him to live, not because of any mitigating effect his surviving might have on my circumstances, but because I really had nothing against Arty in the end of the day. When he died I expected a rough time from the screws, but, as I say, it never came to that.

Why did I plead guilty, you might reasonably ask? Why did I not fight on? Why did I allow people to keep the impressions so skilfully crafted for them? What about my name? Our name? What about my pride? I learned something that day in the estuary. It was that there are things bigger than pride. If I had fought the

223

charge, other people would also have been losers; the lesser charge of manslaughter, even though it brought a sentence of eight years, also avoided a protracted trial. What is eight years? Nearly half of them have gone by and there's talk of a review soon because of good behaviour. I don't regret it.

I understand Janet is a legal adviser to a big company out Vancouver way. I have in my mind a picture from the paper at that time of the Moriarity family snapped going through Heathrow. Janet looked at the camera with that great defiance I so well remember. I know she's happy. Some people go through life unhappily because they are forced into a neverending compromise of what they really believe in; rarely do they get an opportunity for choosing presented to them as starkly as Janet did. In a way her break with the old world was something she had decided as Jan Staunch all those years ago back on the Shankhill – Dublin was just a marking time. Mother Staunch, from whom Janet got all her imagination and independence, would have done the same as Janet in another incarnation; she could see beyond pride and fear and all the other trappings that go with mere material possession. Whilst Edwin and the brigadier act out their parade ground fantasies under the gables with their blood-red Ulster hands, the Staunch women fly free – one in actual fact, the other in her mind – unhindered by the prison their men have made for them.

I read newspapers because without them it would be so easy to accept my separation from you as a permanent condition. I was intrigued by the retirement of Sir Trevor Tice, and the end of internment in the North, and the renewal by the British Tory Party of its pledges supporting the link with Ulster into the twenty-first century and beyond. Where did we lose our way in the foothills of history? What happened to the dreams hatched in Iveagh House, or were all the people there just acting out parts as another way of filling in another day? With the cynicism of the detached, I wonder if the words from the mouths of politicians have any meaning at all, or if the noises they make at us, like those you use to settle down a dog, are based solely on expediency. Prisoners don't vote, but I have followed you doing so twice since those times: once to remove Maguire and his cohorts and once to put the cohorts, without Maguire, back in. But he's not gone forever. Cyril Maguire knows that just beneath the skin lie the hidden bruises of history. He knows when to press them and when to wait. I'm sure he's this minute oiling his way around his midland hinterland, doing what he does best: trading in half-forgotten hurts. His hinterlanders know the game. They need a Cyril Maguire to redress for them, even after generations, the injustices they were made to suffer. Maguire knows their need. He'll be back.

There are simple comforts to be had when you get over the first indignity of freedom denied. I had a visit some months back from a Dublin journalist, a nice young lad with a beard on him like Methuselah. Two months before he had been with a film crew in the Yemen. He told me of one evening in a gaslit cafe in the mountain city of San'a – when his group were doing what the Irish are meant to do at sundown: drinking and singing – and of the tall, bearded European in dark glasses at the edge of the circle who followed each bar and phrase. The journalist brought his chair over and they began to chat. It was all questions about Ireland. The journalist's answers, no matter how detailed and long, were never long or detailed enough. Then, when the party was disbanding, he asked about me.

You know the inquiry that took place and how the captain of the ferry, the only witness in the end, stated that the explosion had had to kill all those in its immediate orbit. The boat was searched in Yemen three weeks later when it arrived, and our ambassador to Saudi Arabia flew down specially to be present. That satisfied the Departments of Foreign Affairs and Justice. It satisfied Interpol. The Government of Yemen had no record of Vincent Ashe entering their country, they said. We gave the young journalist a cup of tea here and he went back to Dublin with his memory of an evening in a faraway land tidied into a recess of his disappointed mind.

Perhaps the inquiry was right. Perhaps he could not have survived, although I was eight feet from Nona when she jumped and I'm still around, so to speak. I'm not surprised that Vincent still straddles the border between substance and shadow. I once thought that exile for him would be worse than death, but I have since realised that I was wrong. Vincent's Ireland, the Ireland he for years made me a small part of, was the Ireland in his head. The blood and chains and the storms of outrage were all something he had persuaded himself had been stolen from him personally. The theft was in his mind. There is no Ireland like the one Vincent loved or loves, no docile race, no poor, ravaged woman straining to give life between her thighs. We all reconstruct within each of our heads the cosmos. It is, in a way, our duty to so do. The painter and the engineer do it on a canvas or in a bridge, the Vincents do it with innocent life. Were there really a lover needing his help, Vincent would be not her champion but her bully. Love for him, if love it is, must be shown in domination; his pleasure comes from control. Ultimately he must kill his love. And if Vincent is today somewhere in the Middle East, then the long courtship with the thing he has created continues, hindered not by deserts or oceans or time.

Hope is a rich memory in the making. People give you hope, and God knows what I would have done without your love and support. There are other people too: Brother Walter, for example. He met me for five minutes only, yet his was, I think, the first letter to reach me in here. (Angie's was a close second, but that was when the trauma of events was still fresh; I got another letter, from South Africa, at least two years ago. She wrote to tell me she was getting married there.) Brother Walter's voice was as I remembered it from our brief encounter in St Paschal's: friendly, helpful; harmless, people down the country would say. Belfast was much the same; the spuds were good that year, the apples were bad; next year it would be the reverse, you could bet your bottom dollar on it, Brother Walter said. He revealed himself in tender glimpses of life given to God. I wrote short letters describing the regime here, not because I thought he would be interested, but more to ensure the arrival of his letter in return. I heard about disease on fruit bushes in the same breath that told me of Father Patrick's headstone: 'Hail, Glorious St Patrick', it said. Brother Walter had just come in from it and, what do you know, it was snowing – big, soft flakes, the first snow of that new year. Among rambles up the Clare Glens forty years before were snippets about the death of Father Superior and how Father Blaise was settled in Rome and how, even though offered the choice of coming back home to St Paschal's on the Valley Road, Father Blaise had refused.

There exists in the upper echelons of power a peculiar weightlessness about matters inconvenient which also happen to be unprovable. Nona Lane, a terrorist, had died because bits of her had been found; the man alleged to be Vincent Ashe had not been and he still remains wanted for murder. The fate of Adam Coleraine has never been dealt with because to do so would entail the preparatory step of admitting to his existence. There was no search because no one was missing, no warrant because no one was wanted. The ferry captain had a habit of being the worse for drink so his tales to the media about another man on the deck became easy targets for official scorn.

I have mentioned that the lack of any rancour towards me by the rank and file has resulted in little privileges like visits out of time and my mail being allowed come and go uncensored; but I was somewhat surprised when one of Brother Walter's letters alluded to this state of affairs. I confirmed generally the position to him and thought that was the end of it. Six weeks between Brother Walter's letters became a minimum, often stretching to eight. Summer came and went. I became captain of the prison handball team. It was all a game.

Then that Christmas came an envelope addressed in Brother Walter's writing, the postmark Belfast. Inside, a single sheet. 'My dear friend, I think of you often. Was it all worth it? My answer is, Yes! Someday perhaps I can explain.'

Celebration on your own is a doubtful indulgence. I ran my thumb along the ink characters and tried to read the mind from the slant of the hand. 'Yes!' was underlined with a stroke of great affirmation. I looked at the paper held up to the light for a watermark; there was none, but he would have thought of that. Neither was there a smell. Writing back to Brother Walter, I enclosed a page saying, 'Yes. It was.'

Over the next eighteen months, his pages grew from one to two, to five, to twenty. I have no idea where they come from, nor would I say if I had. He evades nothing. Whereas before I would have hesitated to write and tell you everything as I have, Gilly, the frankness of Adam's letters has inspired me to do so. He has taught me that the truth, though often ugly and painful, is seldom unrewarded. There is so much to understand. He values every day, those of long hours with birdsong on waking and sleeping, or those whose nights begin in the middle of an afternoon. He takes each in their season as they come, like good and evil.

227

Adam has dwelt long on evil. He used to see it as something outside him, something to be avoided at all costs and which you normally observed in someone else – but who wakes up of a morning chuckling villainously to him or herself, I am evil? Adam discovered that omnipresent in everyone are good and evil, they are the opposites that produce the tension that gives us free will and distinguishes us from animals. He prefers to think of them as light and dark. Light and dark are present in all manifestations of man. More, if God is the creator of such a strange species in his own image – albeit a species he is unable to control – then God too must comprise light and dark, good and evil. Adam wonders what Father Patrick would think of that!

The same human spirit that I observed – that I felt! – in the sunshine on my last day in Belfast is for Adam the prevailing of light. He sees people this way now, although he worries that to do so invites the suggestion that he sits in continual judgement. He does not, anymore than someone describing the skin colour of another is judging them. Counsell dealt forever on the dark side: he brought dark to fight dark and made dark in the process. He had no qualms about what he did or had done – the villain is never a villain to himself – and what Adam saw in Counsell as arrogance might, in another, be described as heroic commitment. Vincent was similar. He and Counsell would have got on swimmingly had fate popped both of them up together in the same active service unit or regiment.

Alison walked an uncertain path between light and dark. Adam sees her as his project. Yes, Alison, he does. Someday soon, when the files on MI5 with 'Coleraine, Adam' on them have gathered so much dust that his name will be obscured, then he and Alison . . .

Angie is light, albeit cold. Pom and Becky Cocozza belong to the warm light. Adam's mother? Zoe? Strange, they seem to come together as a pair nowadays, a pair walking hand in hand in a surprising shadow land, not that they could possibly for Adam be dark in themselves, like a Counsell, but as if some part of them had been claimed by this shadow that they are now walking through.

Adam has become the temporary keeper of our hope. He sees not Zoe's death as the crucial moment any more, but Nona's. Zoe died in the zenith, for Adam, of her perfection; Nona died, Adam's seed in her, and the door of immortality opened a chink big enough to let a waft out. Nona is all bright for Adam, even though she dealt on the dark side. Adam heard Ashe reveal Nona on the ferry and, at that moment, for the first time in his life, he felt compassion. What a time for happiness! He felt it must have been like that at the birth of the universe, when each second with the coming of the light went on for a thousand years. Happiness. Nona's each step to the ferry's side one of joy. Adam's smiling at her when, paused before her leap, only she could see his face. Nona's shining peace when she heard him, peace that only he could see. Peace. Adam's peace when he called out to her, 'I forgive you!'